HOLLYWOOD AND VENAL
Stories with Secrets

Written by
NAT SEGALOFF

Illustrated by
THOMAS WARMING

Library of Congress Catalogue-in-Publication Data:
Segaloff, Nat, 1948-
Warming, Thomas, 1969-
Hollywood and Venal: Stories with Secrets

Published in the USA by:
BearManor Media
4700 Millenia Blvd.
Suite 175 PMB 90497
Orlando, FL 32839
www.bearmanormedia.com

Paperback ISBN 978-1-62933-556-8
Hardback ISBN 978-1-62933-557-5
BearManor Media, Orlando, Florida
Printed in the United States of America
Cover Illustration by: Thomas Warming
Text design by: Robbie Adkins, www.adkinsconsult.com

Dedications:

For Nikki Finke, who takes the big chances
–Nat Segaloff

To my parents, Ina Lise Larsen and Kai Warming for their eternal love and support.
To Nikki Finke for everything in between.
–Thomas Warming

TABLE OF CONTENTS

PREFACE

Like the Sphinx, Hollywood is a mystery wrapped in an enigma, except it's also dipped in tinsel. This is not accidental. Just as it takes a battalion of lawyers and accountants to untangle a film's profit-and-loss statements, so has Hollywood created an alternate history on top of its already fabricated reality. The stories in this book are an attempt to tease a little truth from the Gordian knot that the American motion picture industry has tied around its own past. They exist because of Nikki Finke, the fearless reporter whose Deadline Hollywood website debuted in 2006 and almost immediately sent the industry's venerable trade papers, *Variety* and *The Hollywood Reporter*, into shock. They needed studio and network advertising to stay in business and were known to do a little stroking along with their coverage; Nikki didn't. She took no prisoners and soon developed a reputation as a prickly, no-nonsense, sometimes vindictive, but always well-informed trade journalist. In that way she was different from such legendary Hollywood gossip columnists as Hedda Hopper and Louella Parsons. Like them, she had power, but, unlike them, she always got her facts straight.

Ducking personal publicity, Nikki let her reporting do the speaking. When she sold Deadline Hollywood to Jay Penske, the new owner of *Va-riety*, in 2009, she agreed to cease covering Hollywood news. Instead, she devised the website Hollywood Dementia and, joined by insiders from all walks of the industry, covered Hollywood as a state of mind. HollywoodDementia.com® began in 2015 with no shortage of anticipation. "There is a lot of truth in fiction," she told the *New York Times* at the time. "There are things I am going to be able to say in fiction that I can't say in journalism right now." Added Patrick Goldstein of the *Los Angeles Times*, "everyone [in Hollywood] is secretly full of trepidation about what Nikki's new site will be like. Will it be literary short stories, or will it be fiction as a thin disguise for the truth?"

This book is the result of the freedom that Nikki provides and the deep knowledge she possesses of Hollywood history. I cannot speak for the dozens of others who have written for her, but my fiction is based, to varying degrees, on fact. I spent five years as a studio publicist, fifteen as a critic, twenty-five as a producer-writer, and my whole life as a movie fan and historian. The short stories that follow are romans-à-clef. If you have the key, you're ahead of the game. If not, enjoy them for what they are.

Acknowledgments: Writer Gregory Mcdonald was a friend and mentor. He once explained to me, "In a novel, you start with a lie and, by the end, you tell the truth." I also appreciate the friendship and counsel of Harlan Ellison who insisted, "I always lie, except when I'm lying." Truth was Harlan's demon as well as his mission. Since I started writing fiction, I have come to understand both of these men better than when I was writing non-fiction.

Virginia Meyn, my college rhetoric teacher, was the first person to encourage my writing. I don't know why it's taken me several decades and twenty previous books to thank her. Likewise, my eighth grade English teacher, James Batory, is to thank for introducing me to short stories. He would have us rest our heads on our desks for the last ten minutes of each class period while he read to us, starting a new selection each Monday and finishing it on Friday. No one ever skipped Mr. Batory's class.

Thomas Warming is not only a fine artist, he channels what I write with such sensitivity that I am honored to have his work illustrate my words.

Ben Ohmart is a remarkable and daring publisher and I thank him for his support and, at times, his indulgence. Robbie Adkins, who perfectly and attractively presents this published work.

Finally, I wish to thank those whose counsel and inspiration have informed this enterprise: Norma Barzman, James Bridges, Jean Rouverol Butler, Tom Carlile, Steve Chalke, Helen Colton, Christopher Darling (for "Glossary," in particular), Jean Porter Dmytryk, Susan Toth Ellison, A. Alan Friedberg, Paul Gonthier, Frank Goodman, Bernard Gordon, Callard Harris, Jane Badgers Harris, Marsha Hunt, Daniel M. Kimmel, Elizabeth Lauritsen, Norman Lear, Robert Lees, Stan Levin, Roger L. Memos, James Robert Parish, Arnie Reisman, Ben Sack, Allan Taylor, Mike Weiss.

It is my hope that, from among the lies that follow, there can be found some truth.

-- Nat Segaloff,
Los Angeles, 2019

PART I:
CORRESPONDENCE, COARSE

The old Boston politicians were wise. They held onto power by living by the motto, "Never write when you can speak, never speak when you can nod, and never nod when you can wink." This is how the Irish stayed in power in a Brahmin town that didn't want them there in the first place. This is how they seldom got caught with their hand in the till. This is how power perpetuates itself.

Hollywood is no stranger to power. The moguls who built and perfected the system may have been crude but they knew how to wield influence and bend others to their will. This, despite being largely illiterate and dependent upon more educated people to do their bidding. Someone was always on staff to untangle their English; very seldom would you find any of them incriminating themselves with anything as clumsy as a memo. A search through studio archives shows an endless flow of missives, notes, contracts, scripts, and, yes, memos, all of which seem to have been vetted. In short, crass as they may have been, they were not fools.

Modern executives have a different operating ethic. They follow the advice attributed to Secretary of State Dean Acheson, "A memo is written not to inform the reader but to protect the writer." In what has become a CYA (Cover Your Ass) industry, it's deemed more important to keep your job than to do it. In 1991 Jeffrey Katzenberg, then the head of Walt Disney Productions, wrote a 28-page memo in which he described the state of the film industry and offered suggestions–no, decrees–for how to improve it. Although it was intended strictly as internal communication, the memo was almost immediately leaked and faxed around town in an attempt to slap the opinionated but astute Katzenberg into his place. Katzenberg may have been brash and presumptuous, but time has validated many of his observations. What was considered scandalous at the time, however, was the phenomenon of a man having written opinions. The memos in this section prove how dangerous it is to put anything in writing.

"Memo from the Corner Office" is a somewhat less serious take on an executive (Bradford "Buddy" Newborn) who thinks he knows it all but clearly doesn't.

Speaking of Disney, "Walt's Last Wishes" expands on an urban legend that has haunted the Magic Kingdom ever since its founder's death in 1966. There are numerous reasons why Walt would never have left posthumous filmed instructions to his corporate inheritors, but everyone knew that he was at the forefront of technology, so why shouldn't he have found a way to see into the future from out of the past? His memo will either set the record straight or bend it into a pretzel.

"Night Shoot" is a bizarre e-mail exchange between a production company and the hapless employee they dispatched to supervise a risky shoot in Eastern Europe. Perhaps it was naïve of anyone to think that they could deal with Dracula on his own turf, but if you work in network television long enough you can get arrogant. (For a while, this humor piece was even considered for development as a reality TV series. Talk about life imitating death.)

Finally, "I Want to Thank the Academy" is a tragic sequence of communications between a bitter filmmaker and his harried publicist. Over the years many people have used Academy Awards acceptance speeches to promote a personal agenda. Doing so almost always draws fire from those who believe that the Oscars are a place to celebrate the movies, not air dirty laundry. Somebody should tell that to Corliss "Corky" Monroe, the man with bile on his brain.

MEMO FROM THE CORNER OFFICE

TO: All Employees of Persistent Pictures
FROM: Bradford "Buddy" Newborn
RE: Studio Philosophy and Production Slate

We're all proud of the eight Oscars that Persistent Pictures won last night under Bob Cutner's management, and I know we all hope he gets to use that taste and leadership skill at another company now that he's suddenly moved on to make way for me. Since arriving to head the studio, I've seen many of you in the hallways, in the valet parking lot, and as I walk through the commissary on the way to my private dining room, but this is the first chance I've had to introduce myself since my father, Bradford Newborn, Sr., bought the studio in that hostile takeover you all must have read about. To quell some of the rumors and wisecracks I've been hearing through our advanced phone monitoring system, I am well aware that movie making isn't anything like the shoe business. It just so happens that shoes are only one of the many manufacturing interests of Newborn International. We also make small home appliances ("Nothing larger than a breadbox" is our motto), custom-printed T-shirts, and breath strips. We had a major investment in the Miami Majors, an ice hockey franchise that I was in charge of running until last year when it folded. On that regard, you can ignore those rumors and take it from me that the Majors died because of poor public support, not because of that lawsuit from 12-year-old Jimmy Brewin after a puck got

sucked up into the Zamboni and shot into the stands. (Little Jimmy is doing well, by the way; he loves his new nose, mouth, and mansion.)

We're going to have a full company meeting on the 10th on Stage G (the Petie Pettigrew stage, for those of you who grew up loving the *Petie and His Friends* series) but, in the meantime, I wanted you to digest this memo.

Persistent Pictures, like every other movie studio today, is facing tough times. Not only does it cost an arm and a leg to make our movies, you then have to spend another arm and a leg to release them. Then, if they fail, you lose your ass. This is why they make so many sequels and reboots: nothing is riskier than a new idea. Well, we're going to buck that trend. Don't worry, we're not going to do original movies. No fear of that. I may have been made last night, but I wasn't born yesterday. Instead, we're going to combine the best of sequels and reboots and create brand new original derivative works.

Not only that, my friends at the Harvard Business School have done a study (at great expense to my father) and determined that the opening weekend is what decides the fate of new movies but that, if they make it to a second weekend, their success is assured. Therefore, from now on, we are going to release our films on their second weekend.

The B-School study also ran the numbers on sequels and found that the biggest complaint about sequels is that they are too much like the first film. That's why, from now on, we will plan on making the sequels first. That way there won't be anything to compare them to.

Piracy is an ongoing problem all over the entertainment industry. Research has shown that the more popular a film is, the more it gets pirated. For example, *The Dark Knight* stands as one of the most pirated films of all time, while *Jack and Jill* and *Grown-Ups* are two of the least pirated. The lesson is obvious: if you don't want your film to be pirated, it has to star Adam Sandler, and if you can feature him in a double role, all the better. This is why we are pleased to announce that the talented, lovable Mr. Sandler will soon start shooting Persistent Pictures' Christmas release, *Robin Hyde*. In this mash-up of *Robin Hood* and *The Strange Case of Dr. Jekyll and Mr. Hyde*, Adam (I love this) will play the heroic Robin of Loxley. When the dastardly Sheriff of Nottingham dies, Robin gets a magic potion from an alchemist and turns himself into the Sheriff so he can infiltrate King John's court and speed the return of Richard the Lionheart. But Maid Marian comes between Hood and the Sheriff, and poor Robin has to keep changing back and forth to prevent her from seeing through his disguise.

Robin Hyde is a romantic action fantasy, but we are not afraid of being boldly socially relevant either. Inspired by *"Straight Outta Compton,"* my roommate from freshman year pitched me a timely story about a black rapper who agrees to teach a white actress how to talk and act black so she can play the heroine in a movie that would otherwise star an African-American actress in the role. Of course, they fall in love, except that she is out of place in his world and he is just as out of place in hers. We're adding songs now (both hip-hop and real music) making it a cross between the classics *Pygmalion* and *Imitation of Life*. We're calling it *My Fair Be-yotch*.

Among the challenges we face at Persistent Pictures is entering the tentpole market. At first, I didn't know why a movie studio would be making outdoor camping equipment, so I asked our sports manufacturing division to start designing tentpoles. Imagine my surprise when somebody explained to me what a "tent pole picture" is. I laughed so hard I almost didn't fire him. As Persistent's first foray into the summer blockbuster sweepstakes, therefore, I have green-lighted what will become an instant classic: *Jurassic Dick*. *Jurassic Dick* will have all the thrills of CGI dinosaur movies like *Jurassic Park 1-2-3* and *Jurassic World* but it's anchored in a bona fide classic: *Moby Dick*. Did you know that *Moby Dick* has been filmed at least six times? It's so popular, they even novelized it into a really long book (except they had to change the big white dinosaur into a whale because of copyright problems). There's even an actor named Moby Dick who is a grown-up (only they call him an "adult film actor" but I guess that means the same thing) and we are currently in negotiations to have him star in our family version.

When it comes to science fiction, no one will be able to beat *The iPad of Dorian Gray* in which a vain but incredibly attractive young man sells his iSoul to the iDevil in exchange for eternal youth while his selfie is imprisoned in an iPad. Part of the deal is that a character named Siri keeps giving him wrong answers to his questions because he has a Scottish accent. Our story analyst tells me that the spec script resembles a mixture of *The Portrait of Dorian Gray* and *Pinocchio*, and we're not sure whether to do it as a feature cartoon or a reality series. Your input would be appreciated.

Ron Przewlocki in our visual effects lab came up with a great idea: combining the classic sci-fi stories *The Invisible Man* and *The Time Machine* into *The Invisible Time Machine*. These are two of the most popular books ever written by a man named H.G. Wells. We've hit on the novelty of making it about a time traveler who nobody can see. That way we won't have to spend a dime on visual effects! Obviously H.G. Wells was a genius because he not only wrote these great books but he made *Citizen Kane*. (Note to story department: how's the work going on *Citizen Kane II: Rosebud Lives*?)

One of the first things I learned when dad asked me to take over this great studio was that no one person can do it all. I am so impressed with all of you. When I walk through these hallways at night, going through your trash cans and desk drawers, I am constantly reminded of the talent pool we have at our fingertips. Please don't get upset about my interest in your private lives; it will help me make decisions in the coming layoffs.

Many of you have put questions into our new "Ask Buddy" suggestion box. Dad said this will be a great way to let me in on what you're thinking. In fact, as soon as my graphologist finishes matching the handwriting on the suggestion forms with the signatures on the back of your paychecks, we'll put the box into operation. Among the more helpful ideas I've read so far are "why can't we go back to free parking," "must the air conditioning be turned so cold that it makes my nipples hard," and "I am a Nigerian prince being held prisoner." On the other hand, I'm not yet an expert on technical filmmaking terms, so could one of our crew members please tell me what it means when someone tells me I have a "cranial-rectal inversion"? Also, what's this about needing a glass navel?

I have been setting aside an hour every day to entertain pitches from USC and UCLA film students. Although I trust our story department as if it was made up of my own relatives (which it is, LOL), it never hurts to ask members of our prime audience what they'd like to see on the silver screen. Here are some early survey results:

- *New Girl in School*–When the gorgeous Bathsheba Schwartz enrolls at Hardy High School as a senior, all the guys line up to take her to prom: Troy the ROTC guy, Gabriel the animal lover, and Boldwood, the agricultural major. She flirts with them all, and melodrama prevails until there is only one survivor. This could be the dating movie of the year. (*Far from the Madding Crowd* meets *Ten Things I Hate About You*)

- *Dances with Wolverines*–An idealistic college anthropology student goes to work for Dr. Xavier and leads the mutants in a revolt against the bigots who want to convert them with ex-mutant therapy. (*Dances with Wolves* meets *The X-Men*)

- *Breadfruit!*–(Animated film) A new take on the classic *Mutiny on the Bounty* told from the point of view of the vegetables gathered by the ship's crew. Meet lovable Eddie Eggplant, luscious Melanie Mellon, the prickly Andy Artichoke, and the wacky Larry Locoweed as they turn a deadly cruise into a zany voyage. Voices by Gilbert Gottfried, Sarah Silverman, Billy West, and the late Marcel Marceau.

- *Asshole: The Kanye West Story*–This will be the greatest movie ever made. (Note: Replaces *The Taylor Swift Story* originally scheduled for production.)

- *Fifty Shades of Brown*–A plague of incontinence hits Mother of Mercy Hospital and the entire building is placed on quarantine until the problem passes. Meanwhile, the patients, doctors, and staff have to fill the empty, lonely hours by any means they can fantasize. Based on B. M. Thrower's controversial Number Two bestseller.

- *"Les Metamorphoses"*–Gregor Samsa commits a small crime yet is pursued relentlessly by an exterminator, Javert, through the sewers of Paris and the subway tunnels of Manhattan. He hides with friends and tries to slip about unnoticed, but it's hard to do since he is a five-foot, ten-inch cockroach. (*The Metamorphosis* meets *Les Misérables*).

- *The Exordysiast*–A priest who performs exorcisms is possessed by the spirit of Gypsy Rose Lee and begins conducting his religious rituals in the form of a strip tease. Based on the friendship between H. L. Mencken and "ecdysiast" Gypsy Rose Lee. (*The Exorcist* meets *Gypsy*)

We're all pretty high on these ideas and are starting to conduct market research on them. To that end, we're going to produce previews of coming attractions, show them to focus groups, and see if it's worth making the whole movies. I don't know why nobody's ever tried this before. It was one of my Harvard B-School friends who suggested it, but it seems to be an excellent way of cutting losses early on.

There's a lot to think about here. I've shown this memo to my friends and they think it's full of lots of ideas that nobody has ever tried before for some reason. I hope whoever keeps talking to *Variety* and the *Hollywood Reporter* stops doing so. I want to give the new Persistent Pictures a fair try. Please keep trying. I am trying every day.

Yours in the corner office,
Bradford "Buddy" Newborn

P.S.: Company T-shirts will be given out at the meeting so please bring your shoe size.

TRIGGER WARNING

Political Correctness used to be a way to end discrimination. Now it has become a magnet for it, Two TV executives–a network VP and a show runner–hassle it out in cross-memos that push the envelope.

FROM: Colin Platzner, Standards & Practices, FORUM NETWORK
TO: Byron Messenger, Producer, *Medic Alert!*
SUBJECT: Unacceptable words

We have examined the script for your upcoming episode titled "Fever Pitch" and look forward to viewing the final run-through prior to taping so we can make the customary adjustments. There is, however, one element to which I must call your attention now. When the character of Beverly is introduced on page 5 she is referred to by one of the male Emergency Room interns as being "hot." This reference to Beverly's sexual allure is unacceptable. One of the women on our staff took offense and feels it objectifies the character. Please find another word or, better yet, eliminate it entirely.

TO: Colin Platzner
FROM: Byron Messenger
SUBJECT: Use of the word "hot"

I don't understand the problem with calling Beverly "hot." It is an important plot point that serves as motivation for the hospital staff. We need to leave it in.

TO: Byron Messenger
FROM: Colin Platzner
SUBJECT: Use of the word "hot"

This isn't something I should need to discuss further. In light of the increased sensitivity of viewers–indeed, the whole country–to the ill-treatment of women by men, especially employers, the word has to come out.

TO: Colin Platzner
FROM: Byron Messenger
SUBJECT: Further on "hot"

As regards the word "hot," I would like to point out that there was no network objection with this same script's use of the words "shit," "fuck," "God damn," and "prick" as well as to the incident that motivates the story, which is a gunman running into a 7-11 and shooting four patrons, splattering their blood across the Slurpee alcove. How can violence be acceptable while the word "hot" might offend someone?

TO: Byron Messenger
FROM: Colin Platzner
SUBJECT: Violence

The violence in *Medic Alert!* is a plot device. I'm surprised a man with your experience does not recognize this. For that same reason, strong language in reaction to the crime is also motivated and is therefore acceptable. Yet the word "hot" is gratuitous and sexist.

TO: Colin Platzner
FROM: Byron Messenger
SUBJECT: Language

I have a surprise for you, Colin. I drew you out on purpose. If you go back and actually read the script, you will see that the word "hot" does indeed apply to the character of Beverly. But if your politically correct eyes had read the stage directions, you and they would have seen that Beverly shows up in the Emergency Room with a temperature of 105 degrees, and this is why the intern refers to her as "hot." But I have enjoyed our badinage–unless your people think that word is too kinky.

TO: Byron Messenger
FROM: Colin Platzner
SUBJECT: Badinage

Very funny, Byron. I know what badinage is, and I resent your playing "gotcha." I'm serious. We are all being criticized for things we did in innocence or ignorance years ago. Conscience has a time machine but the public doesn't. You of all people should be concerned about that.

TO: Colin Platzner
FROM: Byron Messenger
SUBJECT: Legacy

I of all people? Need I remind you that most of your programming today wouldn't be allowed on the air if I hadn't kicked the doors open for real language, mature plots, and honest characters with the eleven–that's right, eleven–hit series I produced in the 1970s and 80s. I brought our industry into modern times with *Traveling Man*, *Family Values*, *Newspaper Picture*, *Cop Time*, *Pancho's People*, and their spin-offs. They didn't call me "Messenger the messenger" for nothing. I have nothing to apologize for. This is Political Correctness gone insane.

TO: Byron Messenger
FROM: Colin Platzner
SUBJECT: PC

I'm glad you brought up your old shows, Byron. As you know, we paid a fortune to license them for rerun. There's just one problem. We can't show any of them.

TO: Colin Platzner
FROM: Byron Messenger
SUBJECT: My old series

What are you talking about? Those shows won a total of 23 Emmys, two Peabodys, a WGA award, and a slew of commendations from public service groups across the country. The living room set from "Family Values" is in the Smithsonian, for heaven's sake.

TO: Byron Messenger
FROM: Colin Platzner
SUBJECT: Your old series

Perhaps you need to look at them again. Do you know what they're about? I had the girl make a list. You have plotlines about abortion, homosexuality, mixed marriage, transgender people, gay adoption, workplace discrimination, genital mutilation, kiddie porn, Holocaust denial, religious cults, conspiracy theories, heckler's veto, date rape, white supremacy, and–to top it off–the N-word. What do you have to say about that?

TO: Colin Platzner
FROM: Byron Messenger
SUBJECT: Comment

"The girl"????

TO: Byron Messenger
FROM: Colin Platzner
SUBJECT: PC

Legal Affairs says that it we want to rerun your old shows we'll have to give a trigger warning to let people know that the following program may contain offensive material.

TO: Colin Platzner
FROM: Byron Messenger
SUBJECT: Trigger warnings

You mean, viewers might accidentally see something that might make them a better and more tolerant person or be able to survive in today's world? Trigger warnings are what fearful college professors give to students who have forgotten that they're in college to hear new ideas even if they don't agree with them. Political Correctness is the death of freedom of thought.

TO: Byron Messenger
FROM: Colin Platzner
SUBJECT: PC

Oh, don't cry Political Correctness at me, Byron. You Liberals started it. You were so concerned about people's feelings that you turned everyone into victims. Now everybody plays the race, religion, national origin, disability, and gender card. You gave everyone permission to whine discrimination and blame everyone but themselves. Remember how you used to piss off Conservatives? Now you piss off Liberals. We can't even show a Pepe Le Pew cartoon any more because people complain he's a predatory skunk.

I am enclosing a copy of the Forum Network Guide to Ethics and Standards. I draw your attention to the section that says there shall be no use of the terms "alley cat," "bat," "hot" (sic), "frigid," "broad," "chick," or "'chippie" applied to a woman; "fairy," "pansy," or "nance" applied to a man; "fag," except when referring to a British cigarette; and you cannot say or spell out the N-word, even in a show set in a time period when the word was historically used.

TO: Colin Platzner
FROM: Byron Messenger
SUBJECT: Deja vu

I recognize the list. Most of it comes from the 1927 Hollywood Production Code. Do you mean that all the freedom we won for our industry (and our country) is back to being guided by an 92-year-old censorship lexicon? Why stop there? Why not run a trigger warning in front of the news? If you're afraid "hot" might offend people, you better flash an alert about real things that are offensive like war, murder, climate change, homelessness, racism, and politics. At least my shows are entertaining. Now I'm going to fight even harder for "hot."

TO: Byron Messenger
FROM: Colin Platzner
SUBJECT: Our purpose

We are not running a school, Byron, we are running a TV network. You opened the door so wide that, like Pandora and her box, things escaped that you didn't anticipate. People are being held accountable.

TO: Colin Platzner
FROM: Byron Messenger
SUBJECT: Pandora's Box

If I am going to be held accountable for anything, I want it to be the First Amendment.

TO: Byron Messenger
FROM: Colin Platzner
SUBJECT: lunch

Let's discuss this in person. Lunch? I've been trying to get to a retro place on Wilshire called Dirndl's. It's set up like a 1950s drive-in. The waitresses are hot. Say one o'clock tomorrow? What's your thinking?

TO: Colin Platzner
FROM: Byron Messenger
SUBJECT: The future

#MeToo.

WALT'S LAST WISHES

When Walt Disney passed away on December 15, 1966 he left an artistic and commercial legacy that his successors are still mining. He also–according to persistent rumor–left behind a private film that was to be shown to his top executives exactly one year after his death. When the day arrived, they were led into "the sweat box," the tiny airless screening room where animators used to run their rough footage, and were shown assigned seats. The lights went down and Walt appeared on the screen. He spoke to each of them by name, looking where he had decreed that they sit, and told them exactly what they were to do for the next five years. When the film ended, the stunned men returned to their corner offices after which the sole existing print they had just watched was destroyed on Walt's posthumous orders. Always known for meticulous, even compulsive, planning, Walt had issued instructions for the completion of Walt Disney World in Florida, its expansion into Common Market and Asian countries, and development details for WED Enterprises and RETLAW. He even cautioned against releasing his animated features too quickly on home video, a medium whose commercial debut was a decade away but which his studio contracts had been predicting for decades.

It was therefore an extraordinary moment when the script for this legendary film was discovered between the pages of story conference notes for The Jungle Book, the picture Walt was working on when he died. We present them here for the first time as testimony to the amazing prescience of the man who built an empire upon a mouse.

Walt: Hello, gentlemen. I hope you'll excuse this unusual way of conducting a meeting but I think you'll understand why I did it once it's over. So sit back, relax, have a smoke, and pay attention.

1. Now that I've been dead for one year I want you to go to Forest Lawn and pee on Walter Lantz's grave. I shall never forgive him for taking over "Oswald the Rabbit" from me, even if it did force me to invent Mickey Mouse. At least Oswald was silent, not like that fucking woodpecker.

2. Disneyland will never be finished. It will also never be affordable. Be sure to raise ticket prices every two or three years just when families have saved up enough to go.

3. Am I the only one who finds those big-head characters at the park creepy? I know the kids like them, but there's something not right about a five-foot-tall Mickey with a four-foot head. Besides, when kids come up to talk to them, they're talking to the cast member's crotch.

4. I don't care how many times Michael Jackson goes on the "Pirates of the Caribbean" ride, he can't buy it.

5. If security catches anybody taking drugs at the park, don't call the police, just send them on the

"It's a Small World" ride until they flip out.

6. Burn everything you can find from when we paid the FBI to bury Wernher von Braun's Nazi credentials once he became a hit on the "Tomorrowland" episodes on our TV show.

7. Let me be in the ground at least 18 years before hiring Jews.

8. Be sure to erase the "Suck Mr. Lincoln" tape we made for Benny's stag party.

9. See if you can renegotiate our settlement with Great Britain over Dick van Dyke's accent in *Mary Poppins*. How many times must we apologize for letting J. Pat O'Malley be his dialogue coach?

10. Whatever you do, never re-release *Song of the South*.

11. Anybody who suggests building a Euro-Disney, especially in France, must be fired immediately.

12. Should any of our Mousketeers write a tell-all book, say nothing. We have such good will around the world that nobody will believe it, at least as long as our beloved Annette is still alive.

13. If P.L. Travers ever sets foot in my studio again threaten her with a biographical movie showing what a bitch she was.

14. I read a terrific science fiction book called *John Carter* by Edgar Rice Burroughs. Are the screen rights available? Some day we should turn it into a movie.

15. Be sure to protect my copyrights and trademarks. Once every couple of years find some little day care center that has painted Mickey, Donald, and Pluto on their walls and sue the shit out of them.

16. Keep having our animators slip all those "in" jokes into our cartoon films. People will keep coming back to try and catch them.

17. Would someone please settle once and for all whether Goofy is a dog?

18. Competition is the essence of creativity. The more other companies develop characters that the whole world loves, the more our own people will be inspired to achieve more. Therefore, under no circumstances should you try to buy other companies' comic book characters, characters from science fiction movies, or children's book characters. Our Imagineers and artists are the best; we don't need to co-opt the creativity of outsiders to keep this company great.

19. Princesses are the future. You can't go wrong with princesses. Little girls can get their parents to buy them all that crap, whereas little boys only want air rifles and bicycles, neither of which can

be a good Disney brand. I tell you, go with princesses.

20. There is a time in every child's life when he or she rejects Disney as being baby stuff, but they return once they have children of their own. This means that we lose them between the ages of ten and twenty-five. That's fifteen years when they're giving somebody else their money. See what you can do about this. Buy a TV network or start a sports franchise or something. Use your brains, fellas. What if it gets out that a dead guy is still running the company?

21. If a film drops dead, just add the words "That Darn" in front of the title (as we did with *That Darn Cat*), e.g. *That Darn Lone Ranger, That Darn Tomorrowland,* etc.

22. As you know, I'm not a big fan of sequels. If you tell the story right, a sequel is unnecessary. For this reason, ditch all ideas about making *Peter Pan II: The Puberty Years, Lady and the Tramp II: The Neutering,* or *Pinocchio II: Termites.*

23. I feel the same way about mash-ups. Leave crossovers to the Marvel Universe. As of now, put these projects in turnaround: *Snow White and the Seven Dalmatians, Dumbo of the Caribbean,* and *20,000 Leagues Under Mulan.*

24. No more talk about work conditions being so oppressive that people call us "Mickey Mouschwitz" and "Donald Duchau." Just because we

once looked at turning *The Diary of Anne Frank* into a musical called *Songs in the Attic!* that's no reason to say such things.

25. Some day we should turn Times Square into Disneyland. There's great potential there for characters like "Willie Wino," "Henrietta Hooker," and "Pete the Pimp."

26. As soon as possible, give Chip 'n' Dale girlfriends. People are starting to talk.

27. Land is limited at the Anaheim park but there's still plenty of room for new rides in Orlando. See what you can do with a "Sorcerer's Apprentice" waterboarding experience, an *Alice in Wonderland* fun house, a *Bambi* "where's my mother?" game and maybe even a *Sleeping Beauty* spinning wheel prick ride.

28. Kids love the dinosaurs in *Fantasia,* Look into creating "Evolutionland" that starts with a Big Bang and sends guests through millions of years. So what if it pisses off the Fundamentalists. We lost them when we let gays into the park.

29. Be sure to reset the mouse traps in my office. (Don't let this get around.)

30. Finally, whatever else you do, don't hit "defrost."

NIGHT SHOOT

It was the dumbest party pitch anybody had heard in forty years so, naturally, it sold. Mack Barrett made it as a joke to Colin Beauregard at Tina Reynolds' gathering on Friday night and by Monday morning the network lawyers had the contracts ready. *The Trades* said that Barrett's pitch was at the level of Snakes on a Plane and maybe even rivaled the most sacred party pitch of all time, *Wheels*. (*Wheels* got made when an agent and a writer got high at a producer's house in the middle 1970s and said, "What's the stupidest combination of genres you can think of?" Because The Exorcist and Vanishing Point were raking in nothing but cash at the time, the writer joked, "a possessed car." When everybody in the room stopped laughing at the crassness of it, the host sneaked off to the bedroom and phoned the vice president of production at Columbia. Presto, in May of 1977 *Wheels* hit the screen and became the 19th top-grossing film of the year.)

The show that Mack Barrett sold to Colin Beauregard was *The Real Vampires of Transylvania. It never aired for reasons that are revealed in show runner Josh Combs's production reports. The author would like to thank Mr. Combs's widow for permission to reprint them.*

Friday, April 13:

How auspicious to start a vampire series on Friday the 13th. I'm here in Romania for pre-production. They had us booked at the local Marriott and we announced an open casting call at 10 AM, then realized that we should have made it 10 PM instead.

In line with the network's mandate for diversity, we put out a call for a cross-section of physical types. Of course, all the vampires have to look young, beautiful, and sexy; our shorthand for this is "VILF." Anybody who's old or ugly or both will be cast as villagers. Since we'll be shooting entirely at night, we were afraid we couldn't have any children in the show. Amazingly, all those who have applied so far are at least a hundred years old, yet look like they're nine and ten.

In order to make sure we hire the real thing, we have mirrors posted at strategic spots around the meeting room. (Note: this may eventually pose a problem for the make-up department.) Costuming probably won't be an issue since everyone tends to arrive dressed in period finery looking like a cross between a *Frozen* character and the Ambassador Hotel doorman. Most of the actors say they're from Seattle and are almost all unrelentingly morose. One of the ways we ferret out fakers is inviting them to sample our craft service table. The real ones refuse everything, although we almost had a disaster when one of the less worldly applicants started to eat a blood orange and we quickly told him it was just a name. Rather than risk another such incident, Amazon

Prime is overnighting us a supply of crucifixes (all of those in town are privately owned and jealously guarded).

Sunday, April 15:

Location scouting all weekend. Total letdown. Have you ever tried to find a castle, ruins, and cobblestone streets within union travel radius of a pile of native earth?

Tuesday, April 17:

What's with the anemic budgets? Do they actually think we can knock out 13 episodes for $3 million all-in? That's $200,000 per episode. Okay, it's actually $231,000 but that's not counting the $31,000 we intend to skim. At least the WGA still thinks reality shows aren't written. I just hope our vampires don't go union. LOL.

Monday, April 23:

First night of shooting. Right away we hit a perfect dramatic conflict: Our main vampire pod has a charismatic leader in Baron O'Neil, his consort is Genevieve Tillis, their ward is Steffi Batchelder, and then a mysterious newly minted vampire, Harris Charlton, shows up. Charlton knows all about the others' pasts before they became undead and he seeks to out them as vampires. Lots of possibilities here.

One sad note: we need to hire a new key grip. The one we had died.

Thursday, April 26:

Terrific fireworks between O'Neil and Charlton. O'Neil ad-libbed something that's sure to become a catch-phrase. He said, "By Satan's horns, I curse the shadow you cannot cast." The crew has started to use it on each other. For example, one of the electricians accidentally stepped on the prop man's foot and the prop man cursed the electrician's shadow. We all laughed.

One sad note: the prop man died so we have to hire another one.

Sunday, April 29:

In an effort to get a few pages ahead, the actors have agreed to work on Sundays. None of them attends church so this is not a big deal, although the script clerk complained that she wanted to find a place to worship. Genevieve Tillis offered to show her the town's church as soon as we wrapped for the night.

One sad note: at sunrise the script clerk was found nailed to the door of the church so we're going to have to hire another one.

Monday, April 30

Slight meltdown. One of the cast members complained that another cast member had called him the N-word. In order to be politically correct, characters will no longer call each other "Nosferatu."

Tuesday, May 1:

We had a visit from the local Child Welfare Society about our use of children in the show.

They wouldn't accept that our sweet little Steffi Batchelder is actually 123 years old. The director of the CWS demanded that we cut Steffi's on-set time to three hours and use her only during the day, not at night. Charlton took him aside and explained how we do things. Then he returned and announced that everything would be fine from now on.

We're knocking off early tomorrow so we can attend the funeral of the Child Welfare Society representative. Such a sad coincidence.

Wednesday, May 2:

Bit of fun yesterday. Somebody played a practical joke on Baron O'Neil by putting real garlic bread on the table in our dining room set. Who knew that he was violently allergic to garlic? He sneezed so hard that he turned himself into a bat and flew madly around the room until we removed the offending food. I had the editor save the footage for the outtake reel. Naturally, Baron was embarrassed and apologized but it spooked the make-up lady who was just about to touch up his lips.

More sad news: the make-up lady came down with some sort of rare blood disorder and has gone to the hospital for tests.

Friday, May 4:

End of week two of production and we have become a tight, cohesive unit. The director no longer has to say "action"; the actors might as well be reading his mind. They have hit upon the idea of mixing with the local townspeople to bring fresh blood–that's what Charlton calls it–to the show. Most of the villagers only show up for one episode and then disappear. (You know how boring production is; I guess they can't take it.) BTW, we'll have to alert Standards and Practices that O'Neil considers all of the female villagers to be his "wives." Perhaps we can dub "fiancées" over the word "wives" in Post. After all, we wouldn't want the religious nuts to think *The Real Vampires of Transylvania* is about Satanism.

Happily, the script clerk has left the hospital, is feeling better, and has joined the cast. O'Neil is treating her like one of his fiancées, so we're going to need another script clerk.

Saturday, May 5:

The first episode is edited and ready for uploading. I think you'll be impressed, especially when you hear that we didn't have to spend any of our optical effects budget. It seems that the cast was able to make their eyes turn red and yellow, zoom across the room faster than you could see, levitate, and make objects shatter all on their own. Suggestion: these tricks look awesome in person. Maybe the PR department can set up personal appearances at children's hospitals and church groups for live demonstrations.

Tuesday, May 8:

Sad news to report. Little Steffi Batchelder is dead. Well, not "dead," technically, because she already was. She was taking a nap on a sofa behind the set and didn't hear us when we wrapped at dawn. A beam of sunlight struck her and she turned into ash. We're going to try to work it into the storyline but I don't think we can get away with it because of the FCC's no-smoking rules.

Thursday, May 17:

I haven't written in a while because I've been putting out fires. That's not a metaphor. The villagers have been upset over our shooting here and, starting a week ago, they began gathering outside our production offices with torches, pitchforks, rakes, and shovels. I informed them that we already had a union landscaping crew but I guess they took it the wrong way because they demanded to know what we had done with (so far) four of their wives, two of their husbands, eight of their children, eleven of their pets, and the town Mayor. You know how, when you're shooting a movie, you don't pay attention to the local news? Boy did I feel out of it! I told them I'd ask around.

Friday, May 18:

None of the cast or crew knows anything about all the local disappearances. I reported this to the head villager who grumbled and walked away making veiled threats about telling TMZ. I know that there can often be tension between film crews and the townies, so I reminded him of the amount of money we were dropping here. Talk about ungrateful! If we get picked up for a second season, we're going to have to find a location that wants us.

Wednesday, May 23:

I didn't want to alarm you, but now I can't avoid it. An old man named van Helsing has been making a pest of himself around here ever since last weekend. He looks like something out of a Bergman movie and has been stalking practically everyone in the main cast. I've tried checking him out but when you Google him all that turns up is one conspiracy theory after another. Would you believe it, he thinks that vampires actually exist! If they did, wouldn't we put them in the show? (ROTFLMAO)

Sunday, May 27:

Bad news. Baron O'Neil was discovered this morning with a wooden stake in his heart. His hands were also nailed to the inside of his coffin with sharpened crucifixes, a silver bullet was lodged in his brain, a head of garlic had been shoved into his mouth, and a small vial of Sparkletts holy water was left beside his withered body. The town sheriff called it the worst case of suicide he's ever seen. We're going to have to shut down for a couple of days until we can restructure the story lines. Harris Charlton and Genevieve Tillis have offered to have a child, especially after losing Steffi, but I'm not sure the show is ready to jump the undead shark before it even premieres. Any ideas?

Monday, May 28:

This morning I received a message from van Helsing. He said he was going to dispatch our remaining key cast members one by one unless we made him a featured player. I ran this past O'Neil, Charlton, and Tillis and they weren't thrilled but they didn't want to let the show die. Tomorrow morning van Helsing will move in as the wacky neighbor. Unfortunately, this means that we will have to fire and pay out the character actor we originally cast as the wacky neighbor.

Tuesday, May 29:

The good news is that we won't have to pay out the actor we originally hired as the wacky neighbor. The bad news is that we will have to ship his body home to his relatives in Tarzana. The cause of death has not been determined, but it appears that he cut himself shaving and bled to death.

Friday, June 1:

Our hotel manager is upset. It seems that our crew have been tearing apart their Gideon Bibles and gluing the pages to the windows, doorways, ventilation shafts, and any place that the outside world can find its way into their rooms. Not only that, they have rubbed garlic on all the door handles and bathroom fixtures. The place smells like Gilroy. Tonight before we start I will have a sit-down with the crew and cast and tell them that we need to respect our hosts.

Saturday, June 2:

Well, that didn't work. Boy did I catch an earful. It seems that many of the cast members have been making unwelcome advances to other cast and crew members. It usually stops at hickeys, but I have told everyone in no uncertain terms that even that is completely unacceptable. I directed most of my remarks to O'Neil, Charlton, and Tillis, who seem to be the ringleaders. I am meeting with them privately later tonight to tell them that I would rather shut down the show than keep them involved with it.

Wednesday, June 6:

Dear Mrs. Combs: The producers of *The Real Vampires of Transylvania* wish to express their condolences over the death of your husband Josh. He was a fine line producer just starting to reach recognition. Although we pulled the plug on his series when he died suddenly, we plan to edit the existing footage into a one-off special and run it in his honor on Netflix or YouTube Red. By the way, please execute the enclosed indemnification papers so we can release his body to you for proper burial. Incidentally, we don't recommend immediate interment, we suggest cremation, salting his ashes with garlic, sprinkling them with holy water, and only then interment. Kind regards,

-- Mack Bennett and Colin Beauregard, producers, *The Real Vampires of Transylvania*

I WANT TO THANK THE ACADEMY

TO: VICTOR SPOONER, VP-PR
FROM: Corliss "Corky" Monroe
RE: My Academy Award acceptance speech

Dear Vic, I'm writing an acceptance speech in case I get the directing Oscar® next week. You guided my nomination campaign brilliantly, but I thought I'd try my own hand at writing the payoff if I win. Could you take a look at it to see if it does the job? Thanks. Corky.

"I want to thank the Academy more than I can say. As many of you know, I struggled for four years to get this movie made, including shitting out three zombie pictures for the same company. I consider this wonderful award to be in recognition of my perseverance and strong stomach. Making this film was a bitch. After they said yes, everybody fought me all along the way. You know who you are. You're the vampires who suck the creative blood out of our art. For you, consider this Oscar a middle finger flipped cold and bold for the damage you do. But to those of us who bleed for our art, this Oscar is a glistening reminder that talent and justice always triumph in the end. Thank you."

TO: CORKY MONROE
FROM: VICTOR SPOONER
RE: Your acceptance speech

Very funny. I know you're still bitter that you had to make the Zombie trilogy in order to get a green light for *The Keys of Fate*, but don't you think this is a little over the top, even kidding around with me? Let me put it another way: if you say this,

you'll never work in the business again, not even as a ticket-taker at the Century City AMC multiplex. You'll have plenty of time to get back at people privately, but not on international TV, for God's sake. Just be gracious, thank your agent, your parents, and your producer (in that order) and get off the stage.

TO: VICTOR SPOONER
FROM: CORKY MONROE
RE: Acceptance speech

Of course, I was kidding. You think I'd commit professional seppuku? If I do win, though, I want to say something provocative enough to have people ask me what I really meant. That's what Jane Fonda did when she won Best Actress for *Klute*; being enigmatic at the Oscars gave her entree to talk afterward about what she really wanted to talk about. How about something for me like:

"I want to thank the members of the Academy that voted for me. This award has given me the clout to make more of the kinds of films we're all proud to have represent our industry, not the mindless chicken shit that producers put into the assembly line. Thank you."

TO: CORKY MONROE
FROM: VICTOR SPOONER
RE: Acceptance speech

I think you're missing my point. The Oscars aren't a place to settle grievances, they're where you kiss movie ass and lay the groundwork for the rest of your career. Try to sound more positive, okay? If you can't thank everyone, just say you're too choked up to speak and get the hell off. They'll love you for having a short speech. Now stop messing around and work on heartfelt comments, then cross your fingers, see your clergyman, sacrifice a virgin, or do whatever it takes to win so you can actually have the chance to speak it.

TO: VICTOR SPOONER
FROM: CORKY MONROE
RE: Acceptance speech

Yeah, okay. I guess I'm still pissed off from them telling me I can make the picture, then pulling it out of theatres after one week and selling it to Netflix where I earn zilch in residuals. Okay, here's a whole new version:

"I want to thank the Academy. I'm grateful that you saw the work we all did on the picture, even though we had to stream it to you at home because you couldn't haul your sorry asses out to any of the screenings we set up. At least let me thank you for not fast-forwarding through it."

TO: CORKY MONROE
FROM: VICTOR SPOONER
RE: Acceptance speech

What are you smoking, dropping, or huffing? This isn't funny anymore. Even with their ratings in the toilet, the Oscars are watched by a gazillion people, and none of them will ever buy another ticket to see a guy who runs off the rails. If you can't write a simple, direct, gracious speech, let me do it for you. After all, I'm in charge of your public relations and I'd rather have you do it right than have to clean up your mega-mess afterward.

TO: VICTOR SPOONER
FROM: CORKY MONROE
RE: Acceptance speech

I'm sorry, Vic. I know you're looking out for my best interests. Here's a page-one rewrite:

"This award means so much to me because it comes from my peers: people who know what we go through to make movies. I appreciate the affection you show for me and my work, and I am proud to be in an industry that makes all of this possible."

How's that? Please notice that I didn't say a thing about being forced to work for scale while the producer took his full quotes, and having to use the studio's travel, hotel, and catering deals on the picture even though it cost more and the food sucked. They must have liked the set design because, the week after we wrapped, I saw the furniture from our living room set in the production vice president's waiting room. And I am especially not mentioning that we had not one but two spies on the picture. So when I said, "I am proud to be in an industry that makes all of this possible" I damn well meant it to go both ways.

TO: CORKY MONROE
FROM: VICTOR SPOONER
RE: Acceptance speech

You've got to stop this. Now it's in my mind that you're a loose cannon. Did you put that last paragraph in there to get a rise out of me, or to test the wording for when you ad-lib it from the stage of the Kodak Theatre? Cuz let me tell you something, buster. You are not going to act like that if I have to stand in the wings and shoot you in the heart with a crossbow. I want your word of honor on your children's souls that you'll be a good boy if you win.

TO: VICTOR SPOONER
FROM: CORKY MONROE
RE: Acceptance speech

Don't worry, Vic, it's just me getting it out of my system now so I won't be tempted to say it later. Do you actually think I'd take Mel Grossman across the coals for sticking me with a unit manager who was boffing the script supervisor on the side? Or gripe about how the studio laid off the cost over-runs from their stinking costume epic *Sinbad* onto my budget? Why should I talk about the way they charged me $175 to "ship" the hard drive from master control to the screening room when all they did was press the upload button? Never mind that every Academy member is being screwed the same way. I'm not going to blow the whistle.

TO: CORKY MONROE
FROM: VICTOR SPOONER
RE: Acceptance speech

You knew the job was dangerous when you took it, Corky. Remember that, if you win, you'll be talking to people who are complicit and still make pictures good enough that the industry nominates them, just as they did yours. F'r'chrissake, don't bite the hand that's jerking you off.

TO: VICTOR SPOONER
FROM: CORKY MONROE
RE: Acceptance speech

Don't get me wrong, Victor. I'm not going to use the Oscars as a platform to call in the Justice Department. I remember Michael Moore, Sasheen Littlefeather, Vanessa Redgrave, and the others who used the show as a bully pulpit. I realize–and I think it was Paddy Chayefsky who said it–that the Oscars are all about "Ladies and Gentlemen, this is Mrs. Norman Maine." But, my God, what an opportunity! Just once I'd like to see somebody say, when they accept the Best Picture Oscar, "Nobody wanted to make this film, and now they named it the best of the year." I mean, think of the movies that never won the Oscar: *Citizen Kane, 2001, Raging Bull, Vertigo, The Wild Bunch, Singin' in the Rain, M*A*S*H, Apocalypse Now.* Each of them changed the art of cinema more than *The English Patient* or *The Artist* or *Dances with Wolves,* all of which are almost forgotten today. And what about the directors who were never even nominated: Stanley Kubrick, Sam Peckinpah, Michael Powell, Charles Chaplin, John Frankenheimer, Don Siegel, Buster Keaton, Blake Edwards, Raoul Walsh, Rouben Mamoulian, Preston Sturges, and Fritz Lang. I'm not saying that my picture is in their league, but Jeez, let's have some perspective.

TO: CORKY MONROE
FROM: VICTOR SPOONER
RE: Acceptance speech

Yadda yadda. We can take a film history course later. I hope you win, kiddo, I really do. But don't make a tirade, make a nice speech, I beg you. I'll see you there. You be good. Promise?

TO: VICTOR SPOONER
FROM: CORKY MONROE
RE: Acceptance speech

I promise.

TO: CORKY MONROE
FROM: VICTOR SPOONER
RE: Last night at the Oscars

You did it, you bastard, didn't you? You won and then you managed to go down in flames all within the same minute. I'm ashamed of you. You are so over in this town. You are certainly over with me and my agency.

TO: VICTOR SPOONER
FROM: CORKY MONROE
RE: Acceptance speech

I had nothing to do with it. Swear to God. I had my speech all written out in my pocket, but I couldn't find it, so I just ad libbed. What the hell. I was so nervous, I don't even remember what I said, but then I heard the audience make that weird noise like when something happens on stage that they know isn't supposed to happen, and I realized that I was the one who was talking. Then in the press room afterward everybody asked me what I meant and I didn't know until the guy from the wire service read it back to me and I thought I'd poop and puke at the same time. I'm sorry, Victor, Honest. I don't know how it happened but nobody will ever believe me, will they? Do you?

TO: CORKY MONROE
FROM: MAILER-DAEMON
RE: Undeliverable message

We were unable to deliver your message to the following address: VSpooner@VP-PR.com.

PART II: MOGULIZATION

Critic Pauline Kael maintained, in her snarky way, that anybody who writes about Hollywood is automatically writing satire. It's easy to dump on the larger-than-life figures who live larger-than-life lives making larger-than-life money producing dramas about real, average people. Movie stars are not average. As Cecil B. DeMille once said, if you want the girl next door all you have to do is look over the backyard fence.

The people who ran Hollywood in its early days were not average. They had dreams and the gumption to make their dreams come true. The Louis B. Mayers, the Jack L. Warners, the Harry Cohns, the Samuel Goldwyns, the Jesse Laskys, and the rest were showmen as well as businessmen. It was easy to point out their flaws, but even their detractors had to admit that those ogres loved making movies. Contrast that with today's college-educated bean counters who now hold the reins and hang on for dear life. It is said that today's studio bosses prefer making deals to making pictures. That isn't exactly true, it's just that making a picture requires a commitment, and it's commitment that frightens the current crop of industry executives. In the words of producer-writer-actor John Houseman, "In the old days they used to help you make a movie. Now they dare you."

Offered as proof of Houseman's lament, "Christmas Picture" takes place at the imaginary lunch of four high-level film people who probably never hung around together, but what if they had? In their attempt to create holiday joy they reveal a lot about themselves and more about Hollywood. The fact that none of them observes Christmas is icing on the cookies their assimilated kids probably leave for Santa Claus.

Herschel Wechsler is the subject of "Herschel the Horrible." An embarrassment to the film business, Herschel has aced all the angles and climbed into a position of power, if not respect, by gaming the system and taking advantage of people. Ripe for a fall, his competitors conspire to make it happen sooner rather than later.

"Group Marvelous" is a hate letter to a broadcast network. I'd heard stories like it but couldn't imagine any of them being true. Then I worked at one. Whatever Group M deserved, they got.

CHRISTMAS PICTURE

Joseph E. Levine, David O. Selznick, Samuel Goldwyn, and William Castle took a break from their pinochle game and agreed that what Hollywood needed was a good Christmas picture.

"As long as the goyum are spending everything they have on presents," Levine said, "why can't they throw a little of it our way?"

"After all," added Goldwyn, "Jesus was Jewish, at least on his mother's side."

Selznick wasn't sure. "I admit that a Christmas picture is good for holiday business," he said, shaking his head, "but what happens after December 26? Who wants to see a picture about Santa Claus in January when the bills come in?"

"For that matter," Levine shot back, "who wants to see a picture about the Civil War seventy-five years after Appomattox? If it's a good picture, they'll come whenever you open it. But you gotta have the right ad campaign."

"Amen to that," Castle agreed. "Good ads, but also a gimmick. The gimmick is what brings 'em in. It's called showmanship."

"I know your kind of showmanship," Selznick said dismissively. "Seat vibrators, a nurse on duty, insurance policies, a skeleton that sails over the audience's heads. I never even remember the names of the pictures. What would you do for Christmas, give everybody a piece of the true cross?"

"It brought 'em into the church, didn't it?" Levine grunted.

"All I'm saying," Castle continued, undaunted by his skeptical friends, "is that Christmas is a time of gift-giving, and the wise showman gives something to the people who buy the tickets. Call it a souvenir, call it whatever you want. Give them something to take away and they'll come back for more of it."

"I think we should make a film about a traditional American Christmas," said Goldwyn. "The family sits down to a turkey dinner, then they go to midnight mass, and then they come home singing 'O Holy Night.' Mother and Father tuck their kids into bed with visions of sugar-plums dancing in their heads, then go to the kitchen to make Martinis while they wrap presents and trim the tree. The next morning the kids scramble down the stairs to see what Santa left them, after which they all go out to a movie followed by Chinese food."

"That's a great idea!" Castle perked up. "And inside the fortune cookies is a message that says 'What? You've only seen *Stalking Santa* once?'" I tell you, word-of-mouth is what sells pictures."

"Bullshit," Levine growled. "Word-of-mouth is what kills pictures. In and out is what I say. If I have the right ad campaign I can sell a ham dinner to Hadassah. Our industry is the only racket where they pay their bucks up front and can't get a refund if they don't like the product. In and out, that's my style. As long as it has sprocket holes you can saturate it in as many theatres as you can and advertise the shit out of it. Buy a gross. People will see anything if you sell it to 'em right. Look at boil-in-the-bag rice. What a stupid product. Who needs that? Same with pictures. By the time word gets around that it's a turkey, you're counting your money."

"What about the critics?" Castle said.

"No problem," Levine shrugged. "Just put a freeze frame on the end. They'll call it art and write about it forever."

"Is this the kind of Christmas picture we want?" Selznick said. "In and out?"

"Hey, if it's good enough for Santa Claus, it's good enough for me," Levine said. "Why do you think Santa splits right after he leaves the presents? Have you seen some of the shit that passes for toys these days? It's all made in China."

"China, huh?" Castle mused. "Maybe we can do a Chinese Christmas picture," he said. "Jackie Chan as *Samurai Santa*."

"Samurais are Japanese," Selznick corrected.

"So he converts."

Goldwyn got up from the pinochle table and started pacing. He walked with his arms folded, tapped his index finger against his biceps, and muttered, "Maybe if we turned Christmas inside out." The others stopped talking. "You know how they reverse the point of view these days, like telling *The Wizard of Oz* from the witch's angle? What about *A Christmas Carol* from the point of view of the three ghosts?"

"I already did that in *13 Ghosts*," Castle said, "with a ghost viewer. Red if you wanted to see them, blue if you didn't. Of course, nobody used the blue."

"Okay, then," Goldwyn shifted, "how about the nativity from the point of view of the innkeeper who turned Mary and Joseph away?"

"The anti-Semite?" Selznick said. "Zanuck al-ready made *Gentleman's Agreement*."

Goldwyn was undaunted. "What if we set Christmas in outer space?"

"Somebody already did that, too, and I handled it," Levine snorted. "Didn't you see *Santa Claus Conquers the Martians*?"

"We're getting off track," Selznick said assertively. "In the entire history of show business, nobody does Christmas like the Jews. Who writes the best Christmas songs? Jews. Who makes the best Christmas movies? Jews. Who runs the best toy stores? Jews. We don't even take the day off so all the goyum can come and see us perform. What do you say to that?"

Goldwyn clucked his tongue. "It's too Jewish."

"You sound like L.B.," Levine chided him, knowing that Goldwyn and Louis B. Mayer were still at odds.

"Don't start," Sam said. "Louis always had a thing against Jews on screen."

"Can we please stay away from religion?" Castle said. "Half the audience still thinks we crucified Christ. Let's stick to snowmen, reindeer, trees, and holly."

All four men fell silent. Finally, Goldwyn said, "Maybe if we made a Christmas picture and released it in Easter we'd have the next eight months to play it off."

"How hard can it be?" Selznick said in frustration. "Hollywood makes 500 pictures a year. Why can't we find one that says Peace on Earth, good will toward men, love thy neighbor..."

"My neighbor's an asshole," Levine grumbled. "He puts up his damn Christmas lights the day after Thanksgiving and leaves them through Valentine's day, f'r'Chrissake. People come from all over just to drive past his house. All night long we got horns, rubberneckers, noise –"

"We're getting off subject," said Selznick. "What are the elements of a good Christmas picture?"

"Well," inhaled Castle, "you got your trees, you got your toys, your angels, sleds, eggnog, you got Santa Claus coming down the chimney, you got the kids staying up late to see him, you got a killer on the loose who breaks into houses through the chimney, his glowing yellow eyes shining through the soot covering his horribly burned face. . ."

"Whoa, dial it down a little," Goldwyn said. "This isn't *The Christmas Killer*, it's got to be warm and fuzzy."

"Okay, you're right," Castle said, sending clouds of smoke up from his trademark cigar. "Only he's not burned, he's fuzzy – furry from head to food. He's an evil elf that turns into a werewolf one night a year and the only way to stop him is you have to keep a fire going in the fireplace. The gimmick is that we give away red and green werewolf candles."

"Get a grip, Bill," Selznick said as calmly as he could manage as his Dexedrine kicked in. "Millions of people love Christmas. It's based on a best-selling book."

Goldwyn straightened. "I have a great idea," he said, "It's so good, even I like it. It's Christmas day. An elf comes back to Santaland from his delivery duties. He's tired. He hasn't seen Mrs. Elf and the little elflings. He wonders if Santa has held his job open. He's had experiences in real life and he has trouble relating to his family. His fellow elves who've had the same experiences also can't relate to their families."

"What are you giving us, Sam," geshried Selznick, "*The Best Years of Our Lives* at the North Pole?"

"We're making this much too complicated," Levine said. "The story of Christ is the greatest ever told. I see it now. Jesus is chased all over the Holy Land by Roman legions. He's just wearing sandals and a simple cloth robe but the soldiers are all decked out in armor and leather and they carry swords. We can shoot it in Italy for a song, do it in Italian, and dub it later into any language we want."

Goldwyn and Castle groaned. Selznick held out his hand and calmed the table. "How about Santa Claus takes to the radio to announce that he's calling off Christmas this year because the world's gone to hell, but a little girl's belief in him saves the day?" "That's beautiful," Castle said, wiping away a tear (although it might have been ash). "It's pure and uplifting. What about if the reason Santa did it is that he's possessed by Satan and he wants little Rosemary to carry his spawn?"

"You're not listening to me," Levine grumbled. "This isn't *Rosemary's Baby* with mistletoe. We're not in the gimmick business, we're in show business. I've produced two hundred films and I never had to give anything away to get people to see them."

"I know your track record, Joe," Castle snapped back. "Did you ever even watch half the dreck you produced? I mean, 'presented'?"

"Bill, you're running amok," Selznick said, trying to calm him. "Let's get back on track. I know literature. Charles Dickens wrote a slew of Christmas stories besides *A Christmas Carol.*' There's a gem called *The Cricket on the Hearth...*"

"He better not be named Jiminy,' Levine said, 'or Disney will sue his insect ass.'

"Dickens is public domain,' Selznick continued. "It has everything: a miser, a toymaker, a missing son, a bittersweet love story, and a happy if ironic ending."

"Which one is the cricket?" Levine asked.

"None of them," Selznick said proudly. "He just sits on the hearth and watches everyone else."

This excited Castle. "We could make the cricket CGI. Maybe we can give away miniature crickets. Or maybe those clickers. Yeah, those little metal things you press with your thumb and everybody says it sounds like a cricket but everybody knows it doesn't."

"We're not getting anywhere," Goldwyn proclaimed. "Maybe we should get a bite to eat, relax, and something will come. Who could eat?"

"For some reason I'm not hungry," said Selznick, popping another Dexedrine.

"My sawbones says I gotta lay off the salt and fat," said Levine. "I haven't had Chinese in a while. Anybody know a good place?"

"There's a new joint on Pico in the Orthodox neighborhood," Castle said. "It's called Sum Dum Goy. They have a luncheon buffet."

"Oh, that's just a gimmick," Levine said. Castle wasn't amused at the dig.

"Still," Goldwyn said, "I think something productive might come out of this meeting. I just hope we can remember it."

"Don't worry," Selznick said, putting on his coat. "I'll send around a memo."

HERSCHEL THE HORRIBLE

Herschel Wechsler was like something that comes out of your nose. Most independent producers who strike it big at least make an effort to distance themselves from their bottom-feeding beginnings. Not Herschel. It wasn't that expensive suits hung on his doughy frame as though he'd slept in them. It didn't matter that he sprayed spittle when he talked. Nobody even held his fly-shit toupee against him. It was that he had the kind of face you just wanted to push into the front of a 1958 Buick.

Hollywood has known its share of monsters with good taste. Joseph E. Levine, Harvey Weinstein, Joel Silver, Scott Rudin, and Otto Preminger readily come to mind. Okay, maybe not Otto Preminger. But the others possessed that rare combination of passion, guts, showmanship, charisma, and intelligence that dignified them and their productions despite the controversy they often courted as people.

But Hershel Wechsler was irredeemable. He was such a scoundrel that you didn't even have to use his last name. Whenever you said "Hershel" everybody knew who you meant. Sure, his pictures made money, and you'd think that alone would absolve him of the town's enmity, except he managed to do it in the one way that Hollywood found unacceptable. He did it at the expense of the motion picture industry's dignity. As more than one of his competitors–they bristled if they were ever called "colleagues"–remarked, Herschel always found a way to scrape underneath the bottom of the barrel.

When it came to the time-honored tradition of movie ballyhoo, Herschel knew no shame. His first great success was *While You Were with the Sirens*, a sword-and-sandals import starring a female bodybuilder as Penelope, the wife of Odysseus, who stalls the suitors awaiting his return by taking them to bed in various prime numbers while their son, Telemachus, filled in the blanks. Advertising it as "*Last Tango in Paris* Goes Greek," Herschel was rapped on the knuckles by the MPAA for self-applying "Rated LXIX" to the picture. It cleaned up. He followed it with *Wacky Gulag*, a grim Russian prison camp drama that he hired a popular comedian to dub with irreverent jokes. This time it wasn't just the MPAA, it was Amnesty International that picketed. They never picket. This time they did. The publicity helped it make a fortune.

Eventually even turds want class. Herschel thought he could earn it through charitable work and had his publicist wangle him the Chairmanship of GOA (Guardians of Animals). That lasted until an animal rights activist sneaked onto his Yugoslavian location for *Spy Kittens* and brought back video of cats being tossed through blazing hoops. "They all landed safely in water, didn't they?" Herschel told the press, but the damage was done.

Herschel might have survived the embarrassment if, first, he had the capacity to be embarrassed, and, second, if he hadn't tried for the golden ring. But his craving for respectability spurred him onward, and he set his sights on Hollywood's greatest honor, the Academy Award.® That pitted him against Establishment producers who simply passed the Oscar back and forth year by year like a golden fruitcake among entrenched members of a private club protecting their hegemony.

The Academy of Motion Picture Arts and Sciences® has inviolable rules covering what you can and can't do to go after one of their awards, chief among them being that you have to achieve outstanding merit in your professional field. Over the years, standards have been established to prevent those breaches of propriety that had sullied earlier Oscar races such as boastful billboards, planting fawning newspaper stories, and similar puffery. All of it was designed to preserve the integrity of the awards and the motion picture industry. By the time Herschel thirsted after Oscar, the Academy's ethical standards were so restrictive that it would take the law firm of Findem, Fukkem, and Forgettem to see the loopholes in the award procedures. So Herschel tested them by starting small: in 1995 he managed to win the "Best Original Song" Oscar for "Look at My Id" from the film *Freud: A Musical Analysis*. It was so banal that in fifteen years it never turned up even in dental offices. Nobody would have cared except Herschel bragged that he had "bought" it by sending a DVD to every Academy member in the days when DVDs were new, and he threw in a DVD player in case the recipient didn't have one yet.

In 2002 he held champagne brunches for *L'artiste Silencieux*, a French drama about a mime that he distributed in black and white (it had been produced in color), replaced the dialogue with subtitles (it had been shot with sound), and positioned as the foreign language art film of the year (despite being silent). When word leaked out about his chicanery, instead of admitting anything, he doubled down by announcing, "you missed the flash-frames of all the genitals." Within 48 hours the DVD went platinum.

His most subtle ruse was purposely misspelling the phrase *For Your Consideration* as *For Your Consternation* for the Academy campaign for the rom-com *To Whom It May Concern*. For the price of a single, one-page display ad in the Trades, he got a week's worth of free publicity wondering whether the error was deliberate.

What enraged the moguls in the executive suites of competing film companies wasn't that Wechsler outdid them in ballyhoo – secretly they marveled at his chutzpah – it was that he was so blatant, even gleeful, about his ability to bamboozle the industry. The shovel that broke their backs was when Wechsler went around Hillcrest Country Club proclaiming that he was going to win the Oscar® for *The Irish Doctor*.

Shot in Morocco with an English cast, an American script, and a Chinese director, *The Irish Doctor* was an endlessly pretentious story about a mysterious medic whose life flashes in front of him while he dies following a car crash. Herschel hit upon an advertising campaign that crossed over from the art houses to the multiplex market by convincing middle America that they could be enriched by seeing it when, in fact, they were just being bored. Over Hillcrest's matzo brei and lox, Herschel made the mistake of boasting that he could pull the same trick on enough Academy members to give him Best Picture.

"Everybody's onto your schemes," lectured Johnny Armstrong of Sony Classics. "The lunches, the tchotchkes, the home visits by your stars, even sending your poor assistant to fetch people's laundry. If you've got an Oscar-worthy picture it'll sell itself to the voters."

"Oh yeah?" Herschel said between spittles, "What about *Doctor Dolittle* back in 1968? Best picture against *Bonnie and Clyde*, *In the Heat of the Night*, *The Graduate* and *Guess Who's Coming to Dinner*? In a year with *Point Blank*, *Two for the Road* and *In Cold Blood* in it?"

"Those were the old days when studio employees voted as a bloc," said Mel Landis of Fox. "How do you think we got *The Towering Inferno* up there in '74 opposite *Chinatown*, *The Conversation*, *The Godfather, Part II* and *Lenny*? And *A Woman Under the Influence*, *Blazing Saddles* and *Young Frankenstein* got shut out. People want to protect their jobs."

"Those days are over," Herschel agreed. "Independent guys like me now have a chance, and I'm not gonna blow it. Mark my words: *The Irish Doctor* is gonna win the big one or my name isn't Harry Walters."

"But your name *isn't* Harry Walters," Johnny Jacobson of Paramount said. "It's Herschel Wechsler."

"I'm changing it after I win the Oscar," Herschel shot back, "Like S.P. Eagle became Sam Spiegel. I'm going to stage an Academy campaign that'll make Sherman's march to the sea look like a sightseeing trip." With that, he stood from the table, brushed matzo brei off his Hawaiian shirt, and left.

When he was safely gone and the waiter had hosed down the spot where he'd been sitting, Jacobson turned to Landis. "He may have a point. No matter how many screeners we send out or showings we host, people vote not only their likes and dislikes but what they think is best for the industry. He's barely spending a dime while we're going broke fighting the free press coverage for his stunts."

"I don't see how we can get around the rules," Armstrong shook his head. "There's a certain leeway to get nominated, but after that you can't even serve food at screenings. I've heard people joke that if they give you a free lunch, you have to throw up on the way to your car."

"How the hell does he plan on doing it?" Landis said. "The Academy ought to disqualify him."

"We'll find out when *The Irish Doctor* gets nominated," Armstrong said. "And I mean 'when' because I have no doubt that he'll buy enough ads to get that pretentious piece of shit into the running now that there's ten slots."

"Do we draw straws for which of us files a complaint with the Board of Governors?" Jacobson asked with a gleam in his eye.

"No," Armstrong said. "Knocking him on the ropes for one picture won't do the job. The man is a greasy spot on the industry. He enters the room by oozing under the door. We have to kayo the sonofabitch forever. Whatever it takes, we must out-Herschel Wechsler Herschel Wechsler. And not get caught."

Having thus called a peremptory strike, Armstrong, Landis, and Jacobson charged their own lunches as well as each other's to the budgets of all of their studios' current releases, and left the club.

Meanwhile, Herschel Wechsler was already at work jamming *The Irish Doctor* down the Academy's throats. The first "For Your Consideration" ad in the trades–double-truck, of course–said, "What? You've only seen *The Irish Doctor* once?" and listed nightly screenings all across LA and the Valley where Academy members and their families could attend for free–with complimentary refreshments, of course. He also made arrangements with theatre managers to allow the voters' kids to sneak into any other movie in the multiplex, creating a sense of obligation on the part of the Academy member. But it was when he sent out bottles of Jameson's Irish Whiskey that the calls started coming in, many of them from people in recovery programs who resented his effrontery. This, naturally, garnered free publicity in the mainstream press. Rather than apologize, Herschel announced an "Irish Doctor Cocktail" consisting of a shot of Irish whiskey and a dash of bitters served over ice with a lollipop instead of a stirring straw (because doctors always give kids lollipops after a shot). They were an instant sensation at barrooms everywhere.

Back at Hillcrest there was an emergency meeting. This time Jacobson, Landis, and Armstrong were joined by Lew Friedrich, Fred Sumpter, and Carl Blandings of Warners, Universal, and Disney. "Talk about bad taste," Blandings began, "wasn't it Herschel who proposed *The Day the Clown Cried* action figures?"

"We all know Herschel's excesses," said Sumpter definitively. As the grand old man of the industry, everyone deferred to him. "And let's face it, there have been times when we've come fearfully close to his tactics as we tried to save some of our own stiffs." He looked at Friedrich. "I still remember how you gave out paperweights with real bullshit in them to promote *Home on the Range*." He looked at Jacobson. "My kids still talk about the cheesecloth condoms you sent to the press to get attention for *Baby Maybe*." He saved his coldest gaze for Armstrong. "And aren't you still paying civic fines for running a monkey for the Santa Monica School Board to plug *Teacher's Pest*, convincing the liberal voters to support him because he's a Simian-American?"

"We've all sinned," Armstrong waved dismissively, "but those were only against the public. They expect us to pick their pockets. Herschel Wechsler is a pimple on the ass of the entire motion picture industry."

"We know we can't beat him at his own game," Friedrich said, "because he makes up new rules as he goes along."

"Then find a way to make him overplay his hand," Sumpter declared. "Make him do something so crass he'll get his brouhaha caught in the wringer. Nobody leaves this table until we find a way to neutralize Herschel Wechsler."

It took an hour and a half but Armstrong's idea was so brilliant that, later, three people would claim credit for it: tell Herschel Wechsler he's nominated for the Jean Hersholt Humanitarian Award®.

"Are you out of your effing mind?" was Landis's reaction. "Herschel likes people the way a cannibal does. The Academy voters'd never go for it."

"They don't have to," Armstrong said. "The Hersholt is voted by the Board of Governors."

"That's even tougher," Friedrich said. "The last thing they want is controversy."

"Oh yeah?" Armstrong was ready. "They gave a career Oscar to Kazan, didn't they?" The table fell silent. "Here's what we do. We tell Herschel there's a move to get him nominated. The rules don't apply to the special awards. He'll be so fired up that he'll take his mind off *The Irish Doctor* and press his own self-destruct button."

Sumpter had not yet reacted and his stillness finally drew the others' attentions. "I'm on the Board of Governors," he said solemnly. "We cannot be lobbied."

"You mis-heard me," Armstrong said respectfully. "I said we tell *Herschel* that he's nominated but we don't tell the Board of Governors. He'll go crazy trying to chase it down."

"What if he calls one of you and asks?" Landis said to Sumpter.

"All of our deliberations are secret," the elder statesman said proudly, a smile starting to un-freeze the corners of his mouth. "Compared to the Academy, a Grand Jury meets in Madison Square Garden."

Knowing that Herschel wouldn't trust the news from any of the executives, Armstrong leaked it to the Trades and let them start the rumor by calling Wechsler's office. Naturally he was surprised, naturally he was honored, and naturally he was hooked. The first ad appeared 48 hours later: "I want to thank the Academy," signed "Herschel Wechsler." That's all. Nice and vague, and yet it sent word throughout Hollywood that his name was in play for something. But for what? Knowing that Herschel couldn't keep a secret, the press descended.

"Can't a fellow thank the Academy out of the blue if he wants to?" he said often enough that he almost managed to sound genuine instead of coy. "Sure, *The Irish Doctor* is eligible for Best Picture, but there's more to it. I love the Academy. They do good stuff. Why shouldn't I honor them?"

The press, having been burned more than once by Herschel's stunts, remained skeptical. "Are you in the running for some award?" one reporter asked. Herschel tried to be cagey. "I'm glad you asked that," he began. "I'd love to be considered for a major award given how much I've enriched the industry. Just having my name in front of them is an honor enough."

It was that last sentence that bit him. "The Academy does not comment on its Governors awards procedure," Fred Sumpter announced tersely, adding that he could neither confirm nor deny that Herschel was being considered. That only further whetted Herschel's desire. When the picture nominations were announced a week later, Herschel was so consumed with his personal lobbying that he paid scant attention to the Academy campaign for *The Irish Doctor*. The picture languished.

"The Academy honors the industry and Herschel Wechsler honors the Academy," his next two-page ad read. This time the showbiz columnists joined the press in asking that was behind Herschel's scheme.

"It's no scheme," the producer insisted. "People watch the Oscars and the special awards and forget about the Academy the other 364 days of the year. I looked it up. They also have a library, they preserve film, they hold screenings and seminars, and do community outreach. I look forward to a closer association."

This time the Academy's silence was broken by others who joined the conversation with appropriate outrage. The Trades, who had no trouble accepting the ads, explained that they generally cut Herschel a lot of slack because he always made such good copy. The *Los Angeles Times* editorialized about Herschel's self-aggrandizement in the face of neither evidence not logic nor reason. And the Hollywood Foreign Press announced that there were not enough goody bags on all of Canon Drive for Herschel to buy their DeMille Award.

The final blow was struck by the Los Angeles Critics Circle that devised a one-time-only Emperor's New Clothes Award for *The Irish Doctor*. They took one of the faux Oscar statuettes sold in Hollywood Boulevard souvenir stores, wrapped it in gauze, stuck a thermometer up its ass and promised it to Herschel if he'd have the guts to accept it in person at their awards dinner.

But it was when Academy members began returning *The Irish Doctor* screeners broken in two and dumping out of the film's streaming downloads halfway through that Herschel started to believe the blowback whispers. The clincher was the MPAA's anti-piracy division informing him that none of the illegal file-sharing sites wanted his film. After that, when the Academy announced its official recipients of the Thalberg, Sawyer, Hersholt, and other Governors awards omitting him, Herschel knew he had gone too far (when, in fact, he had never been going at all). When the Oscars were handed out, his office said that he was vacationing in shame at an undisclosed foreign location. *The Irish Doctor*, though nominated for seven awards, lost in every category.

At the Governors Ball after the telecast, the six men who had engineered Herschel's self-defeat–Armstrong, Landis, Friedrich, Jacobson, Blandings, and Sumpter–toasted each other.

"Oddly enough," Johnny Armstrong said, "I kind of liked the guy. At least he was colorful, not like the Harvard-type 27-year-old Jasons who run things today with no sense of style or history."

"You're not getting soft, are you, Johnny?" Mel Landis said.

"Not on your life," Armstrong countered. "Our industry was built on ballyhoo, but we always delivered the goods. Herschel was all ballyhoo and no goods." With that said, each of them carried his drink through the maze of celebrants to rejoin his own party at their tables. Each was surprised to find a beautifully wrapped gift at his place setting. Nobody else at the table had one. "A waiter brought that here especially for you," Jacobson's wife said. "He just put it there and left."

"How odd," Jacobson half-mumbled, taking out the card. As he read it, the color drained from his face. His wife took it gently out of his hands and looked at it blankly. "What does, 'I want to thank you instead of the Academy' mean?" she said. "And who is Harry Walters?"

GROUP MARVELOUS

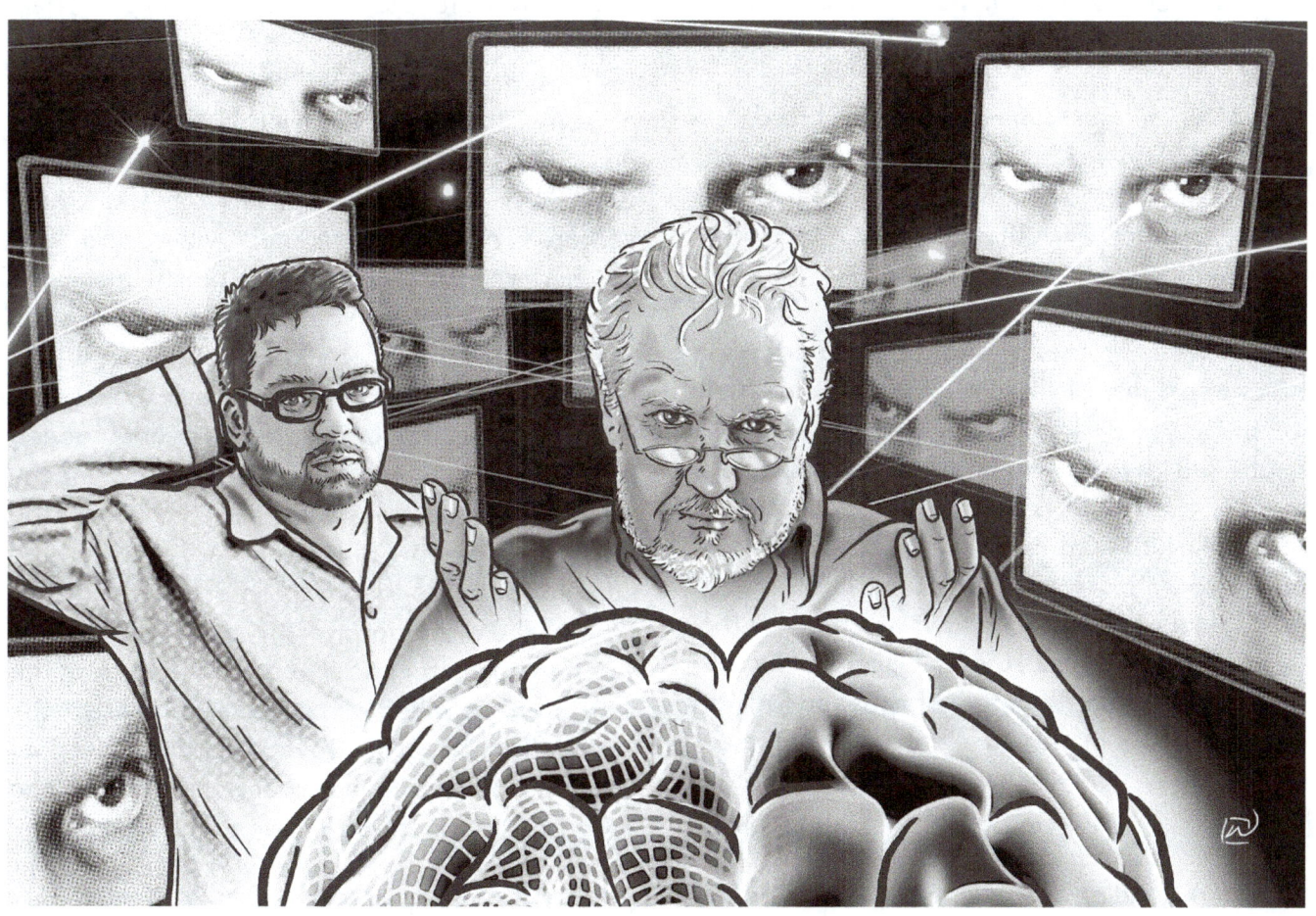

**You and a Guest are cordially invited to
Celebrate the acquisition of
Matheson Broadcasting Corporation
by
Collective Investment Systems, Inc.
On Friday, April 30, 1999
at the
Hornet's Nest Lounge, Hotel Bickford
Philadelphia
7:30 to Midnight
R.S.V.P. Dick Blasingame, x230**

All these years later I can't bring myself to throw away my invitation to the party celebrating the sale of the TV station where I'd given thirty years of my life. The party–and what happened that night–was sixteen years, eleven months, and five days ago. But who's counting?

Working for Group M–Matheson Broadcasting Corporation–was harder than it needed to be. The job itself wasn't bad, it was the way they treated you. They used the "management by fear" philosophy: rather than compliment you for work well done, they made you feel thankful at the end of every day that you hadn't been fired. For example, they would take out blind "help wanted" ads in *Broadcasting* magazine to trap employees who were sending out resumes. If they found that one of their workers was looking to change jobs, they would summon him to personnel and say, "If you're not happy here, you can quit."

They recruited the most talented people and then ignored them. When there was about to be a baseball players strike, they assigned Greg Dwinell, the sports reporter on the 6 and 11, to go out and find an expert to interview. When Greg reminded the News Director, "Hey, I'm an expert, that's why you hired me," they told him, "Yeah, but you work for us. We want a *real* expert." Talk about irony.

If you worked at Group M, you needed a sense of irony. That's why we called it "Group Marvelous." Our station, WPHY-TV in Philadelphia, was Group M's flagship outlet. Every day was an adventure. The level of paranoia was so high that you daren't ever turn your back on anyone; if you wanted a promotion, you had to stab your competitor in the front. The company medical plan had a special provision for psychiatric counseling because, well, sooner or later everyone needed it. There was even a rumor that the company went through ashtrays and trash cans to test the saliva on cigarette butts and cardboard coffee cups for diseases that might interfere with work. One of the more noteworthy corporate gambits was a memo categorically banning the use of the word *foreign*, which was considered divisive; the word *international* had to be substituted. First infractions for using "the 'F' word," as it came to be called, were a write-up. Subsequent uses engendered a $25 fine, then a $100 fine, then dismissal. Only when the memo was leaked to the press were the penalties removed, but abuses still went into people's personnel files. ("Oh, I have some international matter in my eye," became the standard joke.)

But the most insidious management technique was in full force at company parties like the one at the Hotel Bickford. Believing in *in vino veritas*, the executives made it a point to stick to ginger ale (which looked like Scotch and soda) themselves at company bashes while encouraging the employees to get drunk. Most of us knew about the trick, which you ignored at your peril.

Group Marvelous had come about through the grit and luck of George Kidwell Matheson, an electronics engineer who discovered how to safely build heating coils into metal cookware. When America was being wired for electricity during the New Deal, his Matheson Griddle and Waffle Maker took the country by storm. From there he expanded into toasters, washers, light bulbs, electric blankets, and other household appliances. The slogan "You Can Be Happy If It's Matheson" became a national mantra. In the late 1950s, after grousing at the size of his TV advertising bills, he decided to get into broadcasting so he could run his own ads for free and overcharge his competitors to run theirs. Group M soon had stations in five major cities. Each was affiliated with a different network and Matheson was a genius at playing ABC, NBC, and CBS against each other, even daring to pre-empt their programming for local events such as sports, telethons, and prime-time specials. George showed just enough public service spirit to deflect attention from the fact that everybody who worked for him thought he was a shit.

When, in 1999, George tired of television, he wangled a merger with Collective Investment Systems. He left his legacy at WPHY: Dick Blasingame.

As General Manager, Blasingame was the perfect TV executive. When he said Yes he meant Maybe and when he said Maybe he meant No. We called him the foam rubber brick wall. He was not the fastest arrow in the quiver; I once pitched him a special about NASA and the United States space program. His only comment was, "You forgot to explain who Neil Armstrong is. I don't know him and neither will our audience."

It was in this corporate atmosphere of support, cooperation, bonhomie, and irony that the April 30, 1999 party took place. The date, it occurred to me later, was Walpurgis Night, otherwise known as Witches Sabbath, an Old Country tradition when the dead rise in search of souls. Not a bad metaphor for television, eh? Typically, we had learned of the acquisition by reading it in the paper, not from our own company. And so, like high school seniors in that limbo between the end of finals and graduation day, we began the evening hoping for a bright future while worrying whether we would survive getting there.

Just to be safe, I didn't bring my wife, and I was surprised that most of my co-workers also came stag. It was as if we expected combat.

Charlie Ryder staked out his territory at the buffet where he had already vetted the anonymous entrees. "Like airplane food, when in doubt, go with the chicken," he told me. "As long as you can figure out which is the chicken."

I ignored him. "What do you hear?" I asked.

"Some people see the glass as half-full," he said. "Others see it as half-empty."

'How do you see it?" I probed.

"This is Group Marvelous. It's a dribble glass."

I liked Charlie. He ran the station's film library which, in those pre-digital days, was 16mm. When a print came in, he would screen it, put bleeping tape over the profanity, and decide where the commercials would go. He's respected now, but when he began at WPHY in the 1960s he became famous for cutting "Rosebud" out of *Citizen Kane* so he could cram it into a two-hour time slot. The only reason they didn't fire him was that he knew movies better than anybody and loved working late. He never married.

"I have a feeling the party's over," Charlie said. "You can tell by the buffet. They're already cutting back."

Art Crankshaw, one of the studio camera operators, nodded in agreement. "Before the sale we were corporate, but at least we were local. Now we're going to be run by people who've never been to Philly and the only hoagie they've ever heard of is Carmichael."

"Over at Channel 5 they give out bonuses" Charlie said. "Here they give out pink slips. At Channel 5 they never fire anybody."

"No," I said, "but they got rid of Karl Flanderson anyway."

"Karl who?"

"Karl Flanderson, the worst floor director in Philadelphia history. Dumb as a bag of doorknobs. He was so slow cueing talent that the whole news anchor team looked like Bambi in the headlights waiting for his signal. But they couldn't fire him because of affirmative action."

"Then how did they get rid of him?" Charlie asked. Art looked at me knowingly.

"They made him director of the year," I said, "and took out newspaper ads praising him. The next day he got a job offer from NBC. The network hired him away"

"Genius," Charlie said.

Art laughed at a private memory, then shared it. "Does everybody remember the Brent Major Memorial Piss?"

I did but Charlie had missed it.

"First day we got those new wireless microphones," Art chuckled, "Brent does a standup in front of the police station. When we cut back to the studio, he excuses himself to go inside and use their bathroom. But he forgets to turn off his transmitter, so we hear him go in and we roll tape." He paused for effect and snared a stuffed mushroom off a passing tray. "I think he was pretty cool about it when it turned up in the Christmas party joy reel. Blasingame loved it so Brent had to go along."

"Was Brent Major really as stupid as they say?" This from Melanie Sibeski, the community outreach manager, who heard us and sidled over.

"Worse," I said. "The kind of guy you'd send to the hardware store for a left-handed monkey wrench. But you wouldn't do it because he was also the nicest guy in the world."

"The nicest guy in the world who earned two

million a year to sit there and read news he didn't understand," chimed in Brenda Ross from payroll. "I know because I cut him his paychecks. And he was sexy, too. Women would mail him their panties and house keys with notes saying when their husbands would be out of town."

"Did he ever take 'em up on it?" Melanie asked.

"Never," Charlie and Brenda said together. Added Brenda, "he was as square as they come. And like I said, a super nice guy and happily married."

"Tell 'em about the colored paper," Art prodded.

"Oh, that," Brenda grinned. "Absolutely true. I saw it. When they typed his scripts, they would put the happy stories on green paper, the sad stories on blue paper, and the violent stories on pink paper. That way, Brent would know whether to make a happy face, a sad face, or a concerned face."

"What's he doing now?" Melanie asked.

"He and the missus moved to Texas and he's raising horses," Brenda said. "When he left, he told me, 'Time to get off the needle.'"

"I didn't know he was a drug addict," I said.

"He wasn't," Art said. "He was a fame addict. But he got over it."

Across the room, laughter interrupted our reminiscences. Dick Blasingame and his sales staff were enjoying a private joke. Sure enough, they were drinking ginger ale. As if drawn by the same magnet, we all stared at them.

"Dick's a survivor," Charlie said. "You remember *Moon and Teeth*?" More head shakes.

"*Moon and Teeth*," Charlie savored the words, "is probably the most notorious triple-X porno film since *Deep Throat*. It's set on Noah's Ark–is anybody still eating?–and none of the cast goes to waste."

Brenda blushed and excused herself. Melanie stayed to listen. This symbolized the difference between the payroll and community outreach departments.

Charlie continued. "This was in the days when TV stations signed off the air at 2 AM with the Star-Spangled Banner while the overnight crew stayed on duty to maintain the pre-solid-state equipment. One night, Blasingame brought in a hot 16mm print of *Moon and Teeth* and threaded it on the film chain."

"Wasn't that risky?"

"The station was off the air. But the transmitter was still on. You never want to touch the button that sends the signal out."

"You wouldn't be telling this unless –."

"Bingo," Charlie said, "Only it wasn't Dick Blasingame. It was some unnamed engineer who hated Dick Blasingame because Dick Blasingame was being, well, being his first name. And presto, *Moon and Teeth* goes out to the fifteenth largest market in the country. But wait. That's not the news. The news is that, while it's running, the phone doesn't ring even once. Then, when it's over, the phones light up."

"I bet hell broke loose," Melanie said.

"No," Charlie marveled. "Everybody who called just wanted to confirm that they had really seen it. Nobody ever said a word to the FCC or the newspapers. Even the other stations didn't report on it; I guess their night crews were watching it, too. Blasingame just took the print and gave it back where he got it. Case closed."

"That is what I call luck," Art said. "Some people just have the sun shining out their ass."

With that, at the front of the lounge, Blasingame tapped the side of his glass to bring the room to silence. "I just got news from Valhalla," he began, air-toasting the home office. "As part of the CIS acquisition of Group M, I'm moving to New York to be the new Vice President of Programming."

Applause. Cautious, be-careful-what-you-wish applause, but applause nonetheless.

"This is a great move for me because I'm from New York and I miss the pizza. Meanwhile, I'm pleased to announce that I have personally hired a remarkable man to replace me. He comes with the very highest recommendations. In fact, used to work here as a floor director, and he rose through the ranks, always being hired away by one station after another, and now we have him for a five-year-contract. Many of you may already know him. Karl Flanderson." In the silence that followed, somebody dropped a pan in the kitchen. Or maybe it was a bag of doorknobs.

"Tomorrow is now today at WPHY," Blasingame continued. He stopped speaking, and there followed the kind of silence you hear at a grammar school Easter pageant when parents aren't sure if the play is over yet or if the kids have just forgotten their lines.

Flanderson spoke. "I'm happy to be back," he began. "I always considered WPHY my home, and I'm thrilled that so many of you are still here. I know what you're all thinking and I first want to say that no one is going to be fired or pushed out, and that I intend to pick up where I left off."

Within two weeks, a procession of us were summoned to the personnel office to be asked if we were happy here. Ironically (there's that word again), among the first to quit was the personnel director. I held out until I landed an assistant professorship at Temple. My courses included writing for television and philosophy of management.

Just after I started teaching, I bumped into Dick Blasingame at a university reception following a broadcasting seminar. I introduced him to the Dean of Faculty who, it turned out, had worked at Group M several years before Dick arrived there. Dick asked me how I liked academia. I said it was just like television, only without the stupidity.

"Give it time," said the Dean, sipping his ginger ale.

PART III:
SWEET REVENGE

It is often said that everybody has two professions: whatever they do for a living, plus being a film critic. The major difference is that, if you do something for a living, you need to know what you're doing, whereas any damn fool can write a review (a notion furthered by the metastasizing of film criticism thanks to social media). True film critics have studied the medium, know its history, have seen uncountable numbers of films, and have a facility for expressing their well-thought-out opinions in language that consumers can understand. It isn't easy, but that doesn't stop people from doing it.

"Critical Thinking" is an example of the love-hate nature of film criticism. It's a frustrating profession. Critics do not create, they react. This frustration sometimes makes them provocateurs; in fact, there actually was a troublesome critic who rubbed a powerful exhibitor the wrong way but, when the exhibitor tried to neutralize her, he accidentally made her into a star.

The story that causes dropped jaws, however, is "The Curious Case of 'Rapture in Rimini.'" It's really two stories, one, the efforts of a creative publicist to outwit the censors and open the country's hottest film without getting everyone arrested for pornography; and, two, bribing a major critic to help the process by pandering to her ego. The theme of revenge doesn't just run through the story, it is the story.

They say that survival is the best revenge, and if that's the case, you have to hand it to Bernie Saffran, the hero of "Age of Anxiety" and its sequel, "Bernie Beats the Grey List." Writers are the shit-ons of the film industry. Nobody works until they've done their job, and yet the moment they turn in their script they are deemed unnecessary. When you're a writer and you turn 41 in Hollywood, you're considered passé by a town that wants to attract youth dollars and thinks that only young writers know how to make it happen. The irony is that just when you get good at something, they won't let you do it anymore. Bernie managed to game the system the same way blacklisted writers did during the 40s and 50s; he partnered with a front, a younger man who fit the image. Then he got lucky, and he used that luck to help other over-40s re-enter the business. Maybe it's wish fulfillment more than revenge, but the wisdom that threads through both "Age of Anxiety" and "Bernie Beats the Grey List" is worth considering, especially by people who plan on reaching middle age and want to hold onto their careers.

Contrary to the widely held belief, revenge is not a dish that is best served up cold. Rather, it's a dish that is best jammed down the throat of the person who has wronged you. Keep reading.

CRITICAL THINKING

Jensen Hirsch had the second most dangerous job on the newspaper. He was the film critic. If he'd held the most dangerous job, war correspondent, he might have at least got some respect. But film criticism, as *New Yorker* editor Harold Ross once told Nunnally Johnson, "was for old ladies and fairies," and Jensen Hirsch was neither.

"Look at it this way," Hirsch liked to say whenever anyone dismissed his job as cushy, "a film critic is the only person on a newspaper, magazine, television, radio station, or website whose job is to criticize an advertiser. Sports writers, political columnists, and beat reporters can say what they want and nobody can ever do anything about it because those folks don't advertise. But God help the journalist who takes on supermarkets, car dealerships, furniture stores, real estate, or movies."

Damn it, he was right. Film and theatre criticism is almost an S&M relationship between people who buy advertising for their shows and those who draw a salary for saying if they're worth seeing. Directors or actors might call or write him to complain, but they were always polite, cautious that that Hirsch would be reviewing what they did next. The only ones who routinely griped were theatre owners whose box office was dented by a negative Hirsch review. Even then, they were making so much on advertising kickbacks and inflated operating costs that they usually held their tongues.

Nevertheless, every now and then some angry exhibitor would call the publisher to complain and threaten to pull their advertising unless Hirsch was fired. Sometimes they even did cancel their ad buys, but they would always skulk back a few days later after the studio raised holy hell. In such cases, Hirsch's editor, Russell Pelota, would summon Hirsch and warn him that next time could be the one that got him fired.

"Do you want me to like everything?" Hirsch always said. "A critic who likes everything likes nothing."

"No," Pelota said, "But why can't you just stress the good parts and minimize the bad parts?"

"For the same reason that good news doesn't sell papers," Hirsch countered. "People buy the *Sun-Herald* to read me drag a rotten film across the coals. If I spelunk for praise of *Transformers 6* and commend it just because it has no visible splices, that's not damning with faint praise, it's praising with faint damns."

Time and again, Hirsch would quote his way out of such confrontations. He knew he was right, and he knew that Pelota knew he was right, but he also knew that Pelota was looking for a way to stop the aggravation. The only way to head it off, Hirsch figured, was to create a firestorm so huge and so obviously a threat to the *Sun-Herald*'s First Amendment freedom that Pelota would have to grow a set and support him.

There was only one man to do this: Max Pouch.

Max Pouch owned all the major cinemas in town, something like twenty of them. He was always good to write stories about because he reminded people of the colorful moguls who had founded Hollywood. But Max Pouch was an exhibitor, not a mogul. He produced nothing. All he did was show the movies that other people made and then hold onto as much of their ticket money as possible. He was brash, he was crass, and he was uneducated, but he was also successful because he entered the theatre business at just the right time. (Legend had it that he won his first theatre in a poker game when another player defaulted on a huge IOU). Before long, he came to believe that he had a God-given gift for choosing hits. That's the way he put it; "I have a God-given gift for choosing hits." The fact that Pouch Theatres played every damn movie that was released made this technically true. He even began to boast that he could tell if a movie was going to be a hit by watching only the first twenty minutes. Then fifteen. Then ten. After a while his employees joked (behind his back, of course) that he could pick a hit by looking at the film while it was still in the can.

But Max Pouch had a weak spot. He could not take personal criticism. And he spent so much money buying advertising in local media that he never had to face any.

It was on the night of the advance preview of *Simon Says*, a new frat house comedy starring the screen's "top grosser" (meaning vulgar), Bobby Krakauer, that Jensen Hirsch planned to take his best shot.

Lines formed an hour early at the Pouch Plaza twentyplex but Hirsch liked to linger in the lobby with his critic colleagues rather than go into the auditorium, confident that there was a row of prime seats reserved for them. He wanted to engage Pouch in front of people who could write about it. The moment he saw Pouch and his entourage enter, he turned his back and pretended not to know he was there.

"I hate Bobby Krakauer films," Hirsch said loudly when he knew Pouch was near. "The man literally sucks the energy out of any movie he's in."

"It's nice to know you're entering with an open mind," chided Chris Morgenroth, the studio publicist, trying to be cheerful. She knew the film was critic-proof.

"And *Simon Says* is playing exactly where it deserves to be," Hirsch continued as the Pouch party approached from the rear. "A crappy film in a theatre that deserves better. Why has Max Pouch let his flagship theatre go into the toilet? Maybe crap like this reminds him of his youth. How sad. With all his money, you think he'd show a little taste. I guess it takes one to know one."

"One what?" Pouch said from behind Hirsch. Hirsch could feel his hot breath on the back of his neck. He turned.

Max Pouch was an impressive man, the kind you wouldn't enter an elevator with if you saw he was the only one in it. A husky five-foot-ten, he had a bulldog face showing each of his sixty years, icy grey eyes that stared through you, and a cologne that wrestled with his thick cigars for aromatic dominance. He was the anti-Semite's idea of a Jewish movie mogul all the way from his cantilevered nose to his diamond pinky ring.

"'Smatter, you don't like my theatre?" he barked. He said it "thee-AY-tur." Not only did he never whisper, he never had to.

"Never mind if I do," Hirsch said. "Do you? Look what you're doing to it."

"What's your problem?" Pouch challenged.

"I don't like your taste."

Pouch considered this. "Well, tough shit," he said, "I don't like yours. Or you."

"People disagree with critics all the time," Hirsch said with clear condescension. "That's your prerogative."

"You just gotta show off with big words, don-cha?" Pouch said. "Well here's a word for you: get the fuck out of my theatre."

"You can't throw me out," Hirsch said. "The Shubert Law."

"What the hell is the Shubert Law?"

"The Shubert law says that because I'm a critic and I need to see this show to do my job, you can't bar me."

Pouch looked at Chris Morgenroth. "Is this as-shole right?"

"Yes, Mr. Pouch," she said. "Mr. Hirsch is right. You can make him buy a ticket instead of getting in for free, but you can't keep him out."

"We'll just see about that," Pouch said, calling. "Security!"

Nobody came.

"You don't have security any more," Hirsch said, tauntingly. "Just like you don't have projec-tionists. The most you've got is two scared ushers with pimples."

"No problem," Pouch grunted, and picked up Hirsch by the collar. He dragged him across the lobby, kicked open the side door, and tossed him out onto the sidewalk. "You come in here again and I'll show you what 'two thumbs up' really means." Pouch then took out his silk handker-chief, wiped the critic off his hands, and waltzed through the lobby. The other critics didn't know what do or where to look. "How's that for a five-star review?" Pouch smiled at them. "Show's over, folks. Time for the movie." They all filed inside docilely.

Predictably, the picture stank, but none of the critics had the guts to say so. Equally predictably, Pelota called Hirsch into his office the next day.

"What the hell did you pull last night?" the ed-itor brayed at Hirsch, then said, without waiting for an answer. "You picked a fight with the fifth largest advertiser in the paper, that's what you did."

"He didn't pull any of those ads, did he?" Hirsch said confidently. "I checked with Advertising on the way in."

"No, he didn't pull the advertising," Pelota con-ceded, "he pulled you instead." He gave Hirsch what looked like a handbill. "This is going up in all the box offices in every Pouch Theatre in town and he's even sending it to his competitors in the suburbs. You happy now?"

The handbill showed a photo of Jensen Hirsch with the words, "Do not let this man buy a ticket or get into this theatre."

"What about the Schubert law?" Hirsch said. "That's on my side."

"I checked. It only applies to live theatre where you can only see it in the one place. But you can catch a movie anywhere. Pouch can indeed keep you out of his theatres in this town."

"What about freedom of the press?" Hirsch asked.

"Oh, this press is free," Pelota said, opening his office door as a signal for Hirsch to leave. "But from now on your movie tickets are not. If you can't do your job any more, I'll find someone who can."

"Am I fired?"

"Not yet, but if you don't shape up and remember where your paycheck comes from, you will be. Now get out."

Hirsch went home, fed his cat, and turned on the oven, preparing to climb in. He was a film critic. What else could he do? He'd heard all the jokes about his profession: "'Critics are like eunuchs in a harem," Brendan Behan had famously said, "they know how it's done, they've seen it done every day, but they're unable to do it themselves." And from Ernest Hemingway: "Critics are men who watch the battle from a high place, then come down and shoot the survivors." He even once floated his own definition: "A critic is someone who writes about taste for people who have none." None of that mattered right now. Despondent, he went for a walk. A long walk. He got back at sunset and heard the phone ringing through the door. He rushed to answer it.

"Is this Jensen Hirsch?" the urgent voice said. "This is Tony Rogers from Channel 4 News. Turn on your TV and stay on the line." Hirsch did as he was told. When the picture came on, it was Max Pouch being interviewed in front of the Pouch Plaza 20 box office. Behind him, the poster with Hirsch's picture was taped to the cashier's cage. "Stand by for a live interview," Rogers said. "I've

been trying to reach you all day."

"About what?" Hirsch managed.

"Here we go," Rogers said, and then, "This is Tony Rogers with a live exclusive interview with *Sun-Herald* film critic Jensen Hirsch. Jensen, how does it feel to be banned from Pouch Theatres?"

"No problem," Hirsch managed. "I'll just see the movies somewhere else."

"But you'll miss advance screenings, free tickets, and special previews."

"In that case, I'll enjoy watching them with the public. They're the ones I'm writing for."

"Do you think you'll be fired for insulting a major advertiser?"

"I feel confident that my editor, Russell Pelota, and the publisher will support me in this First Amendment challenge," Hirsch said stalwartly.

"Then I'm afraid I have a surprise for you," Rogers said in his best interviewer's voice. "The *Sun-Herald* has announced that you've been relieved of your duties by order of the publisher. You're fired. Now back to our studio."

The line went dead. Hirsch looked at the TV screen. He saw his picture with a big "X" drawn through it, then the camera panned right as the co-anchor chirped, "In other stories..." and Hirsch realized that he had suddenly become yesterday's news. The only thing worth less than yesterday's news is yesterday's reporter.

When the phone rang at 7 the next morning, Hirsch wasn't prepared to be civil. A film critic's eyes don't even clear up before the crack of noon (note to publicists; schedule 10 AM screenings at your own risk). "Is this Jensen Hirsch?" the cheerful woman asked.

"Please, no interviews. What time is it?"

"It's time to talk to Brandon Nelson," Miss Cheerful said. "From FLM-TV."

"You don't have to spell it out," Hirsch mumbled. "There are no children listening."

"That's the kind of wry humor Mr. Nelson is looking for. Hold please." Before Hirsch could scratch himself awake, a razor-voiced man acted like they'd known each other for years.

"Jensen Hirsch, Jensen Hirsch–I love the sound of it. This is Brandon Nelson. Call me Brandon."

"Call me still asleep," Hirsch managed. "What time is it?"

"Time to talk," Nelson said.

"F'r'Chrissakes, doesn't anyone where you are know what time it is?"

"It's a little past 7 AM your time. And your time is what I want to talk to you about," Nelson continued with all the enthusiasm of a Jesus freak. "How'd you like to come work for me?"

Why not play along? "What do you do?"

"I run FLM-TV. We're the top movie network after HBO, Showtime, Turner Classic Movies, Hulu, Amazon, and Netflix."

"That puts you somewhere between the test pattern and the farm news, doesn't it?"

"Ha ha ha, that's the kind of humor I'm looking for. Look, Jensen, your photo is all over town. Max Pouch has banned you. You're a celebrity. Read the papers–all of them except yours. You've become the most famous critic in America over-

night. There's only one thing to do: on-camera reviews for me. What do you say?"

There was only one thing Hirsch could say. "Is this a prank call? Is this Bob on the City Desk busting my cojones?"

"I love it," Nelson giggled sharply. "No, it isn't. This is your lucky call, is what it is. Max Pouch isn't a factor on network TV. No local account is. When can you start?"

Hirsch mentally computed how long it would take him to pack, sublet his apartment, grab his cat, file a change-of-address with the Post Office, and throw himself a going away party.

Russell Pelota's voice drew him back to reality.

"Are you listening to me, Jensen? Pelota said. Hirsch shook his head and focused on the editor's dour face. The network offer was only a daydream.

"You haven't heard a word I've been saying, have you?" Pelota snarled. "I said you're not fired yet, but you will be if you don't remember where your paycheck comes from like everybody else around here. Now get out."

The next day Jensen Hirsch reported meekly to his *Sun-Herald* desk. Bob on the City Desk didn't say hello. Hirsch went online. He had to find a non-Pouch cinema in a nearby town that was playing *Simon Says* so he could catch the matinee and still make deadline for his review, which would run a day late because he had been tossed out of the preview and couldn't see it locally.

But first he had to write a letter of apology to Max Pouch. After all, he had a cat to feed.

THE CURIOUS CASE OF
RAPTURE IN RIMINI

It was the film that everybody wanted to see and it was Frank Webster's brilliant idea not to show it to them. *Rapture in Rimini* was the art film of the year, the year being 1973. It starred Alton Benning, widely considered to be the greatest actor of his generation, and was directed by the visionary Giovanni Scanzani, who was at the forefront of the Italian cinema's return to romanticism after decades of gritty neo-realism. But that wasn't what anybody was really talking about, not once they got past the first sentence and lowered their voices to a whisper. What *Rapture in Rimini* was really about was "the peanut butter scene." Because it was the peanut butter scene that made *Rapture in Rimini* more than just a foreign language film that only students and arty types would line up to see. The peanut butter scene was where Alton Benning took two fingers--one for each Oscar he'd won over the years—dipped them into a jar of Skippy, and used them to lubricate his way into Daria Schell, the young actress playing his mistress. That kind of thing may have been nothing new for habitués of 42nd Street groin grind houses, but *Rapture in Rimini* wasn't intended as pornography. It was art. The problem was, the law didn't always know the difference in the early 70s and this posed a monster threat for General Artists, the company that planned to release it.

Movies got cheaper to make in the early 1970s and there were more of them coming out. The old-line studios such as MGM, Fox, Paramount, Columbia, and Warner Brothers were chasing their own frightened tails against an explosion of releases from ad hoc independent companies. It was a vitally exciting time. Film schools were churning out directors. Everybody was reading reviews and being choosy. People no longer went to *the* movies, they started going to *that* movie. Tentpole films weren't even a fantasy in Michael Bay's eyes (he was still in grade school). Tickets were $2 in major cities, half the price of a new record album, meaning that moviegoers could afford to take chances, even if the major film companies could not.

General Artists had guts. But, then, little guys have to. They staked a million dollars on the American distribution rights to *Rapture in Rimini*, pretty much everything they netted from handling *Rock It Out*, the previous year's surprise hit starring the rock 'n' roll group, Maiden Ant. But they were also nervous. The Motion Picture Association of America's Ratings Board had slapped the picture with an "X," restricting audiences to those over seventeen, which automatically halved the dating crowd. This placed General Artists at odds with AmericaWide, the financial conglomerate that had bought them five years earlier as a "leisure time" division. Ari Volpe, who founded and headed General Artists, was assured of independence on paper, but he was also aware of the pressure that AmericaWide could place on him by phone. For example, they were refusing to allow their name or corporate logo to appear on the film, its publicity material, posters, trailers, or ads. They said it was a matter of public image, yet the banking giant didn't care what people thought of them when they redlined whole neighborhoods of minority residents. Pundits said they were more allergic to peanut butter than to poverty.

Faced with a potentially obscene movie being locked out of theatres and attracting only the raincoat crowd, Ari Volpe bit the bullet and called Frank Webster.

Master press agent Frank Webster was an expert at putting asses in the seats. What remained to be seen was whether he could keep General Artists' asses out of jail. Webster was known for his ideas, his follow-through, his enthusiasm, and his devotion to his clients. He could also be a total jerk. In his late forties, he had started doing agency work in the 1950s but quickly realized that his button-down colleagues were so afraid of their accounts that they were blind to innovation. Typical of their cowardice was the famous "Don't press the Prestige" TV commercial for bathroom tissue. For starters, nobody ever calls it "bathroom tissue." It's called toilet paper, okay? And since this was an era when both television and movies still couldn't show a hopper in the bathroom, the housewife models handling the product also couldn't show what it was used for. The most they could do was bunch it up and rub it against their faces to show how soft it was. Who tests toilet paper against *that* cheek? Prestige Bathroom Tissue customers, that's who, as long as they were on TV.

Frank determined to quit just before the ad campaign started, but he wanted to do it in a way that would spread his name along Madison Avenue. He planned his move for a kick-off party that his client was throwing at Delmonico's. After everyone was pretty well lubricated at the open bar, Frank announced, "Gentlemen and Gentlemen, may I have your attention, please?" When he got it, he continued, "We're all proud of the work we did on the Prestige bathroom tissue account. It's a quality product, and that makes for a quality campaign." (Wary applause.) "So, just for fun, I'd like to show you one of the campaigns we decided *not* to use." He pulled a large storyboard from behind one of the restaurant's curtains and hoisted it onto a table for all to see. "This shows how much love and creativity go into supporting our client even if the buying public may not yet be ready for such a visionary campaign."

The room was primed and nervous as Frank held up the large storyboard. Each frame showed the same two adjacent bathroom stalls with the doors closed and dialogue balloons above them:

Stall 1: "Excuse me, sir, but do you have any toilet paper over there?"

Stall 2: "No I don't."

Stall 1: "Well, then, have you got change of a ten?"

Stall 2: "Whoa! I said I didn't have toilet paper. What I *do* have is Prestige Bathroom Tissue. And you know what you can do with it."

Stall 1: "I sure do. Wow, it works great. It's Prestige for me from now on!"

Announcer (voice-over): "Prestige Bathroom Tissue. The number one tissue for your number two problem."

Frank didn't want to work again on Madison Avenue anyway, he told the bottom of his Scotch glass.

*   *   *

Frank found a new calling with film companies. Fearful by nature, they were anarchists compared with the careful, all-white, Gentile ad agencies. United Artists on Seventh Avenue, Columbia on Fifth Avenue, Fox on Avenue of the Americas, and Paramount on Broadway were always eager to see what a new "tub-thumper" could do. Since each picture was different, each needed a new idea to sell it to the public.

Instead of getting stuck in another staff job, Frank embraced freelancing: if a Vice President of Publicity hires an outsider as project coordinator and the film is a smash, he can take credit for a wise personnel decision. If it drops dead, he can blame the freelancer. What made companies forget Frank's failures was that he was always careful to kick ten percent of his fee back to the executive who hired him.

He had been doing this for just over a decade when Ari Volpe of General Artists called him in to handle *Rapture in Rimini*. Frank knew about it from the trades, and this, combined with the fact that he had had a good year, made him ask to screen the picture before deciding whether to represent it.

"What are you, a critic?" Ari asked.

"What are you, a pornographer?" Frank shot back. He and Ari had that kind of relationship.

"It's not pornography," Ari said. "Scanzani won the Palm d'Or a Cannes five years ago, f'r'Chrissake. He makes challenging films, not dirty ones. You'll see. There's a lot more to this than peanut butter."

When he watched *Rapture in Rimini*, Frank agreed. The film drew him through an emotional wringer. Alton Benning played a middle-aged man (just like Frank) arriving at the realization that he might never find a woman who could love him as much as he loved her (just like Frank) who meets just such a woman in Daria Schell, who is dying. The peanut butter scene was nothing. The one that put Frank away was near the end when Schell lay in her hospital bed while Benning read her the riot act for dying. He had never seen any actor, let alone one with Benning's power, so emotionally naked. He wasn't just angry at Schell for leaving him, but also at everyone he had ever loved all his life. It was about whether 'tis better to have loved and lost than never to have loved at all, or whether love is an addiction which, once triggered, produces only pain and suffering. Fortunately, the film had long end credits because Frank needed the time to compose himself.

"I'll do it," he told Ari, stopping by his office on the way to get a drink, "but on one condition."

"Don't ask for more money," the executive cautioned. "We know we can only play it off in the big cities and we'll be lucky to break even."

"On the contrary," Frank countered. "You're going to make a bloody fortune. I'm going to make *Rapture in Rimini* the must-see film of the year.

But I need complete control over everything: the ads, the screenings, the critics, everything."

"Are you sure you don't want to personally carry the prints to the theatres?"

"I'm serious, Ari. I had no idea the picture packed such a wallop. All anybody is talking about is—you know."

"Peanut butter," they said together, sharing a knowing laugh. Then Frank grew solemn.

"My job—make that my mission—will be to make people *talk* about the film while *thinking* about peanut butter. We have to give them an excuse to see it. It will be the motion picture equivalent of people saying that they read *Playboy* for the articles."

Ari was brief. He held out his hand: "Deal."

* * *

Dan Torgeson and Arnie Fuchs owned JT Theatres, a small chain of art houses in Manhattan, smaller than Don Rugoff's Cinema 5 and as well-respected as Dan Talbot's New Yorker. Their patrons trusted them; many automatically came to JT Theatres without even knowing what was playing there because they were invariably pleased with the attraction. They were plugged-in and resourceful; they had even made a hit out of *Teenage Summer* despite its "X" rating by stressing the social issue of unsupervised suburban teens rather than wrapping their publicity around the film's climactic rape scene. They revived the Marx Brothers by positioning them as

anarchists instead of comedians. They had been celebrated by the press as visionary exhibitors geared to the emerging film school generation of the late 1960s and early 1970s. Then the old-line film companies took notice of the youth market and, one by one, either absorbed the independent distributors or priced them out of business. Suddenly Arnie and Dan found themselves dealing with the very studio behemoths they had been trying for years to avoid.

In that regard, Ari Volpe's General Artists was a cinematic demimonde. Ari had passion but lacked clout, and, while he yearned to count the big theatre chains among his customers, he couldn't dismiss the loyalty of independents like Arnie and Dan. The word was that *Rapture in Rimini* could break the majors' stranglehold and reestablish the art house circuit. That is, if they weren't all busted for porn.

Dan Torgeson was a mensch but, alas, it was Arnie Fuchs who closed the deals. He had the best poker face Dan had ever seen. He used it to stare down critics, distributors, unions, and, especially, theatre managers whom he suspected were skimming concessions money. He was also alleged to have a sense of humor, but even Dan had trouble finding it. Arnie Fuchs was smart but his wisecracks sounded like dictation and half his jokes needed footnotes. That's how smart he was. His self-awareness was so lacking that he once cleared the room at a testimonial roast by reading his scripted insults with the seriousness of a judge on the Nuremberg tribunal. So when Ari

Volpe told him that JT Theatres had been awarded the exclusive New York engagement of *Rapture in Rimini*, he reflexively asked, "Why? What's wrong with it?"

"Nothing, Arnie," Ari assured him. "You bid for it, remember?"

"Yes, but I never thought we'd win it. I figured one of the big chains would beat us out."

"Well, they didn't," Ari said. "It's a picture that needs special handling."

"In other words," Arnie said, "It's a stiff."

"It's expected to do *very* well," Ari continued. "So well that we've hired a special publicity consultant to handle your engagement."

"Do we have to pay extra for him?"

"Relax, Arnie, you need us and we need you. We want to give the picture a big opening that'll sell it to the rest of the country."

"What if we have legal trouble? The world has changed since *Teenage Summer*. The 'X' rating has come to mean porn."

"It's not a dirty movie!" Ari insisted. "It's an artistic picture."

"Then you can visit us in an artistic jail."

"Tell you what let's do," Dan interrupted on the extension. "Let's get a print and screen it for a judge. If we can get a declaratory judgment, that lets us off the hook."

When the call was over, Arnie turned to Dan with the same cold stare he fixed on managers he caught palming tickets. "Thanks for undercutting me," he said.

"Back off, Arnie." Dan held firm. "This picture can make us big-time players. I just want to be sure we don't get raided. We can file a brief for declaratory judgment with the court and charge the cost back to General Artists." He grinned. "The only question is, whose brother-in-law do you want to handle it, yours or mine?"

*   *   *

Frank Webster was informed about the judge's screening and, as Ari predicted, carried the film himself to JT Theatres' Cinema 1. Dan and Arnie introduced him to Superior Court Judge A. Reginald Berwick.

"A publicist, eh?" the jurist said. "I'm not looking at your picture for purposes of publicity, I'm looking at it to see if it meets the U.S. Supreme Court's definition of obscenity."

"I'm not looking for publicity, your honor," Frank assured him. "In fact, I'd just as well ask you not to tell anybody else. I'm confident that you'll find the picture acceptable. Mature but acceptable."

"You wouldn't be trying to influence my legal opinion, would you?"

"Me? A mere public relations expert? Why, your honor—" he said, holier-than-thou.

"Don't start," Berwick grinned slyly. Friendly, but slyly.

Berwick took a seat twelve rows back, on the aisle. Dan and Arnie planted themselves five rows behind him, far enough away to make him think they weren't watching him, yet close enough to listen for any moans, or, worse, snores. Frank stood guard at the doors of the auditorium in case anybody tried to enter from Cinema 2. The Judge didn't take notes and sat so still while the picture played that Dan wondered if he was asleep. When the lights came up, he trudged solemnly up the aisle.

"I don't know what to think," he said. "I'm not a censor and I believe in the First Amendment. No way is this an obscene movie. The question is whether it violates local community standards, and I don't mean the community that likes chunky versus creamy."

Dan tried to be helpful. "Our prime concern is *Jacobellis versus Ohio*," he started, "where the theatre manager was arrested for showing an allegedly obscene film, Louis Malle's *The Lovers*, but was exonerated when the film was cleared."

"Don't tell me my precedents," Berwick grunted. "What makes this picture so powerful is its rich characterizations who do and say things that are offensive, and because of that, it's more disturbing. Why the hell couldn't they have it be about a serial killer who disembowels children? The ratings people have no problem with hate, only love. Do you validate parking?"

After Berwick left, Dan and Arnie took Frank to lunch where they used their forks to chase their food around their plates.

"As I see it," Arnie began, "we have two problems: the commercial and the legal. I feel confident that Judge Berwick will clear the way to show the picture. The bigger deal is how to get people to see a movie that's going to make them want to slash their wrists on the way home."

"I have a solution to the second," Frank said. "We don't let them see it." He let it sink in. Dan spoke first. "I see you share Arnie's sense of humor."

"We take a page from Mike Todd's playbook," Frank continued, describing the famous showman as, "a master of ballyhoo. Todd once bought out an entire week's performances of one of his shows just so he could put a 'sold out' sign in the box office. When audiences found out that they couldn't buy tickets, they figured it was a hit, lined up to buy advance tickets, and the show ran for six months. People always want what they can't have."

"But this is a movie," Dan said. "People just wait until it comes to the suburbs."

"This'll never make it to the suburbs if it doesn't go through the roof here, and, even if it does, some local morals group is gonna try and close it. Nah, we gotta pry people out of their suburban sofas and draw 'em intown. So listen. I want to set up a series of screenings right here. Nighttime screenings, which means you'll have to cancel some shows."

"um–"

"I'll need your complete contact list. Not just the critics but the editors, opinion makers, radio and TV people, goniffs, hangers-on, relatives, friends, every freeloader in town. I'll invite some of them to pre-release screenings."

"*Some?*" Dan asked.

"You're catching on," Frank smiled. "If anybody complains that they were left out, you blame it on me. We'll make everybody so eager to see the picture that, by the time it opens, it'll be all over town."

"What about the critics?" Dan asked.

"Leave the critics to me. If I work it right, I can leverage them for or against whatever the judge rules."

"The critics can't be bribed," Arnie said.

"Who's the most important critic in town?"

"That'd be Connie Stone," Arnie said.

"That'd be right," Frank agreed. "Connie is dedicated, honest, and incorruptible. Dozens of other critics look to her. She has her own group of acolytes called Stonettes."

"Connie Stone doesn't have a price," Arnie said. "That's what makes her so respected."

"Did I say I was going to offer her money? I'm going to offer her something worth more than money. I happen to know that she's in a struggle right now with another critic on her paper for who gets to write the lead reviews. I have a way to solve our art problem and give her an edge, and it won't cost us a penny." Frank smiled even more slyly than the judge. "Just wait."

*   *   *

"I want my own private screening," Connie Stone stated flatly. "It's not a matter of ego because I don't have any. I just don't want my colleagues trying to see how I react or what my friend and I say to each other. Oh, I'm bringing a friend."

"Won't a private screening anger your peers?" Frank asked in his best holier-than-thou voice.

"They're not my peers!" Connie slammed, "they're only my colleagues. I don't care if they share my opinions, but if I make a good comment, I don't want them sharing that."

When Frank greeted her at the screening (she did bring a friend; she often quoted her friend in her reviews), he handed her the cast and credits without the usual press releases. He also handed her the most trusting face he could muster. "I have to tell you something off the record," he started. "There are some people who think this movie is obscene. That it violates local community standards. We even—and this is *really* off the record—have a judge looking at it so we'll know ahead of time whether we should prepare to be raided." He paused for effect and leaned closer. "Your review could be very important."

Connie tried not to reveal her interest, but a slight pink glow spread across her face.

"I'm not begging you to like the film," Frank said, "because that would be a serious breach of ethics for both of us. And in no way am I offering you any compensation if you do." He took her elbow and led her a few feet away from her companion. "What's important is that I know you'll take it seriously. You know Alton Benning's work. You know Giovanni Scanzani."

"We had dinner three years ago at Cannes," Connie announced.

"Yes, yes, yes," Frank agreed. "Giovanni agrees with me, and he says hello, by the way," Frank lied, "What I'm saying is that, if you do happen to like the film, and if your review should validate its artistry and establish that it's not a dirty movie—oh, this is silly."

"What's silly?" she asked.

Frank smiled at an inner joke, which she mistook as modesty. "A picture like this needs quote ads from well-known critics. I know that never in a million years would any reputable critic write just to be quoted in a movie ad (he lied again). But what I'm saying is that, if you do happen to write a positive review, instead of using just a quote, we might run the entire review in all the newspapers in all the twenty-two key cities where we open the film."

Connie sighed, then caught herself in progress and turned it into a cough.

"In fact, even if you don't *like* the film, I know that you, above all people, will *understand* it. Your views, your scholarship, and your impeccable reputation would go a long, long way toward persuading everybody, including courts across the country, that *Rapture in Rimini* is a work of art."

"I'll take your words under advisement," Connie said, suddenly becoming the stern schoolmarm, and Frank wondered if he had over-gilded her lily. He escorted her and her friend into the theatre, closed the doors, and phoned the projectionist to start the show.

*   *   *

Giovanni Scanzani didn't like the idea of some strong-willed American press agent taking charge of his movie. He complained to Alton Benning, and Alton Benning had his assistant phone Ari to expect a call from the mercurial actor. Ari canceled lunch to be ready for it, and, unlike his legendary behavior while shooting his movies, Benning actually called on time.

"I want to be among the first to congratulate you on your magnificent portrayal," Ari told Benning when they connected.

"And I want to be the first to tell you that I will never work for you again if you mess up Giovanni's movie," Benning responded. "In fact, I will not give a single publicity interview."

"With all due respect, Mr. Benning," Ari cut in, "you haven't given an interview for any of your work in over twenty years. And when you do, all you want to talk about is air pollution."

"Fair enough, but if I was ever going to give another one, it would be for this picture."

"With even more respect, Mr. Benning," Ari continued, "when General Artists picked up this picture we didn't have a lot of competition. Your last three pictures tanked, and, regardless of how brilliant you are—and you are magnificent in everything you do—you don't have the clout to demand anything."

"Do I have to come over there and teach you a few things, Mr. Volpe?"

At this, Ari dropped all pretentions of politeness. "You listen to me, Benning," he seethed, "for once you have a distributor who's not going to dump your picture in the drive-ins or cut it so it makes sense. *Rapture in Rimini* is one of the best films I've ever seen, and we intend to treat it like that. If you and Mr. Scanzani cared as much about your picture as we do, you'd come down off your mountain or swim from your little tropical island or wherever you hang out between paydays and take an interest in your own goddamned work. You're getting a percentage of the gross, f'r'Chrissake, and if you do anything to damage those grosses I'll sue your high-maintenance ass back to when you were a spear carrier for Orson Welles."

"This isn't over yet, Mr. Volpe."

"Yes it is, Mr. Benning." Ari Volpe hung up before Benning could, surprised that he had vented to the most acclaimed actor since Brando. Then he threw up in his trash can.

*   *   *

The invitations went out on Friday, and on Monday morning the complaints started coming in. The invitations were not only numbered, they were for one-only and had small print saying that they were not transferrable. The critics, of course, each received one. Their editors, advertising salesmen, columnists, and sub-editors sometimes did, sometimes didn't. Most of the calls weren't nasty, they were just awkward, with people coyly asking if perhaps there had been "some oversight" in not inviting them to screenings of *Rapture in Rimini* while admitting that there was no reason why they should have been invited'

Pre-release invitations are strange currency. It isn't about money, it's about status. People get used to them and before long consider them not a favor but a right. Frank knew he was upsetting the web of payoffs that General Artists and JT Theatres had established, but he also knew that it would snap back in place once he left. He described it to Dan and Arnie as being like a dinner party that you'd heard about but aren't invited to: "There's no way you can call the hostess and ask that you be added to the guest list, so you can either brush it off or lie about it afterward by saying that you were busy so you had to refuse."

"Nothing makes people say 'yes' faster than telling them 'no,'" Frank assured Ari, whose secretary, Jackie, was getting the brunt of the calls (Frank invited her). "This is just what we want."

Indeed, the next day it was all over the papers that General Artists was picking and choosing who they were inviting to see *Rapture in Rimini* in advance of its opening. The comments themselves produced reactions from readers asking why critics felt entitled, why the film company was being so tight, and all opinions in between. Dan and Arnie kept referring calls to Ari and Frank, and Ari and Frank made it a point not to return them.

*   *   *

Judge Berwick was having trouble writing his declaratory judgment. As practiced, a declaratory judgment is a legal opinion written by a jurist rendering a verdict without a trial, giving potential litigants a sense of what might happen if they went to court. At issue with *Rapture in Rimini* was whether the film might be obscene under the community standards of the movie-going audience in New York. On that question, the answer was a bold, "Are you fucking kidding?" But as the film went to play off nationally, less worldly communities might have different standards, so what Berwick wrote here might be called into question. He didn't want to risk that. He was also aware that an "X" rating would prevent the film from being advertised on radio and TV and in many newspapers who equated the "X" with pornography. *Rapture in Rimini* was clearly not pornography.

So he asked to screen it again, and this time to bring his wife and in-laws. "I call it the mother test," he explained when he asked Frank to set up the showing. "The picture can be perfectly acceptable to you and the guys, but when you've got your mother sitting next to you, you develop a heightened sense of propriety."

Meanwhile, Dan and Arnie were hearing from their own families.

"I keep telling everyone it's not a dirty movie," Gladys Torgeson said, "and they all say, if it isn't, why does it have an 'X' rating?"

"It's to keep kids out," Dan explained. "Tell them that *Midnight Cowboy, Medium Cool, A Clockwork Orange, The Devils* and *If...* were also 'X'-Rated when they came out."

"I did, and they said so were *The Miracle of Love, Sin with a Stranger* and *Teenage Summer*."

"Serves me right for marrying a fellow film student," Dan half-joked. "Did you explain that—"

"—it was before the porn industry adopted the 'X'? Yes, I did, but then they brought up peanut butter."

"I've been getting feedback, too," Arlene Fuchs said. "Mostly from my people at the Prosthesis Foundation who are afraid to hold any more benefit premieres at the theatre if we get smeared with an obscenity charge."

"Nobody's being charged with anything!" Arnie said. "F'r'Chrissake, nobody's even seen the goddamn picture."

"Maybe we should," Arleen said softly. "That way, we can speak from authority."

*   *   *

By the last week before *Rapture in Rimini* was set to open, it had already played a week of screenings, fifty chosen people at a time in a theatre that sat four hundred, with Frank Webster diligently at the door wielding more power than a bouncer at Studio 54.

"Sorry, but the invitation says no guests and not transferrable," he told the sales director of the local NBC affiliate.

"Bobbi said you wouldn't mind," the man said.

"I don't know Bobbi,' Frank told him, 'and from now on she's off my list, Besides, your station wouldn't run commercials for the film, so why should I let you in to see it?"

"Professional courtesy."

"You tell your station to start acting professional," Frank said so others in line could hear him, "and I'll show you some courtesy. The picture opens next Friday. Buy a ticket." Then he turned to the others in line, several of whom were melting away rather than face similar humiliation. "Please, all legitimate invitation holders come this way."

On the Sunday before opening, Connie Stone published her review. It wasn't just a rave, it was an apotheosis. Phrases such as "it changes the art of cinema" and "the nakedness is internal as well as external" bespoke a money review. Frank phoned her at home with his gratitude.

"Nothing to thank me for," she cooed. "The film is a triumph in every way. My friend said she hoped it wasn't just about peanut butter, and she was right. But it is about—well, you read my review."

"And so will everybody else," Frank said softly. "I already sent it to the advertising department. They're checking with your newspaper now to see about licensing it for national use (he left off saying "just as I promised" but his tone of voice did the job). Anybody who hasn't heard of the film now will certainly hear about it. For that matter, anybody who hasn't heard about you will hear about you, too."

When Frank reported this to Ari, the executive smiled, and Frank added, "and it only cost us ten thousand dollars to neutralize her."

"That much?" Ari asked.

"That's what a full-page ad costs in the *New York Times*."

"I tried bribing a film critic once," Ari said. "It didn't work."

Frank shifted into his teaching mode. "You don't need money," he started. "Some critics just want to be quoted."

"I hear you," Ari said, "Where it gets costly is when you actually have to write them a check."

"Good lord, you don't pay them a lump sum at once, do you?" Frank was astonished.

"Cash is always preferable, but you can't write it off your taxes."

"No, no, here's how you do it, Ari," Frank explained. "You agree on a figure and a payment schedule so it doesn't look fishy. Then, once they deposit the first check, you never have to come through with the rest. They're tainted."

"Don't ever leave me, Frank," Ari joked.

*   *   *

Connie Stone's review did Judge A. Reginald Berwick the favor he was looking for. By pronouncing *Rapture in Rimini* an artistic triumph, it quashed any concern over community standards and allowed him to decree from the bench that the picture did not meet the U.S. Supreme Court's murky threshold of obscenity. He handed down his declaratory judgment on Monday, the day after the Stone review.

Across town, Arnie and Dan were ecstatic. *Rapture in Rimini* was set to open huge even though fewer than a handful of people had seen it.

The next surprise was when Alton Benning landed in his private jet at JFK airport to hold a press conference to complain that his film was being sold as pornography. When informed by the attending press (who managed to get past their awe of seeing the reclusive actor in person) that *Rapture in Rimini* had just been adjudged both legally and artistically not obscene, he responded, "That's what we intended. The real obscenity is not found in love but in Mankind's actions against himself and God's world. I'm speaking, of course, about the obscene pollution of our air by industry, rampant technology, wastefulness, and our own profligacy."

"Is that why you flew in on your own private jet instead of a commercial flight?" one reporter asked with temerity.

"What I do is a symbol, not the reality," Benning countered. "Go ahead and mock me, but I sacrifice myself on the altar of Truth. For when the end comes it will be revealed that indecency of the human spirit is at the core of our suffering, and levity is all we mortals have to stifle the onslaught."

He paused for the drama of the moment, as he had done to such effect in his most memorable performances. But those had all been scripted, and this one was not. He made a few more Joycean statements, then excused himself to get back on his plane to return to his island home with clean air half a world away.

The newsfilm of Benning's airport encounter generated more calls about tickets. With the film set to open in two days, Dan and Arnie considered running it on both Cinema 2 and Cinema 1. Ari talked them out of it.

"We need a long run," he said. "We need to milk this puppy enough for it to penetrate the heartland." Arnie immediately asked for a revision of booking terms and an increase in studio contribution to advertising. He got both.

Romance in Rimini played for a record-breaking six months at the JT Theatres Cinema 1 in Manhattan. Frank was right; after two weeks, word of mouth negated anything having to do with peanut butter and it became the must-see movie for people dealing with middle-aged ennui.

Needless to say, those who had been shut out of advance screenings saw it on their own and lied that it was their second time. Connie Stone's newspaper rewarded her by making her their permanent critic rather than have to share six months on, six months off with a peer (make that a colleague).

AmericaWide rewarded Ari Volpe at contract renewal time by stripping him of his executive power as payback for publicly associating them with an "X"-rated film, even one that was an artistic and commercial hit. A year later he left with four top General Artists executives to start their own company.

Alton Benning was widely rumored to be an Oscar® contender for his remarkable performance, but for some reason he began distancing himself from the film that revived his career, gained weight, and opened a soap manufacturing company.

Dan Torgeson and Arnie Fuchs leveraged their success into a number of high-profile bookings that straddled the line between art and commerce. They were eventually pushed out of business when the major film companies decided to open up their own "independent" subsidiaries and strangled the art house market.

Frank Webster gave up publicity once film companies started spending $40 million to open a film instead of using their creativity. "It's no fun any more," he told columnist Liz Smith before disappearing into retirement.

By 1990, *Romance in Rimini* was on cable TV where anybody could watch it, including children under seventeen.

AGE OF ANXIETY

Bernie Saffran made the mistake of turning 41 in Hollywood. Like an ice cube on a griddle, his name almost immediately melted from producers' phone books, studio screening lists, and rosters of opinion makers (whoever they were). He didn't even need to mark the milestone with a birthday party; everybody in town simply knew. His long-time agent handed him off to a trainee. His favorite deli no longer seated him at a window booth (so his grey hair wouldn't scare away younger patrons). Even the multi-pierced sales clerk at The Gap suggested that he might find a more suitable selection at CostCo. Here he was, nine years before he could join AARP, and the town where he had been writing for twenty years erased him.

He didn't think it would happen. Nobody does. Times were changing, weren't they? If a guy could be gay and nobody cared any more, why couldn't he be 41?

But the 27-year-old Jasons who ran the town thought otherwise. (The ones who all hang at the same bars and have the same trainer and dress off the same Armani rack and were all born in that period when parents named the kids Kristin and Jason). "You're only as old as younger people make you feel," Bernie used to joke, but when he hit 41 he became the punch line.

He tried to hide it, of course. He turned his baseball cap backwards. He wore his T-shirt out and let his sports shirt hang unbuttoned over it. He listened to whatever crap the kids listened to over the radio—oops, make that streaming audio.

He even–though it made him choke on his Lipitor–watched "Saturday Night Live" to gauge the lowest common denominator of humor (hell, if Lorne Michaels in his seventies could dictate the taste of demos three generations below him, so could Bernie Saffran).

His new kid agent practiced on Bernie's career. He had him slice off the bottom half of his resume. If anybody asked what he'd been doing before 9/11, he was instructed to say he was in rehab, substance addiction being more acceptable in Hollywood than middle age. He even agreed to be partnered with an up-and-coming young (of course) client whom the agency had signed fresh out of film school. That was Robbie Piersall.

Robbie was 21, good-looking, athletic, and had an engaging personality. His ideas sounded new to those who hadn't seen a movie more than ten years old, and he knew how to work a room. Only problem was, he couldn't write for shit. Once he got past the first act, that was it. His idea of a character arc was discovering something in a dream sequence. It would become Bernie's job to take Robbie's first drafts and rewrite them into something professional. The agency figured that Robbie and Bernie–note the billing–could be a team like Cyrano and Christian (Robbie asked, "Who's Cyrano and does he have to be a Christian?"). As a warm-up before sending them out, their agent, Lance Steele (honest), had them come in for a practice pitching session.

Robbie broke the ice by chatting with Lance about the latest group they'd seen perform and how many Twitter followers so-and-so had and who was starring in such-and-such a picture. Bernie cared little about the flashes in the pan that so consumed Lance and Robbie, but he knew the drill. He had been doing it in his own pitch meetings back when the names they dropped actually had talent. Finally, Robbie introduced Bernie.

"You know Bernie Saffran," he said. "I am so lucky to be working with him. Between the two of us you get ideas and craftsmanship."

Lance had warned them that he was going to play hardball, saying out loud what the development people would be thinking. "There's a slight age difference, isn't there?" he said provocatively.

"I like working with younger people," Bernie said, going for irony. "Everything is always new to them and their optimism is infectious."

"Do you think you can write material that appeals to modern youth audiences?" Lance asked. Bernie was ready for this.

"Audiences don't change. They still want to be entertained and respected. Between the two of us–" he nodded to Robbie "–we write stuff that has broad appeal."

Lance turned his attention back to Robbie. "Suppose a producer says they're re-making *Twelve Years a Slave* set in high school. How would you pitch that?" Robbie went into deep thought. Bernie didn't have to; what he had to do was keep from laughing.

"Well," Robbie began cautiously, "first, I'd take slavery out of it and make it about bullies. Every kid can relate to bullies more than slavery. Bullies get little kids to do things for them, sort of like slaves. They steal their lunch money. They shut them in lockers. Not to take away from slavery, but I think it's easier for audiences to relate to bullies than to slaves."

Bernie no longer wanted to laugh. He wanted to puke. He also wanted to remind Lance and Robbie of the very real evil of slavery, and how it fueled today's institutionalized racism. Where to start? Never mind. Neither of the young men even looked at him. He had become invisible.

"Were you ever bullied in school?" Lance asked earnestly.

"Me?" Robbie smiled it away. "No, no way. But I wasn't a bully, either. I thought it was best not to mix in."

"Do you mind if I say something?" Bernie finally managed. "I was thinking it might be helpful to go over some generic expressions in case someone mentions something as stupid as setting *Twelve Years a Slave* in high school. Phrases like, 'that's an idea' or 'that's something to really think about.' Why dig ourselves a hole appearing to go along with something that offensive?"

"Because *Twelve Years a Slave* set in high school is actually in development over at Endis Pictures," Lance said. "But I guess that means you don't want me to put you up for it."

"Actually," Bernie said, "I'd love to go in and just meet the asshole who had the balls to propose it."

"Okay," Lance said, "let's calm down and take a step or two back. Forget that I'm a D-girl. Now I'm

Lance. How do you intend to present yourself at pitch meetings?"

Bernie figured a little humor would help at this point. "We'll drive onto the lot," he said, "and I'll park in the visitors' section. Robbie and I will give each other a pep talk, and then he'll go in and do the pitch while I wait in the car."

Lance looked satisfied with the answer and turned to Robbie. "Okay, what do you do as soon as you get in the office?"

"Hey, hold on a minute," said Bernie. "I was kidding when I said I'd wait in the car."

"I wasn't," Lance said. "Maybe you'd better let Robbie do the pitching. He relates better. Don't worry, you'll get some of the writing fee, and we'll settle the credit later."

Bernie didn't hear the rest of the meeting. He took Robbie to lunch when it was over–some hip Thai place on Sunset where the music was so loud he couldn't hear the kid say how thrilled he was to be working with an old pro like him. And of course, when Bernie got home, there was a message from Lance Steele saying he was sorry but the arrangement just wasn't going to work out. But Bernie already knew that. He had seen the eyes of Lance's secretary light up when she set them on young, handsome Robbie and then plunge into despair when she saw Bernie standing behind him.

The next day Bernie dyed his hair for the first time. He'd always felt that a touch of salt among the pepper would make him look experienced without appearing old, but now he was no longer

sure. Rather than try it himself–he was afraid to be seen browsing the paint aisle in CVS–he asked his barber, Alvaro, to do it just before closing time and at the chair farthest from the door.

"A lot of people refresh their hair color, Bernie," Alvaro said encouragingly. He was careful not to use the term *dye*. "Think of it as a fashion accessory for your head–like frosting, straightening, or a permanent."

"Yeah, right," Bernie grunted as Alvaro donned latex gloves to prepare his scalp. "You and I both know that a dye job is the last step before a face lift, and a face lift is the last step before moving into the old filmmakers' home."

"You mustn't say that," Alvaro said. "If you can't work in your chosen field, then choose another one."

"That's easy for you to say. There'll always be a job for a hairdresser in a town that's so consumed with how it looks."

"I wasn't always a hairdresser," Alvaro said as he worked the coloring into Bernie's scalp. "My brother and I used to be in business together."

"What kind of business?" Bernie was being polite.

"It didn't have a name, but we called it the reverse collection business."

"Reverse collection sounds like you paid people."

"Oh, no, they paid us. We made them pay. What I mean is, they paid us back the money that they stole from our clients."

Now Bernie was intrigued. "You mean you were debt collectors."

"Not exactly," said Alvaro. "The statute of limitations has passed. And if you ever write about this, don't use my real name."

"You have my solemn word, not to mention my full attention."

"My brother Miguel and I worked for a company whose name I cannot give you, but they were a kind of insurance agency combined with a skip tracer." He looked around to make sure they were the only ones in the shop. "We investigated insurance fraud. When somebody got reimbursed for, say, a broken leg, and later on the company found out that they never had one, we collected."

Bernie went along. "You mean you brought them to court and made them pay you back?"

"No," Alvaro whispered. "If they had been paid for a broken leg but didn't really have a broken leg, we gave them one."

Bernie had been sipping from a bottle of water, and when he heard what he heard, he nearly passed it through his nose. "You mean you broke their leg?"

Alvaro smiled and nodded Yes. "Arms were the easiest. Legs were hard because you had to make them lie down on the curb. Fingers were tricky because you had to bend them back just right or they'd snap off like when you're boning a chicken. Cracked ribs were the easiest, A quick jab and the job was done."

"Oh my God," Bernie managed. "Who else knows about this besides you and your brother?"

"Miguel's dead," Alvaro said reverently. "Anyway, we had to give it up."

"Police?"

"Oh, not police," he said matter-of-factly. "We killed a guy."

By now Alvaro was washing the brown out of Bernie's hair which might easily have turned white underneath.

"If you killed a guy, there's no statute of limitations. Don't tell me any more."

"That's okay. We didn't really do it, but we helped find the guy who did. See, what happened was we decided to branch out from insurance collections into enforcement. A woman called up and said her husband beat her and could we teach him a lesson? You know, the color will get a little lighter the first time you wash it."

"Never mind that, tell me about the woman."

"She gave us the name of the bar where her husband hangs out and we waited till he left and was getting on his motorcycle and we jammed a broom handle in its spokes so it couldn't move and we hit him with another broom handle so *he* wouldn't move, and we told him never to mess with his wife again."

"And that killed him?"

"He was alive when we left but somebody else musta come along and finished him off. And do you know what the really bad part was?"

Bernie shook his newly brown head weakly.

"The woman who hired us to beat up her husband, she wasn't really his wife. She was his mistress. We never saw her again. But boy, she must have hated him. Miguel and me, we got cleared when her real boyfriend matched the description of the murderer, thanks to her."

"Wait, you said you never saw her again."

"We didn't. The boyfriend killed her too because he found out she swore an affidavit that she set us up. Here, let me trim a little around the ears."

Bernie leapt out of the chair and tore off his smock. "If that's the truth, it's a hell of a story."

"Si."

"All these years I've been having my hair cut by a guy who used to break other people's bones?"

"You break bones, too, señor. I have seen your movies. The only difference is that you do it on paper and I used to do it for real."

"Have you ever told this to anybody else?"

"No."

"Well, don't. Alvaro, you and I are going to sell it to the movies. I don't know how much we'll get for it, but it's a terrific pitch. And I know just the person who can do it."

And that is how *The God Guys* reached the screen. Bernie had, of course, kept Robbie's phone number, and he and Alvaro pitched him and Lance the story. Robbie and Lance liked it so much they took it all over town and easily got a deal. When, predictably, Robbie didn't know how to write a shootable screenplay, Lance said he'd have him try again, and this time Bernie did it in secret. It sold. Of course, Bernie got no writing credit (it was just like the HUAC days where blacklisted writers used fronts. Back then it was because they were Red. Now it was because they were Gray) but he and Alvaro got "story by" credit and a large silent share of Robbie's fee.

Bernie got his AARP card at age 50. He and Alvaro lived comfortably on the residuals of *The God Guys* and its sequels. Bernie never dyed his hair again.

On Robbie Piersall's 41st birthday, Bernie would send him congratulations. He figured Robbie, despite all his success, might need moral support at this transitional phase of his life and career. "Welcome to the club, kid" it said.

A week later the card came back "addressee unknown."

But this would not be the end of Bernie's story.

BERNIE BEATS THE GREYLIST

Bernie Saffran thought he was finished with Hollywood because he thought Hollywood was finished with him. At 41, he had felt like *The Invisible Man*: forgotten but not gone. He was stunned, therefore, when, at 45, he started getting job calls. It wasn't that he was suddenly lifted off the greylist. No, it was the stratospheric receipts from *The God Guys* and its two sequels.

His action scripts, based on the sordid revenge tales of his barber, Alvaro, were rabbi'd through the studio gauntlet by Robbie Piersall, a 21-year-old embryo he was forced to share writing credit with. Time and again he sat silently while 27-year-old embryos hung on Robbie's every word when it had been Bernie's writing that had clinched the sale. Once the grosses started coming in, however, the truth leaked out that an older writer could actually write a youth-oriented hit. (It also helped that the two scripts Robbie wrote on his own were deemed unfilmable until Bernie punched them up.)

Like a prisoner suddenly freed by DNA evidence, Bernie found himself playing a new game: he was hot but out of circulation. They wanted him for rewrites, not originals. After a few months of hearing "pass" from a succession of production vice presidents, he finally realized that nobody wanted his ideas, they just wanted to meet him because of the way he had gamed the system. From that point on, he just took meetings for the free lunches.

Bernie wasn't the only good writer in town over 41. Most of them had become script doctors, secretly employed at tens of thousands of dollars a week to fix the scripts of some hot 23-year-old who couldn't tell a noun from a verb but who landed a sale because he drank mojitos with one of those 27-year-old Jasons who worked in development. Bernie knew it was common practice for a producer to buy a script from some hotshot just for the bragging rights, then hand it to someone twice the kid's age to turn into something that could actually be shot. The town was full of script doctors who still had the chops but had lost their new car smell. Bernie took a few of those gigs and happily used the cash to pay off his friends' debts, but what he couldn't get used to was being anonymous.

"Looks like you're gonna have to find another beard," kidded Mel Landsman as he and Bernie sat down at their Farmers Market table across from Bob's Donuts. They were joined by the usual crowd: Leo Crowther, Paul Schumacher, and Perry Blade.

"I'm not going through that charade again," Bernie grumbled. "Not with anybody who uses the term *smash cut*."

"Then you might as well start novelizing all your old specs," Mel said. "After all, they only make a hundred movies a year but they publish a hundred thousand books."

"Publishing's gotten as bad as movies," Leo grumbled as he wiped cream cheese off his mouth. "Same mentality. They all ask, 'Will it appeal to the post-literate generation?' For six months my agent's been trying to sell *The Cremation Squad*. The publishers want a film sale first and the studios want a book sale first. I've been thinking about rewriting it about cats. Cat books, they buy."

"Nah," shot Perry. "When *The Jungle Book* was a hit, I pitched *King Lear* with animals. Lear would be a gorilla, the daughters would be monkeys, and I had a marmoset lined up for the Fool."

"What happened to it?" asked Bernie.

"They decided to do *Hamlet* with penguins."

Paul Schumacher, who usually had a lot to say, was saying nothing. Bernie noticed. "Say something, Paul," he said. "CGI cat got your tongue?"

Paul finished his coffee, placed the paper cup gently on the table, twisted it in his fingers, and looked at each of the others in turn. "Listen to yourselves. Just listen. *King Lear* with animals. Novelizing your unsold specs. Desperately crunching the stupidest things you can think of: *Titanic* in high school with zombies. Shame on you."

"Oh, and you're Mr. Guiltless?" Mel shot back. "How long have you been trying to set up *The Poseidon Adventure* in outer space?"

"We're all pathetic," Perry sighed. "We're all trying to sell pictures we wouldn't watch even on fast-forward. The truth is, our knowledge kills us. The kids who are working today think their ideas are new because they haven't seen anything old."

"It's the bland leading the bland," Leo pronounced.

"Lemme ask you," Paul turned to Bernie. "What was so bad about working with that Piersall kid? Was he a goniff or was there hope?"

"Only a little goniffy," Bernie said, thinking back on their eight-week shotgun collaboration.

"He had the attention span of a fart. It was like when you're trying to fix your car and you ask for a three-quarter inch wrench and he hands you a bottle opener because he thinks it looks better."

"Then how'd you manage to sell *The God Guys*?" Perry asked.

"I took my name off it and kept his on," Bernie said flatly. "In this town, if they've heard of you, you're dead. If you're a newbie, you have a chance. They like discovering people. Go figure."

"Then that's our solution," Paul said. "All we need is a name."

"And shit," Perry added quickly. "We need shit. If shit sells, we'd better write shit. Are we good enough to write shit?"

"But we need a real person to take the meetings," Leo said. "Even blacklisted writers needed a front."

Bernie shook his head. "Not any more. All you need now is e-mail and someone to vouch for you. I may still have a vouch or two left in me. If they won't buy my scripts, maybe they'll buy one by-"-he turned names over in his head-"—Corky Stackpole."

"Who the hell is Corky Stackpole?" Paul asked.

"A character I cut out of an old script. I liked the name but I hated him. He can be our front and we won't even have to cut him in."

"Let me get this straight," Paul said. "We all go home and write shit, then we say we've discovered a great idea from a 23-year-old named Corky Stackpole but it needs work, and we position ourselves to do the rewrite?"

"Exactly!" Bernie said. "I propose we each keep fifty percent of our doctoring fee and pool the other fifty percent in case one of us accidentally writes a good script and nobody buys it."

Everybody agreed, shook hands, and clinked donuts to celebrate. "Here we go, gentlemen," Bernie said, hoisting his honey-dipped in a good luck toast. "We are now in the shinola business."

Smash cut to:

Bernie chose Richard "Dickie" Magnuson as the first recipient of a Corky Stackpole turd. "Corky's new and he's a little weird," Bernie said when Dickie agreed to look at it for old time's sake. *The Mercy Machine* was an old spec Bernie had written when he wasn't spending time on the picket line during the 2007 Writers Guild strike. He knew at the time it was too lousy to take out, and he pitched it as Corky's tyro effort. "He's fresh out of college and bright as hell, but he has that thing where he's afraid to leave the house, what's it called, agoraphobia. So he deals entirely by e-mail." Dickie` bit.

Monday at the Farmers Market, Leo Crowther told the others, "Dickie Magnuson called me over the weekend. He wants me to take a look at *The Mercy Machine*." Bernie smiled and blushed at the same time. "He says Corky Stackpole's characters suck, but he likes the concept of medical school dropouts injecting themselves with experimental drugs and becoming super-heroes."

"Is that a yes or a pass?" Bernie asked.

"I'm getting to that," Leo said. "He asked me if I could do a rewrite. I thought I'd offer it to you first, considering it's yours."

"Nah," Bernie said. "I was written out on it before I even typed 'the credits roll.' Do it with my blessing."

"Oh, and Dickie asked if this Corky kid had anything else he was working on." Once Paul, Perry, Mel, Bernie, and Leo stopped laughing, they all said Yes and split up to go home to dust off their archives.

In Brackett and Wilder's *Sunset Boulevard*, Joe Gillis–the William Holden character–says, while reading Norma Desmond's ill-fated *Salome*, "Sometimes it's interesting to see just how bad bad writing can be. This promised to go the limit." Corky Stackpole handily exceeded the limit. Although the public regards the Hollywood trades as news, insiders know that the industry's chief form of communication is rumor. Within two weeks everybody in the business was talking about Corky Stackpole and, predictably, bragging that they were the only ones who had actually met him in person. The Bernie Bunch (that's what the Bob's Donut table called their cabal) were too busy digging to the bottom of their old zip drives to laugh. Then the complications started.

"Did anyone here send a Corky called *Scarface and Me* to Gerry Colardo over at Warners?" Paul asked. Bernie, who was tracking all the submissions, shook his head No and asked for the logline. "It's about the poor schmuck who was always cropped out of the group photos of Al Capone," Paul said. "In the end he's the accountant who finks on Big Al to the Untouchables." No one had. "I thought it was strange," Paul continued. "Thing is, Jerry didn't want me to rewrite it, he wanted me to consult. He wants to pay me to be his advisor."

"How old is he?" Perry asked.

"Twenty-four."

"Now that you bring it up," Mel said, "Sandi Furnival at Fox asked me pretty much the same thing. She won't hire me to write, but she trusts my judgment. I just signed a long-term consultancy for actual money."

Bernie was baffled. He went around the table. Everyone there was over 41 and each had been asked by a different production executive under 30 to be his or her script taster. "What's happening here?" he asked.

"I'll tell you what's happening," said a voice behind him. It was Jack Schiffer. Jack was carrying his tray to the table that he and his writers' clique occupied near Phil's Deli. "This town has exploded with work, only nobody knows who's doing it."

"What do you mean?" asked Mel.

Jack rested his tray on the table. "The spec market's taken off like I haven't seen it since *The Last Boy Scout* tore Hollywood a new one in 1989. Some kid named Stackpole started it, but now there's more material going around than they can ever develop. So what they're doing is asking older guys like us to do their thinking for them."

"Isn't why they have readers and coverage?" Perry asked.

"Don't knock the work," Jack said, picking up his tray. "Readers have experience with finished scripts, not scripts that need work. It takes a real writer to know when something can be saved and how to do it."

Bernie was at home recycling a half-finished treatment for *The Fountainhead* set in the North Pole when Chaim Yonkel's assistant called from Disney. "Mr. Yonkel wants to know if you'd be interested in rewriting *Second Thoughts*," she said.

"Never heard of it," Bernie said. Now he was getting choosy. He was also stalling till he could search the title and see if it was one of his. "What's the logline?"

"It's a rom-com about a middle-aged couple who win the lottery, lose their child, their house burns down, their jobs get outsourced, and their marriage hits the rocks, but they redeem themselves by watching *My Little Pony*'"

Bernie suppressed a retch. He couldn't help himself. He also couldn't find any record that *Second Thoughts* came from anyone in his group, just as with *Scarface and Me*. "I'm impressed that you'd make a downer movie with middle-aged characters," he managed.

"Oh, we're going to use twenty-somethings," the assistant said perkily. "We'll lose the child, save the house, fix the marriage, keep the jobs, and change *My Little Pony* to vampires."

"Who submitted it?" Bernie finally asked.

"Mitch Rosenbloom," she said. Bernie's heart jumped. Mitch wasn't in either his or Jack Schiffer's group. Bernie and Yonkle's assistant worked out the terms in a few short minutes, although when Bernie said, "I want to know how much you'll pay me just to read that crap," it almost ended the negotiations. Once it was settled, he called Mel Landsman.

"You've pulled back the curtain from the Wizard," Mel said. "I've been getting calls, too. The pabulum has hit the fan. The companies hired young executives who know audiences but they don't know enough about the craft, so they're all hiring old farts like us to cover their asses. It's the biggest CYA scheme since the invention of memos."

"Good God," Bernie said, "we've gone through the looking glass, if you don't mind a little homogenizing of metaphors. What you're saying is that Hollywood is now being run, not out of CAA or UTA or WME or the studios but out of geezer tables at the Farmers Market."

Which is exactly how Bernie explained it to the co-conspirators on Monday morning. "Enjoy it while we can," he cautioned everyone. "All these embryos go to the same trainers, they party at the same clubs, they have the same pill doctors, and they all hit Cancun at the same time of year. Sooner or later they'll realize they all have the same consultants. Until then, let's strike a blow for grownups."

Future film historians would later marvel how, for a two-year period, most of the movies emanating from Hollywood studios appealed to audiences over 30. They would blog how films contained fully rounded characters who dealt with drama in realistic ways. It didn't take long before adults started coming back to movie theatres, leaving the tent-pole films to stream on iPads and Smartphones. Journalists praised the industry for finally appealing to the 60 percent of the population they had hitherto been ignoring. Profits soared from this re-enfranchised market. It collapsed, of course, when the CGI industry complained that nobody needed CGI any more. Meanwhile Bernie was the king of Hollywood.

"It's like Billy Wilder said when he got the AFI award," Bernie told his group over lunch at Norah. "Theirs may be the kingdom, but ours is the power and the glory. Pass the ketchup."

PART IV:
BLACKLIST BLUES

Most people, *if they think about it these days at all, regard the Blacklist as a ham-fisted attempt by Conservatives to rid the country of Liberals, accusing them of being Communists, starting with the movies. It was bald attempt to suppress progressive thought by instilling fear, crushing intellectual freedom, overturning President Franklin Roosevelt's New Deal, subverting the troublesome First Amendment to the U.S. Constitution, and making anti-Semitism acceptable. Although some continue to justify it by insisting that the ends justified its mean, and that Communists did indeed exist in America, by any standard the means did more damage to the Republic than the Communists ever hoped of achieving.*

However you look at it, the Blacklist continues to generate fierce emotions. Its primary victims may be dying, but its secondary victims–their children and other family members–carry the scars. Some offspring of Blacklistees refuse to become politically involved in anything, including voting. Others became more radical. Many ventured into scholarship. None can forget.

It's debatable whether the Hollywood Reds wanted to overthrow America or just wanted to make it more fair and live up to its promise. The real enemies of the United States, they said, were the people who did the Blacklisting, those who
went along with it, and those who remained silent while it was going on. These themes are woven through the three Blacklist pieces that follow.

If history is written by the winners, then Blacklist history is written by its victims. If asked, most will remind us that Communism was, and is, legal in the United States, and so, for the House Un-American Activities Committee to subpoena alleged Communists to testify before them, it was not only an infringement of the witnesses' First Amendment rights, it was a de facto abuse of power. It was also, they say, an admission that these so-called patriots must have thought that America was so weak a republic as to be threatened by a ragtag collection of left-wing radicals when the real danger came from themselves.

As for the Communists who were undoubtedly in positions of power in the State Department, the military, and throughout American life, the same question must be asked: who did more harm, they or the people who trampled on the Constitution going after them. Dalton Trumbo was right; there were only victims.

"A Cocktail of Fear" is a speculation on what took place on November 24 and 25, 1947 when representatives of all the studios gathered in secret at New York's Waldorf-Astoria Hotel to decide how the industry was going to react to the

recent October hearings by the House Un-American Activities Committee into Communist influence in the movies. This is the meeting at which the Blacklist was invented. It's told through the eyes of Nino, a waiter assigned to serve the 48 moguls, mini-moguls, and supernumeraries who so casually threw democracy onto the rubbish heap in order to save their own celluloid empires.

"Collateral Damage" is a perfect example of what happens when loose lips sink careers. An offhand remark by a big star about a smaller one pits them against each other and only gets resolved forty years later in the most ironic way.

The most tragic piece is "Only Scoundrels," an examination of guilt and forgiveness between two unlikely friends. Uneasy times make for uneasy rivals. This is, as Whittaker Chambers called it in his testimony against his former friend Alger Hiss, the tragedy of history.

A COCKTAIL OF FEAR

Nino was used to keeping the secrets of hotel guests but this was the first time they ever made him swear to it on a copy of the Old Testament. The request came as he was setting up his bar in the third floor function room of New York's Waldorf-Astoria hotel. Nino watched in awe as one powerful Hollywood executive after another entered, many greeting each other in Yiddish. He recognized some of them from their previous visits and, most recently, from the spread in *Life* magazine that came out that very morning, November 24, 1947.

"The Movie Hearings," by Sidney Olson, frantically revealed how Reds were trying to take over Hollywood and how the House Un-American Activities Committee had summoned a gallery of star witnesses to expose it. Many in the October 10-20 hearings had testified willingly, but others noisily refused, triggering the gavel of HUAC Chairman J. Parnell Thomas. Ten writers, directors, and producers who refused to discuss their personal beliefs and associations were called The Hollywood Ten and sparked debate all across the country and the political spectrum as to which side was right. Now the hotel suite was filling with studio brass who had not only been friendly witnesses but shared Thomas's impatience with the Hollywood Ten, who were now being called The Unfriendly Ten.

"We're not supposed to be here," said the man Nino recognized as Barney Balaban, head of Paramount Pictures. "When you get the heads of all the movie companies in one room, it's called restraint of trade."

"Who's restraining trade," said Harry Cohn of Columbia Pictures. "We're just talking business."

"That's the point," chimed in Albert Warner, whom everybody called The Major. "The Justice Department is already investigating us for monopoly in how we make, distribute, and show our films. Whose idea was it for all of us to meet like this anyway?"

"Mine," barked Nicholas Schenck, head of Loew's, Incorporated, the parent company of MGM. "To hell with anti-trust laws. The government has made it clear that they'll look the other way as long as we take a stand against Reds in the film business and how to get rid of them."

That's when all eyes–96 of them, because there were 48 men in the room–turned to Nino, who stood at the bar polishing his highball glasses.

"Anybody care for a drink?" he asked weakly.

"What are you doing here, Nino?" asked Sam Goldwyn. It was more of a question than a challenge; Mr. Goldwyn always stayed at the Waldorf when he came east, and he remembered everything and everyone, even as he crafted a public image as a bumbling illiterate. "I thought you were in the main dining room."

"They assigned me here today, Mr. Goldwyn," Nino said. "They said they didn't want someone who couldn't be trusted."

"Better swear him in anyway," said Cohn. "We didn't tell the press we were here and we sure as hell don't want anything getting out of this room." Nino froze. As a hotel employee of some twenty years, he was used to keeping guest secrets. In a hotel that attracted as many movie stars as the

Waldorf, discretion came with the job. Nino could have taken the demand for an oath as an insult but, instead, it piqued his curiosity about what was to come.

"Anybody here got a Bible?" said William Goetz, president of the newly formed Universal-International Pictures. "It's a hotel, maybe one of those Gideon things."

"Bite your tongue." said Cohn. "Barney, you believe this Jewish stuff, you must have one."

"I have one that'll do," said James Byrnes. Byrnes, a former senator and secretary of state, was working with the movie industry to craft its response to HUAC. "Try this." He produced a copy of the Old Testament and asked Nino to place his left hand on it, raise his right hand, and promise to keep secret what he might be about to see or hear.

That done, the meeting started.

Nino paid close attention while trying to appear like he wasn't. Ordinarily, waiters and bartenders are invisible to their customers, but the men at this Waldorf conference were sharp. If they or their designees could parse every page of script and screen every foot of film for Communist content, as they told HUAC they did, they would certainly notice a hotel employee paying too-close attention to their meeting agenda.

"First, we got to get rid of the Reds," said Spyros Skouras, who had taken control of Twentieth Century-Fox. "I don't care what it takes, we fire them."

"They all have contracts," said Warner. "Remember when we were flush with money during the war and signed everybody to rich deals? Now that television is cutting our revenues, we're stuck with bloated payrolls."

"Not a problem," smiled Skouras. "Just say somebody's a Red and you can cancel their contract. I already had Darryl Zanuck fire Ring Lardner, Jr. for not testifying. Easy and quick."

"This could be a great way to trim our payroll, L.B." Eddie Mannix advised Louis B. Mayer, head of MGM. Mannix was in charge of Metro's operations and knew every expense from toilet paper to hush money. "As long as the government stands behind us, that is."

"The government will," assured Byrnes. "As you know, the U.S. Supreme Court is looking into your business practices. Any time two or more of you gentlemen get together, it's collusion."

"He's right," said Paul McNutt of Eric Johnston's office. Johnston headed the Motion Picture Producers of America, the industry's trade group. McNutt was their lawyer. "If you all fire them at once, you could be accused of conspiracy."

"Except," Byrnes stressed loud and clearly, "for today and tomorrow, Uncle Sam is looking the other way. Do what you have to do to get rid of Reds. Period."

As the moguls took their seats, a tall, bespectacled man seemed to be hovering, watching all of them while, at the same time, losing himself in his own thoughts. Nino made eye contact with him and the man slowly walked over to his bar.

"Something I can get you?" Nino asked.

"Orange juice," answered Dore Schary, new

production head of RKO Radio Pictures and the one man in the room who appeared out of place. "Although in a couple of hours I may ask for a double Scotch." Nino filled a large glass with orange juice and handed it over.

"Aren't you going to sit down with the others?" the waiter asked.

"I want to see who's sitting with whom," Schary said. "It's like a high school lunch room. Look. The Loew's and Metro guys sit together, Paramount and Warner are over there in a cluster, RKO is next to Fox, and Universal isn't sure where to sit. Oh, and Columbia is alone."

"Doesn't anyone like Columbia?" Nino asked.

"Everyone likes Columbia," Schary said, "it's Harry Cohn they can't stand."

"Gentlemen, I'm calling this meeting to order," said Eric Johnston as Schary moved at his own speed to a seat halfway between RKO and Metro. "Whatever intrigues any of us may have on the outside, as long as we're in this room we have to form a solid bloc against Communist influence. Our industry is at a crisis. Ticket sales are down, pressure groups like the American Legion are threatening to boycott our films, foreign territories are refusing to import our pictures, Wall Street is nervous, and the public thinks we take our orders from Stalin. What are we going to do about it?"

"In ten days of hearings last month nobody produced anything in any of our films that was Communistic," said Louis B. Mayer. "Doesn't that mean that we're doing our job?"

"Not according to Ginger Rogers' mother," said William Levy, the RKO sales executive who handled Disney's films.

"I heard her," Dore Schary interrupted. "I was embarrassed when she said that the Bill of Rights should only apply to people for whom it was intended, whatever that means."

"It means no Reds, Dore," said Skouras.

"When we had Ginger under contract, Lela was part of the package," Levy said. "What she doesn't know about the law could keep our legal department busy for months, and it did. We finally got rid of her by having her run a charm school for actresses."

Schary was quick to add, "She raised a talented daughter, but there's no way we should listen to her advice."

"Stop being the college professor, Dore," said Mayer unequivocally. "The solution is clear. Fire them and let's get back to business."

"Easier said than done, Dad," said Goetz. He had married Mayer's daughter, Edie, and loved making his father-in-law squirm. "If we fire them, we'll be, in effect, allowing the government to dictate what we can and can't put on the screen. They're already trying to regulate our business practices. You want to hand them our cameras, too?"

"If it's good for America, it's good for Hollywood," Mayer said. "And that's that."

Schary crossed the room for more orange juice. This time Goldwyn joined him and asked Nino for the same. While Nino was pouring, Goldwyn leaned close to Schary and said, in a low voice, "Dore, you've got to do something. They're going crazy."

"Yes, but what?" The younger mogul asked.

"I don't know, but you're a writer. Think of something."

The phone rang. Nino answered it, "Third floor function room. Yes, he's here." He signaled to Eric Johnston, who took the call. Johnston's face went even whiter than it was normally. When he hung up, the whole room stared at him apprehensively.

"It's from Washington," he said gravely. "Congress has just voted contempt citations against the Hollywood Ten."

"Now it's serious," said Mannix.

"More serious than you know," Johnston continued. "After contempt was passed, Representative John Rankin from Mississippi took to the floor of Congress to criticize Jewish actors like Edward G. Robinson, Danny Kaye, Melvyn Douglas, and, quote, 'others too numerous to mention who are 'attacking the Committee for trying to protect this country and save the American people from the horrible fate the Communists have meted out to unfortunate Christian people.' Unquote."

"This is the man," sighed Balaban, "who has used the words *kike, hebe,* and *yid* on the floor of the United States Congress."

The room went from silent to funereal. Nino didn't dare even slice lemons.

"Is this about Communists," asked Schary, "or is it about Jews?"

"What do you think, Dore?" asked Goldwyn.

"We don't make pictures about Communists," he said. "We also don't make pictures about Jews, except when RKO did *Crossfire.*"

"At Fox we just released *Gentleman's Agreement,*" announced Skouras. "It's about a Jew passing as a Gentile. So far, it's doing business. Of course, the Jew is played by a Gentile."

"It figures," muttered William Levy. "Fox and RKO are the only studios owned by Gentiles. None of us Jews wants to call attention to ourselves. Even when the Nazis took over Europe, we waited."

"Nobody's wanted to see Jews since *The Jazz Singer,*" Mayer pronounced. "Rabbis aren't interesting. Priests are interesting. They have all that stuff."

"Is anybody here surprised?" said Harry Cohn. "Most of the Hollywood Ten were Jewish. Most of us who testified are Jewish. Nobody on the Committee is Jewish. That's what this is about."

"So, what do we do?" asked Albert Warner. "To the anti-Semites, Jew is just another word for Communist."

"We need some kind of statement," Johnston said. "A press release. Call it a peace pact. Something that will mollify the Committee and show the public that we mean business."

"And Dore will write it," promised Goldwyn.

"What?" Schary said, horrified. "Sam, are you out of your mind?"

"It may be the only thing that will modify them," Goldwyn said, sort of. "And if anybody can write it, it should be you."

It was getting late. Nino began closing his bar; he had long since accepted the fact that this was not a drinking crowd. If anything, it was a complaining crowd, but he took that as an extension of the talk he had been hearing whenever Hollywood moguls stayed at the hotel. According to their casual conversation, business was always bad no matter how much money they were making.

Nino was not assigned to the second day of the confab. The drink orders weren't sufficient to warrant it. He went back to the main dining room where at least the tips were better.

When the newspaper extra came out an hour after the Waldorf conference ended on Tuesday, November 25, Nino rushed to the lobby newsstand to buy a copy. It carried the text of what came to be known as the "Waldorf Peace Pact." In it, all the studios agreed to not only fire the Hollywood Ten but to sack anybody else who could not prove that he or she wasn't a Communist.

The peace pact neither mollified nor modified the political climate in America. In June of 1950, *Red Channels* was published listing 151 actors, writers, composers, and others whose affiliations, in the opinion of the right-wing publishers, were too radical to allow them to work in radio, TV, or movies. In April of 1951, HUAC hearings resumed and the real bloodbath began. The blacklist did not end until the middle 1960s. Some of its effects are still being felt.

Nino, who had watched it begin at the Waldorf Conference on November 24 and 25, 1947, never broke his oath. But he also never forgot the lesson of how easily powerful people can be undercut by ignorance.

"It was not," he remembered, "a drinking crowd. Instead of alcohol, they were drunk with fear."

COLLATERAL DAMAGE

When Darryl F. Zanuck phoned Sylvia Horn-ing, she was as pleased as if she was Norma Desmond and Cecil B. DeMille was on the line. "I have a terrific part for you, Sylvia," Zanuck said, even though it had been years since they'd spoken. "It's the perfect comeback vehicle, sure to get attention. Mind if I send it over?"

"Not at all, Mr. Zanuck," Sylvia managed. "I'd love to see it."

"Fine," the mogul said cheerfully. "You haven't lost your acting chops since you left us, have you?"

"Still got 'em," Sylvia said soundly. "I've been on Broadway and touring."

"Good, good," Zanuck said, only half-listening. "Read the material and, if you're interested, have your agent give us a call. Looking forward to having you back."

With that, the head of Twentieth Century-Fox hung up. Sylvia was speechless. She didn't tell Zanuck that she no longer had an agent. Or that she had long since let her SAG card lapse. It happened so fast that she was in shock. After eighteen years, all it took was one phone call and she was off the Blacklist.

A Fox contract ingenue in the 1940s, she had been lured from a New York modeling career at 16 by a studio casting agent impressed with her poise and a glow of youthfulness that shimmered beneath an aura of maturity. Tall and dignified, yet with a youthful smile, she had bearing and class. This kept her from becoming one of the "Four o'clock girls" who used to visit Zanuck's office at that hour every afternoon during which his secre-tary held calls and allowed no access while he enjoyed *droit du seigneur*. To the contrary, the mogul acted almost like her uncle, carefully choosing her roles as well as guiding her social life, clearly trying to make her into another Loretta Young (only without having Clark Gable's love child) or a standby Jeanne Crain in case the real Jeanne Crain wanted more money.

Taking acting lessons at the same time that she was thrown into showy featured roles, Sylvia was being groomed for romantic leads while living modestly and chastely with her parents in a Culver City bungalow. If they seemed overly protective, it was because they were; not only did they have to sign her studio contract because she was under-age, they moved from Manhattan to California to keep an eye on her. If what they'd heard about Tinseltown morals was true, they were determined that Sylvia would not become ensnared in them. For Sylvia's part, she was content to live with her father, Harry, a salesman; her mother, Bess, a housewife; and her younger sister, Susan, who was still in school. Acting was a lark for her, not a calling. She was getting good at it, but she had been raised to respect tradition while keeping an open mind about new ideas; at 16, she was by no means a radical.

Her boss, Darryl Zanuck, respected Sylvia's prudence. She might have followed all the latest clothing or makeup trends, but she didn't talk politics with him or anyone else on the Fox lot, as far as he could tell. She was not a "professional againster" as Jack Warner called James Cagney.

Zanuck himself was known as a pragmatic Progressive, a stance he had adopted while production chief at Warner Bros. where their screen stories were "torn from the morning's headlines" and appealed to populist audiences. For years after forming his own company, Twentieth Century-Fox, in 1935, he kept his eye on that audience, making such socially relevant films over the decades as *Pinky*, *Gentleman's Agreement*, *The Grapes of Wrath*, and *Viva Zapata*, among others that challenged the social order (within reason).

Thus, when the House Un-American Activities dug for Communism in Hollywood with its October 1947 hearings, it was a foregone conclusion that somebody would point a finger at Fox. It didn't stick. Zanuck was the only mogul in town that the Committee couldn't push around. Unlike the other studio heads, Zanuck wasn't Jewish, so Hedda Hopper and the other anti-Semites couldn't rally Christian hackles against him. He was also a real World War II veteran for, while the other moguls wangled sinecure commissions, Zanuck actually saw battle with the Signal Corps and returned to Hollywood with the combat footage to prove it.

Some of his employees, however, weren't so lucky as to escape HUAC. Among those who were subpoenaed was Ring Lardner, Jr., who was working on a picture for producer Otto Preminger. An unfriendly witness who refused to answer the Committee's questions, Lardner was cited for Contempt of Congress. Shortly thereafter, he was summoned to Zanuck's office and fired.

And then there was Sylvia Horning. Unlike the directors, writers, and, above all, stars who were mentioned during the House Un-American Activities Committee hearings, Sylvia's was nowhere near a household name when MGM leading man Jeffery Nason dropped it during his October 22, 1947 friendly testimony. He did it right after he said that Bobby Da Marco "always seems to have something to say at the wrong time" and therefore must be a Communist. Then he added, "and, of course, there's Sylvia Horning." It was so casual that chairman J. Parnell Thomas, interrogator Robert Stripling, and Committee member Richard Nixon didn't follow it up with a question of clarification. It just slipped into the record.

Roy Brewer didn't miss it, though. Brewer, the head of the projectionists' union, hated Reds to the point of appointing himself their personal prosecutor. He vowed that, if HUAC wouldn't go after Sylvia, he would. There were only two problems. First, the public at large didn't know who she was so there was scant publicity value in accusing her of disloyalty. The second problem was bigger: she wasn't a Red. But that didn't mean she couldn't be a Commie sympathizer like so many Hollywood liberals who didn't have the guts to join the Party but still wanted to overthrow the system.

Sylvia knew nothing about this pending storm as she wrapped *Time for Love* at Fox at the beginning of November 1947. She had been going from one picture to the next for the last three years, barely able to have a social life, let alone a political one. Any free time she had was taken up by acting classes and publicity appearances that the studio compelled her to perform. For a while, she was seen everywhere from grocery store openings to contrived "Star of Tomorrow" awards, all in service of establishing her name before the public.

What Jeffery Nason had against her was a mystery. They had never worked together and, moreover, were under contract at different studios. Sylvia didn't even know anything was amiss until the usual Friday script failed to turn up on her doorstep for the weekend read. At first, she thought it was a mistake, so she called up the casting department and was told that she wouldn't be needed on Monday. When she asked the publicity department about posing for fashion layouts, they said the same thing. Concerned, she phoned Zanuck's office. His secretary said, "I think you'd better come in and see him, dear."

When she did, Zanuck cut to the chase. "Sylvia," he said, "are you a Red?"

She was so stunned at first that she couldn't answer.

"And don't give me any malarkey about the First Amendment," he said. "The Unfriendly Ten tried that at the hearings and they're looking at a jail term. I need to know if you're a Red."

"I'm not," she said. "I mean, I'm not even old enough to vote for Wallace, which I wish I could have done, but I'm not Red. I'm not even pink."

"Why would Jeffery Nason name you?"

"I have no idea," she stammered. "I don't even know him."

"Why would your name be on the list?" Zanuck zeroed in. "The list that everybody says doesn't exist but we all know does."

Sylvia could only shrug. Zanuck took a few puffs on his cigar and said, "Let me look into this."

A week later Zanuck arranged a meeting with a certain lawyer who was known around town as a "fixer" who had the ear of the Motion Picture Alliance for the Preservation of American Ideals, the arch-conservative group led by Ronald Reagan that was informally known as the "purge board" by those who came before it. Their office was in a plain looking building with no sign out front, a courtesy, they insisted, to those who visited them to plead their patriotism. Sylvia's meeting was called "informal." If she cooperated, an official one would be set up to start the name-clearing process.

"But I'm not a Communist," she told them in answer to the $64 question ("Are you now or have you ever been. . .?") made famous by Chairman Thomas at the October hearings.

"Unless you admit it, we can't help you," the Board spokesman, Van Armstrong, told her.

"I don't think you heard me," she said. "I'm not a Communist and never have been."

"Then I'm afraid we can't help you, sweetheart," he said. "We don't have a way to help someone who says they're not a Communist, only those who come clean."

With that, the meeting was over. Sylvia was by then 21, unemployed, and under a cloud of somebody else's making.

At home she discussed the bizarre encounter with her parents. "They actually offered to help me lie," she said in wonderment. "They didn't care about the truth. All they wanted was another notch."

"And this is the industry you want to work in?" her mother Bess asked. She had been supportive of Sylvia's dreams but only when they made sense. Her father Harry was more direct. "Who writes their material, Franz Kafka?"

"I don't know what I want anymore," Sylvia said, finally allowing tears. "If I'd done something wrong I'd understand, but I haven't done anything at all."

"What does Mr. Zanuck say?" Harry asked.

"He says his hands are full with employees who actually *are* Communists and he has to deal with them first. He said I'm on the payroll until my option comes up."

"But you're innocent!" her mother protested.

"That doesn't matter," Sylvia said. "If I'm a liability to the studio and they can't put me in any pictures, they can drop me."

Which is what they did in the spring of 1948 despite Zanuck's efforts to find parts for her. Roy Brewer simply decreed that if Sylvia Horning was in a movie, his projectionists would refuse to show it, and that was that.

Banned from Hollywood, Sylvia turned her talents in other directions. They did not make her rich, but they provided for herself and her parents, with whom she lived until she wed. The marriage, to a young entrepreneur, lasted barely a year and ended with neither children nor alimony.

Over the years Sylvia tried a number of times to connect with Nason, whose star remained in the firmament while hers shifted toward theatre and the new medium of live television. Moving to New York, she found work in theatre, which did not heed the Blacklist, and she toured with such productions as *You Can't Take It with You*, *The Male Animal*, and a limited run of Shaw's *Pygmalion* in which she was a sensation as Eliza. On Broadway, which needed star names, hers held no cache, so she transitioned to supporting character roles in a revival of *Major Barbara* and as a replacement Ado Annie in *Oklahoma*. Between stage shows she was cast in television dramas (*U.S. Steel Hour*, *Goodyear Playhouse*, etc.) flying under the radar until someone checked *Red Channels* and found her name.

How does someone survive 18 years as a non-person? By becoming involved in social causes. "Being blacklisted can really radicalize you," Sylvia told a reporter years later. "It made me a strong union supporter, someone who worked for civil rights, and a marcher in some of the first anti-war rallies during Vietnam. It was an easy choice. When they call you a radical, you might as well become one."

It was with that backstory that Sylvia accepted Zanuck's offer to appear in the drama *Time to Care*. It wasn't the lead, it was a maiden aunt, and Sylvia would have to show her age. But she had three good scenes and they gave her back her old dressing room on the Fox lot.

There was only one potential problem. The leading man–the actor with whom she'd have to play her scenes–was Jeffery Nason.

Sylvia said nothing when she heard this. On the first day of rehearsals, at the table read, she studied Nason, sitting across the room, for any glimmer of recognition. There was none. Once production started, not wanting to make trouble, she treated Nason with deference to his stardom and indulged no further than small talk. They did not have lunch together or hang out after wrap. He had his retinue, she kept to herself. Only when they were about to shoot their last scene together did Sylvia search in earnest for a way to ask Nason why he had named her to the Committee. She found it when he complimented her on her acting and wondered why they had never worked together. "I'm surprised I'd never heard of you before this," he said. "You'd think we would have met."

"Truth to tell, Mr. Nason," she began, "I think we must already know each other, but I am also not sure how."

"What do you mean?" Nason said, "and don't you think you should call me Jeff?"

"Did you ever work at Fox while I was there in the 40s?" she asked.

"No," he said firmly, "I was at Metro. Hey, that must be where we met."

"I was never at Metro," she said.

"Yes, you were," Nason insisted. His lined face opened wide. "Now I remember. We did a screen test together. I must say, for someone at the start of your career, you were a little hard to deal with. You thought you knew it all."

"I'm sorry, Mr. Nason," Sylvia said coolly, trying to contain herself. "I've never set foot in Metro and I never did a screen test there or anything else."

Nason shook his head. "You most certainly did set foot in Metro, Miss Hartnett. I remember it as clearly as I remember my dressing room furniture."

Sylvia tightened. Her voice quivered. "For your information, Mr. Nason," she said, "My name is not Sylvia Hartnett. It's Sylvia Horning. Sylvia Hartnett was an ingenue at Metro who was let go for bad attitude. I checked."

"Oh shit," Nason said. "You mean all through this picture I've been thinking you were the wrong Sylvia?"

"I guess so," Sylvia said.

"Well, gee, honey, I'm sorry," he said genuinely. "I guess I'm showing my age. I thought you were Sylvia Hartnett. I won't make that mistake again." He smiled as he turned away. "At least there's no harm done."

Sylvia waited until she got home that night to her one-bedroom apartment. Then she laughed. Then she cried. Then she did both at the same time. Then she got to where she couldn't tell one from the other.

ONLY SCOUNDRELS

We were halfway through Silas Raymond's funeral when I finally realized that the mourner I had been struggling to recognize was the man who had blacklisted my father. I saw him again two days later at Musso & Frank's. He sat alone in a booth, watching the door as if he expected J. Edgar Hoover to burst in and arrest him. Then I thought, no, they won't arrest him, they'll arrest the people he named to the Committee under orders of Silas Raymond.

Silas Raymond was the most notorious Red-baiter of the witch hunt era. Even though he didn't sit on the house Un-American Activities Committee, he walked in goosestep with them. He said he could spot a Red within five minutes, and he decimated Hollywood's creative community with a campaign of intimidation, guilt by association, and outright lies. That's why I went to his funeral; I wanted to make sure the son of a bitch was dead. They planted him at the stroke of noon (though the stroke of midnight would have been more fitting) at Forest Lawn, and I remembered thinking that the low turnout for such a one-time heavyweight wasn't because he was forgotten, it was because he'd outlived all of his friends and most of his enemies. I was one of the latter.

I behaved myself during the services even though I wanted to put a stake in his heart right there in the chapel. I needed to see who would show up to honor him. Among his handful of mourners were, appropriately, his children, grandchildren, and great-grandchildren. And Marcus Gottfried.

That was the name I finally connected with the face I'd seen. A former director, he was in his low eighties, twenty years older than my father was when my dad died. We swapped glances during the services and then went our separate ways. Maybe he was wondering who I was, too.

It was fitting that we both wound up at Musso's, the last surviving great Hollywood restaurant now that Nickodell's was gone. We were survivors, too, of an era. That's what I mulled as I slowly realized that my 1 PM meeting with a Paramount development executive was falling through, and I stared at Gottfried nervously nursing a soda. Who would he be meeting? When it was obvious that both of us were being stood up, I can't explain why, I went over and introduced myself.

"Were you a friend of Silas Raymond?" I asked. He studied me for a long beat before answering.

"No," he said without emotion. "Were you?"

"No," I said. "And yet we both went to his funeral."

Gottfried nodded his head solemnly. "I *knew* him," he said, his eyes drifting off, "but that doesn't mean we were friends."

He neither invited me to join him nor waved me away. "You're Marcus Gottfried," I said. "I'm Joey Samuelson. Burt Samuelson's son." He looked up at me with the searching gaze I had used on him at the funeral. Then the coin dropped.

"I'm sorry," he said.

I wanted to say "You should be," but I saw that I didn't need to. Instead, I said, "Tell me your story." When he hesitated, I added, "You owe me that much. It's more than they let my father do."

"Your father was a good man," Gottfried said.

"Then why did you name him?"

"You don't understand these things," he said, looking around. He was either trying to find a waiter or preparing to bolt. So I sat beside him, uninvited, placed my hand on his wrist, and looked squarely and calmly into his faded eyes.

"Then explain it to me," I said evenly, "because now you're the only one who can."

"I'm expecting a meeting," he said, pulling his hand from under mine.

"It's Friday at 2 PM," I said. "Face it. My meeting isn't showing up and neither is yours. Let's have lunch and dine on the soul of Silas Raymond."

He sighed, then smiled. I'd broken the ice that had been frozen for half a century.

"Let's get something straight first," he said, placing his napkin in his lap. "I didn't *inform*, I *cleared my name*. There's a difference."

"Okay," I led flatly.

"Anybody who knows anything about the Hollywood Blacklist knows that we weren't the ones who did the smearing. We were the ones who got smeared. Like your father, all we did was try to make the world better. We were young, we were idealistic, we had a little money for the first time. Maybe we were naive in believing America would do the right thing if we showed it how, but we did believe in the right stuff. Were we a threat to democracy? Never. Were we a threat to the people who were making our country worse? Look around. Our mistake was that we weren't strong enough to win the propaganda war, even if history has long since settled the score in our favor."

I wasn't expecting that articulate an answer. I had assumed that everybody who named names was a Red-baiting anti-Communist wingnut. In my bitterness, as the child of a blacklistee, it had never occurred to me that some of them might also be disillusioned Lefties caught in a moral crisis.

The Blacklist (I always capitalize it) started in 1947 after the HUAC hearings in October of that year. In November, a group of studio moguls got together in secret at the Waldorf-Astoria Hotel in New York and wrote a statement that triggered the Blacklist. The "Waldorf Peace Pact," as it was called, laid the groundwork to get rid of any employee that anybody thought was a Communist. The big purge, however, started in 1951 when HUAC resumed its hearings and all hell broke loose.

"If you didn't face it yourself, you have no right to judge those of us who did," Gottfried insisted. "Here's how it worked. Once you got your HUAC subpoena, you had to decide whether you wanted to testify or leave the country. If you testified, you could either claim the Fifth Amendment or cooperate. If you took the Fifth, you'd lose your job but you'd become a hero to your left-wing friends, only they couldn't help you because they were out of work, too. You would also be a pariah in the press and at the studios. If you cooperated with the Committee, you would be able to work, but you'd lose your friends.

"I was called before the Committee after being named as a Communist by three people,"

Gottfried continued, "only one of whom I actually knew. He was a studio executive I'd demanded a raise from. Some Red, huh?"

"Did he testify against you?" I asked.

"Not face to face," Gottfried said dismissively. "They never did. As chairman Wood explained between gavel bangs, 'this is a Congressional hearing, not a court of law.'"

Our waiter, Louis, filled our water glasses and hovered, waiting for an order. I said we'd share the stuffed celery and appetizer Frank. Gottfried didn't object. "I love their anchovy dressing," he said.

It seemed like a fair time to ask what the Committee called "the $64 question." If Gottfried got angry and left, I'd only be stuck with a bill for the appetizers. If he answered, I might learn something. So I asked it: "Were you a Red?"

Gottfried laughed. "As Hiram Sherman used to say, 'We're not allowed to tell.'" Then he answered firmly, "Of course I was! I joined during the war when Uncle Sam was extolling 'our glorious Russian allies.' What's more, I'm proud of my Party membership. A lot of Progressives joined the Party because it offered more than either the Democrats or the Republicans. It was the Lefties, not the Righties, who went to Spain and fought the fascists in the Abraham Lincoln Brigade. Look at civil rights, women's rights, labor unions, the forty-hour work week, Social Security–the Right opposed all of them. If anybody has anything to apologize for, it's people who *didn't* join the Party."

"But it was all lies," I said. "Russia lied."

"We didn't know that till after Stalin died," he shook his head sadly. "Communism betrayed us. But when we joined, it made sense."

"Isn't that all the Committee wanted to hear? That you were duped?"

"That wasn't what they wanted to hear," Gottfried said as if I was a moron. "It was about conformity. It was about crushing freedom of thought. It was about control and being afraid to have an opinion. It was also about anti-Semitism."

"Which leads us to Silas Raymond," I said, crunching on a rib of celery as I tried to appear casual. "I know why I was at his funeral. Why were you?"

Gottfried spooned up some of the anchovy dressing before he answered. "Closure."

*   *   *

It's an old story but it needs re-telling lest it happen again. Never mind that Communism was legal and still is. Never mind that the First Amendment forbids government inquiry into one's personal beliefs or associations. The Committee didn't care because America didn't care. Whether you took the First or the Fifth didn't matter. When it was over, you were a non-person. If you wanted to work again, you had to call Silas Raymond.

As Caesar's wife must be above suspicion, so Silas Raymond positioned himself beyond reproach. As an industry leader, power broker, and paid consultant, he formed the Motion Picture Business Council with the cagey lie that, since there was no Blacklist, they couldn't get you off of it, but if you made a sincere effort to repent, they would circulate word that you were okay to hire again.

Raymond constructed his Council with an FBI agent, a union honcho, a corporate lawyer, and a self-avowed expert on Communism (who boasted that he had read scores of books on the subject yet miraculously never fell under suspicion). Naturally, Raymond appointed himself chairman.

My father was one of Raymond's first penitents, or so the plan was supposed to go. This was in 1952. Dad had started as a screenwriter at Columbia just after the war. He'd sold two stories to Harry Cohn who, with typical Cohnian logic, took him off his own stories and assigned him to turn somebody *else's* story into a script. This was Dad's big opportunity, not only to jump from story man to scripter but to leap from $250 a week to $1,500.

The story he was assigned, *Man on the Street*, was a populist fantasy that Cohn thought might lure back Frank Capra, who was smarting from the failure of *It's a Wonderful Life*. It was about a politician running for office who makes wildly contradictory campaign promises figuring that nobody expects him to keep them anyway. Once he gets into office, however, his conscience takes over and he tries to please everybody. It was really only the first half of a story and my father's job was to give it an ending. He did the only thing that made sense: he made the politician a stooge of corporations who sought to benefit from the sham election. Everybody from Cohn to Capra was horrified. "How dare you bite the hand that feeds you?" Cohn said as he fired my father. "Big business makes America rich." So Dad moved to RKO where Dore Schary was putting messages into their films. He was working on a race picture when Schary quit RKO for MGM, Howard Hughes took over RKO, and my dad got fired again when his name appeared in *Red Channels* in June of 1950. His name was cross-referenced with half a dozen organizations he had neither been part of nor given money to. Hughes didn't care.

As with Gottfried, there was no one for Burt Samuelson to sue, no one to talk to. When his subpoena arrived in 1951, we traveled as a family to Washington where Dad was eager to set things straight. When he was finally called before Chairman John Wood, he sat at the witness table accompanied only by his daily appointment book and his conscience.

"A lot of people who I don't know have testified that they know me, and that I'm a Communist," Dad started out evenly. "I wish I had that many friends, just not that kind. If you can tell me where they say they know me from, and when they say they saw me, I can look at my date book and tell you where I was on those dates, and you'll see that they were all lying."

The sound of Wood's gavel at the word *lying* was so deafening it made a "pop" on the recording that the Committee was making. It was also the last calm exchange my father had with the Committee. He said he'd talk about himself but not others, and demanded to be allowed, under the Sixth Amendment, to confront his accusers. "This is not a court of law," Wood said, "if anything, it's the court of public opinion."

"In that case," Dad said, losing it, "this member of the public is of the opinion that since this Committee isn't interested in the facts, or even the truth, it is the Committee that is out of order."

Several gavels later, it was over and we trudged from Washington back to Los Angeles followed by the promise of a contempt citation. From that point on, the phone didn't ring, and, when it did, there were clicks on the line. Letters arrived that had obviously been steamed open and re-sealed. None of my friends would play with me. Even the Avon Lady skipped our house.

One day a big lawyer phoned. He'd represented a lot of the people who had been blacklisted, and now he was suddenly the go-to person if you wanted to get off the Blacklist. He said a Council had been set up so people could clear their names and quash their contempt citations. My father, naturally, asked how he could clear his name when he wasn't the one who'd soiled it. The lawyer ignored the comment and insisted that Dad take down a number. After discussing it with my mother (my brother and I were too young), he decided to call it. This was Dad's first encounter with Silas Raymond.

"We cannot get your job back or clear your name," Raymond began when they met. "Only you can do that. If you give evidence that you want to leave the Party, then you have to name people and come to our side to fight them. Our job is to help you and them find ways to get out."

My father looked blankly at Raymond. ""Okay, then, what do I have to do?"

"First thing is to write a letter saying how you were duped. The more detailed, the better. Say where you were, who invited you, and who you were with."

"But I never went anywhere," Dad said, shaking his head. "I tried to tell that to the Wood Committee but nobody cared."

"Don't try to play us!" Raymond cut him off. His fleshy face, pointed nose, and ice-blue eyes made him look like Halloween was coming. "If you don't have names, we have some you can use."

The chicanery galled my father. "Oh, now I remember some," he said, a twinkle sparking in his eyes. "I used to go to Party meetings with Ronald Reagan, Adolph Menjou, John Wayne, Ward Bond, Robert Taylor, George Murphy, Lela Rogers–"

"Stop wasting our time!" Raymond fumed. Dad had just named Hollywood's key Red-baiters. "Get us the letter within a week and we'll see what we can do. And don't try to be smart. Oh, and incidentally, don't forget the processing fee."

"What processing fee?" Dad asked, confused.

"There's a five-thousand-dollar processing fee for the Council's consulting services."

My father was astonished. "You mean I have to pay you five thousand dollars to get off a blacklist that I shouldn't be on in the first place?"

"How many times do I have to tell you, *there is no blacklist*," Raymond insisted.

My father left the room more confused than when he'd entered. For the next few weeks he called everyone he knew, everyone who might be able to lend him or give him a few dollars. It was degrading to do and sad to watch. Finally, Dad realized where he could get five thousand dollars. One night after the family went to bed he shut himself in the garage with the car running and committed suicide. The insurance paid the five thousand dollars. We used it to move to another city, change our family name, and survive.

*　　　*　　　*

Marcus Gottfried's closure came after a similar ordeal. "As my family and I settled into being blacklisted," he said, "I saw my kids' friends refuse to play with them, people cross the street when my wife and I strolled near, and the mail always arrived a day late because somebody had to read it first. This went on for the better part of a year until my savings were almost gone and I could only find the most menial jobs. As a director, I had to be seen on a movie set, so I couldn't use a front like my writer friends. To get off the Blacklist, that meant that I had to clear my name. I had to go to Silas Raymond."

Gottfried was given the same choices as my father: The Council, the confession, the names, and the shame. "It's hard to say you were duped," Gottfried said, "because it meant that you rejected all the things you were raised to think America stood for. Nevertheless, that was what the routine amounted to. When it came to naming others that I'd been in the party with, that's where I froze, and they knew it. If I didn't remember enough of them, Raymond said they'd be happy to provide me with more. I asked what good it would do to name someone I didn't know, or who I wasn't sure was in the Party, and they said it didn't matter, the whole point was to clear *my* name and let others worry about theirs. They even suggested I could give them names of people I didn't like. They didn't have to be Reds, they just had to be troublemakers. Raymond said that a lot of people had taken the opportunity to settle old scores." Gottfried's throat went dry so he sipped the last of his soda. "Your father's was one of the names they gave me. Since he was in *Red Channels* it was automatic. I'm sorry. After forty-five years, I'm all out of tears."

Marcus took my hands in his and at last looked me squarely in the eyes. "You may not believe this, but when I left that room, I felt as imprisoned as when I'd gone in. They congratulated me for helping defeat the enemies of America, but I saw that the real enemies of America were those who sit on Councils like theirs.

"Two days later the newspapers picked up word of my exoneration and the phone started to ring again. That is, it rang from agents and producers. My friends stopped calling. I had been told to expect that. What I didn't expect was that I didn't even get any calls from the friends who had urged me to clear my name."

"Yeah," I said. "The Right doesn't like informers any more than the Left does."

"I didn't *inform*!" Marcus insisted. "I didn't tell them anything they didn't already know."

It's hard not to be judgmental about people like Marcus Gottfried; nobody has the right to criticize someone if they themselves haven't stood where he did. "Did you have to name my father, though?" I heard myself asking. "Couldn't you have skipped him?"

"I'm sorry, kid," he said. "I didn't even look at the names they gave me. They just wanted names."

"What've the years been like since then, Marcus?" I asked.

"Every now and then somebody leaves a room when I enter or asks the waiter to move him to another table. I've gotten used to it. My name turns up in books written by people who were blacklisted, and I get interview requests now and then, but I turn most of them down because all anybody wants to talk about is the Red stuff and not my movies. They're surprised to learn that the Hollywood Ten were the only ones who went to jail, and it was for contempt, not for Communism. The rest of us are still in jail, if you follow me."

He hadn't touched his appetizer, nor had I made it through more than a first bite of mine. He took his napkin and wiped his mouth, then dipped the corner in water and wiped his hands. The symbolism was perfect.

"You know what?" he said with finality." I don't care anymore. I didn't become a right-winger after I cleared my name. I still vote liberal. Clearing my name allowed me to work, allowed me to keep making contributions to my art, my industry, and my country. Some people have said that I did the wrong thing, but an artist has to keep working. Judge the art, not the artist."

I knew the meeting was over, but I wanted more. "Would you mind if I gave you my phone number? Next time we can talk about your movies."

"Tell you what," he said, brightening. "Turner Classics is running two of them tonight. Robert Osborne even interviewed me. You want to come over? I've got a small place on Whitley. My wife died ten years ago and it's a little messy, but how about it?"

'Why not?" I said. History is history. I squared the tab and we left Musso's. Marcus was pretty spry for a guy in his eighties.

"Did you have any more contact with Silas Raymond after that?" I asked as we walked.

"None," Marcus said. "I think he held a bunch of government jobs. Somebody or other was always appointing him to something. You didn't hear much about him until he died."

"I did," I said. "I found myself face to face with him a couple of years ago. Remember the Elia Kazan Oscar scandal? There was a Blacklist exhibit at the Academy after that and he came to the opening. He was ever so old by then and in a wheelchair. He wore white gloves to protect his fragile skin. I had to admire his grit in showing up to a collection of his enemies. It was the first time I'd met him."

"What'd you think of him?" Gottfried said as we stepped into the elevator.

I told Marcus how, like most villains, he was banal in the extreme, and, in his nineties, had become soft-spoken but no less emphatic about his rightness. Hoping to offer him a chance to make a mea culpa in light of history's condemnation, I began by complimenting him on his courage when organized crime was trying to take over Hollywood just before the Red scare. He nodded his thanks, and then veered into JFK assassination conspiracy theories. Why he chose me to hear this monologue I shall never know, but the wilder and more paranoid it got, the more I began to understand his actions during the Blacklist period.

"People who see villains behind every tree tend to be afraid of what they may find in their own forests," I mused. "What was he so afraid of all those years ago, and how did he and his kind get so many others to listen? That's why I had to see who'd come to his funeral."

The services had been held in one of Forest Lawn's smaller chapels. After the blessing, two young men stood to sing his praises. They were from one of those arch-conservative colleges that the right wing invents to legitimatize its think tanks, publishing houses, and lecture circuits. A family friend also spoke about how, when she needed it, dear Silas was able to give her five thousand dollars in cash toward her debts. Finally, a representative of the unions praised him for cleaning the Mob out of the locals, although–and I may be reading too much into it–the union man seemed to be just going through the motions, considering how many of these same union's members were driven from work by Raymond's tactics. I thought about standing and telling everyone about my father and asking why Silas Raymond had to go after him. But I don't think Silas Raymond even knew. That was okay. What bothered me was that he didn't care.

When I told this to Marcus Gottfried as we began watching his movies, he disagreed. "I think he cared very much. He cared about this country and did what he thought he had to do to save it. We all did. What we failed to grasp was that, in trying to save the country, we destroyed what it stood for. The show's starting; you want a beer?"

PART V:
NOW IT CAN BE TOLD

It's a widely held misconception in Hollywood that pictures about Hollywood don't make money. For every The Player, A Star is Burn, or Sunset Boulevard, there's The Oscar, Alex in Wonderland, Day of the Locust, or Won Ton Ton, the Dog Who Saved Hollywood. Truth is, if you look at a list of movies about movies, they're just as successful as movies about anything else. But let's face it, Hollywood is more interesting. From scandals involving movie stars to production accidents, and from meteoric rises to stardom to horrifying tales of plummeting fame, behind-the-scenes movies about the picture business can be riveting.

The thing to remember about the picture business is that anything you say about it is true. Maybe not your truth, but somebody else's. "Nobody's Oscar" is a spin-off from the story of Dalton Trumbo, the prolific writer who could not claim his 1956 Academy Award for The Brave One because he was blacklisted. It was finally presented to him in 1975, the year before he died.

"Firing Forsyth," is a cautionary tale about star attitude that nearly wrecked a picture. A frighteningly accurate portrait of the power politics between an actor and director who used to be friends, it serves up a challenging lesson as to why some films get made, others don't, and some of those that get made get made badly.

More fun is "Deal Picture," a story that not only takes studio thinking to task but acknowledges the time in every filmmaker's career when it was actually joyful to make movies and not a bureaucratic challenge.

It's clear while reading "The Publicist Who Thought He Was a Star" that Hollywood attracts scoundrels. Bobby van Arnold is a larger-than-life (by any definition) scallywag who happens to be doing movie publicity but could also run the studio if anybody had the gall to let him. There are simply some people for whom the rules bend by themselves, and Bobby is one of them.

The finish to this section is "Bad Penny," about a loser who gloms onto a winner. Like the definition of its title, John Clampett (an invented name, to be sure) keeps turning up no matter what the central character (who is strategically unnamed) does to escape him. John is never more than an irritant, and never malicious, but his presence is a constant reminder that no good deed goes unpunished.

NOBODY'S OSCAR

There stands in silent solitude, in a glass case at the Wilshire Boulevard headquarters of the Academy of Motion Picture Arts and Sciences, a lonely Oscar statuette. It carries no name plate and its hollow eyes stare in gilded silence at the countless people who pass it every day without so much as a moment's curiosity. The Oscar belongs to Harper Monroe Farrow, yet Harper Monroe Farrow has never claimed it. That is because there is no such person, male or female, living or dead, as Harper Monroe Farrow.

The Academy, in its unyielding discretion, has never spoken of their orphaned Oscar. Should a new employee notice it, he or she is told only that it must remain under lock and key because, by Academy rules, it can go only to the person who won it. And nobody has ever stepped forward.

Some have speculated that it must belong to the prolific Ben Hecht, who famously wrote or rewrote some 100 films during his colorful career and was rumored to have maintained a cadre of apprentices churning out first drafts that he would polish before attaching his name and a hefty invoice. Others say Farrow could have been any of a number of contract writers who were bored with the studio dreck they were forced to work on but who couldn't take credit for the winning script because they would have been fired for moonlighting. Still others insist that "Farrow" is a pseudonym for a Hollywood insider who wanted the truth to come out but dared not use his own name. Any or all of these explanations could be true.

Let's go over what is known and what must remain guesswork. Harper Monroe Farrow won the Academy Award® for Best Original Screenplay in 1939 for *Beyond Utopia*. Official records, of course, show that *Gone with the Wind*, written by Sidney Howard (but rewritten by Ben Hecht and others) won the statuette. Not to take away from David O. Selznick's achievement, but Farrow's script for *Beyond Utopia* must have bettered Selznick's juggernaut or it wouldn't have won. But you won't find a copy of it anywhere, not in the Academy's library or at the Writers Guild. You can't see the film, either, because all prints were destroyed. Finally, at this late date, anyone connected with the production has most certainly died.

If Harper Monroe Farrow was the pen name for a newspaper writer lured to Hollywood at the dawn of sound (like Hecht, Herman Mankiewicz, and others), he or she should have more credits. If we surmise "she," it would fit the career of Marjory Doyle, a feisty sob sister who worked on Hearst's Chicago *American* under the legendary editor Walter Howey. Doyle was chased out of Chicago for some of the things she wrote about the Capone mob and for years the rumor was that only a fix from the Chief--William Randolph Hearst himself--saved her life. Hold that thought.

Farrow might also have been a disgruntled whistle-blower who, when he or she was rebuked by law enforcement authorities in Hollywood's pocket, wrote a screenplay shedding light on the moguls' collective malfeasance and circulated it to force the government's hand.

Or it could have been simple coincidence that a first-time writer, working on his or her own time, invented a story that accidentally paralleled a horrific secret, and all hell broke loose. The one thing that all of those possibilities share is the growth of unions in the motion picture industry and the film companies' resistance to them.

Many a writer languished in Tinseltown on a good salary during the Depression years. The income gave many of them–and other studio workers who enjoyed full employment while the rest of America struggled–the security to envision a world that wasn't beholden to bankers or corporations but was run by the people who actually did the work. It was during this time that the Communist party gained entree into the movie industry. What baffled the studios was that money wasn't usually the main demand by organizers such as Herb Sorel, Ted Ellsworth, and William Littlejohn, it was better working hours, proper screen credit, and ending managerial duplicity.

The founding moguls were angry. Their Eastern European roots led them to see the careers of stars, directors, writers, and craftspeople as a gift, not a right. They fought back at union organizers with lockouts, intimidation, fire hoses, and, on at least one occasion, gunshots.

Harper Monroe Farrow could not have been unaware of these events, but in all probability did not take part in them; if she had, she would have been gleefully outed by any of the self-appointed patriotic watchdogs of the era like Myron Fagan, Elizabeth Dilling, Roy Brewer, or Vince Hartnett.

It was probably her ability to quietly observe without taking sides–good reporter that she was–that inspired her to write *Beyond Utopia*.

From remnant reports, *Beyond Utopia* was a Ruritanian romance set in a kingdom run by a benign regent. Or perhaps he wasn't so benign because, like King Louis XIV of France, he invited all his noblemen to move into his vast castle (as Louis did Versailles). At first the dukes and earls preened at living with the King. But very soon they realized that their proximity to the throne allowed His Majesty to spy on them more easily. In reaction, they talked of rebelling. But the King was smart; he knew that putting all his nobles under one roof would cause them to conspire against one another instead of him, and his rule remained intact.

Farrow set her story, not among royals, but among gangsters (thus suspicion falls on Doyle), for she suspected that gangster films, which had been sanitized by the Production Code in 1934, would come back into style. In her telling, an itinerant knight from a nearby realm insinuates himself among the nobles and rises to organize them against the big boss. What he doesn't tell the nobles, however, is that, at the same time, the big boss is paying the enterprising knight to keep the nobles disorganized and fighting among themselves, thereby preventing the very rebellion he has been empowered to bring about. To take the bite off the subject, Farrow made it a comedy.

At first, Selznick International Pictures was interested, but soon dropped out because, having made *The Prisoner of Zenda*, they didn't want to return to Ruritania. For a moment RKO romanced the script, but they had their hands full with Ginger Rogers' mother which put their sense of humor, to say the least, on hold. The bigger studios were out, even Warner Bros., which had made its mark with gangster movies, because they were, in fact, already putting several into production like *The Roaring Twenties* and *Brother Orchid*. Then there was the problem with the Production Code, which demanded punishment to those who broke the law, and a comedy about such things didn't satisfy their unbending morality. So Farrow took her script to independent producer Max Wollcroft, who had made his fortune in the millinery business, and who backed it with his own money. To save costs, they shot *Beyond Utopia* in Canada where the union movement had not taken hold, and whose economy was delighted to accept Wollcroft's American dollars. (Note: Additional speculation suggests that Max Wollcroft wrote the script himself under the Farrow name.)

Farrow and Wollcroft could not have known the can of worms they were opening. A few years earlier, Willie Bioff, one of Al Capone's operatives, had left Chicago for California with his sights on bringing the Mob to Hollywood. By 1937 he had installed his flunky, George Browne, as head of the town's leading union, the IATSE. Bioff and Browne had already toyed with the Mob's chief fundraising tool, the shakedown, by hitting the Balaban & Katz Theatre Circuit for a payoff that would make B&K employees drop a demand for pay raises, effectively screwing their own union members. Before long they were threatening strikes against the film companies (almost all of which owned theatres at the time) if the moguls didn't pay up. It was a simple rate card that Bioff and Browne offered: $50,000 a year from each of the major studios and $25,000 per year for the minor ones to make union problems go away.

If the Mob was surprised that the moguls were such eager collaborators, they never said so. The logistics of the payoffs were bizarre (one of the bagmen was allegedly MGM's lawyer), but the result was just what the companies wanted: Union problems ceased, even if it meant getting in bed with gangsters. Whether Farrow knew about the shakedowns when she wrote *Beyond Utopia* is unverifiable. Whether Wollcroft did is equally speculative. Ignorance is probably a safer bet than courage when it comes to Hollywood. Anyway, it didn't matter. *Beyond Utopia* flew under the radar while it was shooting, but once it rolled into post-production it was clear that Wollcroft and Farrow were holding a bomb with a lit fuse. When the first answer print screened at the lab, there were more people watching it from the projection booth than were sitting in the seats out front. To qualify for Academy Award consideration, Wollcroft personally four-walled a downtown theatre for a week's run, but strategically took the smallest newspaper ads possible. He wanted it visible, but he didn't want it seen. (Note: This is what suggests that it was the work of a Hollywood insider.)

When the engagement closed, Wollcroft brought the single print back to his office where there was a stack of messages waiting for him from all the film companies. Naively, he thought they were distribution offers.

"Whose do I return first?" he grandly asked his secretary, Elizabeth. "These are all from people I've never been able to get on the phone, and now they're all calling me."

"Why not start at the top?" Elizabeth said, and dialed Louis B. Mayer at MGM.

"Of course I want your picture, Wooly," Mayer said in his most avuncular manner. Wollcroft's nickname wasn't Wooly, but who was he to argue with L.B.? "I'll pay you top dollar."

"That's very generous of you, Mr. Mayer."

"Call me L.B."

"Okay, L.B. But I'd rather take a lower advance against a percentage of the gross."

"That's not how we do business, son," L.B. said warmly. "This is MGM. We will buy you out. You'll never get a better deal anywhere else, so don't even bother phoning the others."

It struck Wollcroft as strange that L.B. would know he had more calls to return.

"In fact," Mayer continued, "I'm authorized by everybody on your call list to make a preemptive offer."

This didn't sit right, either. "What do you mean by 'everybody' and 'preemptive offer,' L.B.?"

"Let me lay it on the line for you, Wooly." Wollcroft could hear Mayer's throat tighten. "*Beyond Utopia* will not be released. It's bad for the indus-try. It's bad for everyone in the industry." The mogul seemed to swallow the phone, his mouth was pressed so close to the handle. "And it's definitely bad for you."

Wollcroft collected himself before replying with equal intensity, "It sounds to me like you're afraid *Beyond Utopia* will be a hit."

"Oh, it'll be a hit all right," Mayer threatened. "But not the kind of hit you're thinking of."

"Thanks, L.B. I'll take that as the best review I could ever get."

"You don't know how deep you're in, sonny," the mogul said, sharpening his voice. "And from now on you better call me Mr. Mayer." He hung up.

When Wollcroft got home that night there was a very large man waiting for him in his driveway.

"You the guy who made the picture?" the hulk asked.

"I like to think of film as a director's and writer's medium," Wollcroft said magnanimously. "I'm only the producer."

The large man pulled out a pistol and jammed it in Wollcroft's gut. "I like to think of this gun as my medium, and if you don't want me to use it to it to blow your guts out, you'll burn everything connected with your stinking movie."

"I can't do that," Wollcroft foolishly argued. "I have distributors, theatres, audiences waiting to see it. I have a lot of partners."

"I'm the only partner you gotta worry about," the large man said, his blue eyes squinting iron-ic contrast to his twisted mouth, "and I think you need to leave the movie business and go back into women's hats before I fit you with a pair of shoes, size eleven cements."

"You've made your point," Wollcroft said. "I'll take care of it."

"I'll help you," the large man said. It was not a friendly offer.

That night *Beyond Utopia* disappeared. The cut nitrate negative, all the outtakes, trims, and soundtracks, and the sole print all went up in the same fire that burned Wollcroft's house to the ground. The producer stood watching it with the large man, whose name was Albert, holding a can of kerosene. Then they went to Farrow's address.

Harper Monroe Farrow was not a crusader. She was also not there. Nor, in fact, did she ever return to her address. Either she had been tipped off and fled town, or she was only using the address as a mail drop, or maybe somebody else was, because, once Albert gained entry to the bachelor unit, he found nothing but a trash can with the original typed copy of the script plainly plopped into it. He immediately confiscated it and sent Wollcroft into the night, dazed but still alive.

Beyond Utopia might have remained only a Hollywood rumor had it not been for the people who worked on it and those to whom they had proudly described their association. When it was never released, they fumed. Like the Jacquerie in France during the Hundred Years War, word spread. Only a few crew members had saved their script copies - the custom in those days was to drop pages in a trash barrel on the soundstage once they were shot - but tantalizing fragments turned up here and there so that even the trade press, who existed by grace of studio support, had to pay attention. By the time Oscar ballots went out for the films of 1939-a year still revered as the finest in Hollywood's history-the movie that nobody could see had become the one that everyone was talking about.

Frank Capra, outgoing President of the Academy, who had leveraged his prestige in 1935 to save the organization, panicked. It seemed unfathomable that anything-certainly not an independent movie-could unseat *Gone with the Wind*. Nevertheless, Capra demanded Wollcroft provide a print. The producer could not. Capra requested a meeting with Farrow, but no one knew where-or even who-he or she was. The plot not only thickened, it congealed. For a time, Capra considered forgetting the whole thing, but when write-in votes started arriving (this would be the last year that tallies would not be held confidential), it threatened a firestorm. This was a film that not only held the industry up to ridicule, it could bring about indictments. And yet everyone seemed to know about it.

Finally, a clever staffer (whose name has been lost to time and discretion) had an idea. A special award of merit would be announced for the writer of "an unnamed film" who "boldly addressed matters of artistic merit in ways that challenged the status quo." The award would be presented apart from the February 29, 1940 Oscar ceremony and the golden statuette would be held at the

Academy for the writer to collect in person. It was a combined honor and sting (not unlike the Academy keeping "Robert Rich"'s 1956 Oscar for *The Brave One* on hand for its blacklisted writer, Dalton Trumbo, to claim whenever he decided to reveal himself).

Rather than use one of the statuettes already assigned to the awards ceremony, the Academy co-opted one of its generic Oscars used during rehearsals. This explains why the name plate would remain blank and why the inventory for the 1940 ceremony was not affected.

While the cognoscenti were looking for Farrow and the film, the government went after Willie Bioff and George Browne. Robert Montgomery, head of the Screen Actors Guild, could not be intimidated when Bioff attempted to take over his union, and called the Feds. An investigation showed that Twentieth Century-Fox's co-founder Joseph Schenck had tried to deduct his company's payoff from his taxes as a business expense. Schenck was convicted of tax fraud and sentenced to a year and a day in the pen unless he turned State's evidence, which he did, and Bioff and Browne were brought up on charges. That left the unions free to flirt with Communism, but that's another story.

Needless to say, Harper Monroe Farrow never surfaced if he or she even existed in the first place. There are persistent rumors that she went back to writing sob sister columns for Hearst, while others say she got out of the writing game entirely and took up real estate in the postwar LA land boom. The IATSE has long since been cleaned up, and the moguls who conspired with Bioff and Brown found mobsters who were worse than Capone: The House Un-American Activities Committee. Again, they caved.

The looming question is why the Academy hasn't removed its unclaimed Oscar since nobody knows whose it is anyway. The answer might be that those who *do* ask about it need to be told why it's still here—and why Harper Monroe Farrow is not.

FIRING FORSYTH

Brendan Forsyth was a green-light machine. Ever since he shot to stardom opposite Ryan Howson in *Gangsters Two*, the pair of them playing two lovable rogues, he had become one of those rare Hollywood commodities who was popular with both the public and the critics.

He was also smart. He had a social conscience and supported many charities, but he kept a low donor profile so as not to distract from their work. He was selective with interviews. His marriage was stable and the press cut him and his wife, Barbara, respectful slack.

His ability to choose projects was remarkable. He famously passed on the starring role as the ship builder who rescues all the passengers in the disaster picture *Sea Doom* because it was the builder's design flaw that put everybody in jeopardy in the first place. Rather, he wanted to play the captain of the rescue liner because that was the only guiltless character in the whole script. (Interestingly, Ryan Howson had no qualms playing the ship builder, and the re-teaming made box office history.)

He would even take a supporting role if he thought it could help the picture get made. That garnered Brendan a lot of good press, but it also earned him the reputation among his fellow thespians as "the most dangerous actor in Hollywood" because how could any of them go up for a minor role if they knew, at any point, Forsyth might swoop down and capture it? And yet the guy was just so likable that you had to forgive him. What other big star would have played the fire-man for barely ten minutes in the children's movie, *Cathy's Kitten*? (Because his daughter loved the books, that's why.) Or the voice of a paranoid caller on the TV series *Shrink Rap*? (Because the sitcom was his guilty pleasure, and it set off a trend of celebrity audio cameos.)

So when Brendan Forsyth agreed to take on the hotly contended role of Dr. Bob Doherty, an alcoholic surgeon who climbs on the wagon to save a president's life in the medical thriller *Operation Death*, it was seen as another daring decision by the iconoclastic star. Producers Adam Hoffman and Charlie Greene were thrilled; Larry Cooper, the retired surgeon who'd written the bestselling novel, was honored; and director Allan Spanner was eager to work with a fellow he had begun his career with twenty years earlier when they were both struggling actors.

Dr. Bob Doherty was a demanding role, no question about it. Bright, handsome, personable, skilled, and dedicated. The trouble was that, when he drank, and he drank a lot, he became dull, dumb, argumentative, and dangerous. His worst trait, when he'd been hitting the bottle, was that, at a certain point on a binge, he could drink himself sober. There was no other way to describe it. One moment he'd be slurring his words and falling against the furniture, and then, suddenly, miraculously, he'd throw back another shot of vodka and he would act like a teetotaler. In the story, it was in the latter state that he was pulled from his bedroom by the Secret Service and ordered, against his protests, to remove a piece of shrapnel—an old Vietnam War injury—that had shifted in President Mason Anderson's heart and threatened to kill him. In the long and complex operation, during which Doherty relives his tormented past, the alcohol in his system stars to wear off and he cannot separate his memories from the surgery he is performing. He has to have another drink, quick, but he can't leave the operating room. In the tense climax, President Anderson's future hangs on whether Dr. Doherty can resolve his past and do his job.

Larry Cooper's book was widely considered to be autobiographical, although the author, who admitted that he was a recovering alcoholic, insisted he had never operated while drunk. (There was also speculation whether he had actually written the book himself or had hired a ghostwriter.) Not only had *Operation Death* topped the *New York Times* best seller chart for three months, it inspired public discourse on the problem of physician substance abuse, the results of which were that a lot of at-risk people sought help.

Director Allan Spanner was excited about the project. "Brendan and I did the summer stock number back in Illinois when we were just starting out," he told an interviewer. "It was immediately apparent that he was a better actor than I was. But it was also clear that I was a better director than the one we had at the Springfield Melody Tent, and that's where our career trajectories separated. Can you believe it's taken us two decades to find a project we can both work on together?"

Producers Hoffman and Greene shared Spanner's sentiments. The pair already had an enviable string of action films to their credit and they were looking forward to adding this dramatic credential to their track record. "It's taken us years to find just the right property to attract Brendan Forsyth," they enthused to the trades, "and when he accepted this complex and rewarding part, we knew we had the opportunity to enjoy a remarkable experience."

For his part, Forsyth was characteristically silent, even though Spanner, Cooper, Hoffman, and Greene all begged him to attend the kickoff press conference. He sent his regrets from Tennessee where he was doing a charity reading of *Inherit the Wind* as a fundraiser to fight the encroachment of Creationism into public schools. But he did send notes on the book for Spanner to use when adapting it. "Doherty is basically a good man," he wrote in a six-page memo to the director-screenwriter. "The book makes it clear that he descended into alcohol as a response to his powerlessness to save his daughter, Andrea, from leukemia. People cope with tragedy in different ways; Doherty does it with a bottle.

"Moreover," Forsyth continued (perceptively, Spanner thought), "he is both a perpetrator and a victim of the surgeon's 'God complex.' But it cuts both ways. How can God save other people's lives when he can't even save the life of his own child? This is complicated by his unusual ability to appear sober at the worst point in a bender."

One thing Forsyth didn't bring up in the memo, or, for that matter, in any discussions with his agent or the producers while negotiating his fee, schedule, and perks, was that this would be a stretch for him. Like Burt Reynolds, Bruce Willis, Mel Gibson, and a handful of other stars that critics didn't take seriously while they made light comedy and action pictures, nobody ever thought of offering Forsyth textured dramatic roles. That's why *Operation Death* was drawing so much interest months before cameras were scheduled to roll. Everyone knew Forsyth could handle it. The question was whether Forsyth knew it.

*   *   *

"The hardest thing to play is drunk," Allan Spanner told Roy Hillier's USC acting seminar. "Look at Ray Milland in *The Lost Weekend*. That's one kind of drunk. Look at Charlie Chaplin in 'One A.M.' That's another. They're both wonderful performances, and Milland even won an Oscar, but if you met either one of them in a bar you wouldn't buy it. If you want to see a realistic drunk scene, watch any Highway Patrolman's dashboard camera when they pull somebody over for DUI. The harder that people who are drunk try to act like they're sober, the more drunk you know they are. It's all about trying to be in control while being out of control."

Hillier and his fifteen students were entranced by Spanner, who had brought a scene with him from his script for *Operation Death*. It was only three pages, but they would give the students an exercise and Spanner a chance to see and hear his work-in-progress on its feet. The scene fell early in the story when Doherty has had one too many and his daughter drops by the house unexpectedly to tell him that she is pregnant.

"There's a disconnect that I'll reveal to you after we've run it once," Spanner explained as he called one boy and one girl to the riser in front of the classroom and handed them copies. "She's happy about the news and wants her father to share in her excitement, but his joy is dulled by drink, so he internalizes it, bringing a scrim down between them. Let's give it a spin."

ANDREA
What's the matter, Daddy? Aren't you happy for me?

DOHERTY
Of course, I am! It's just – I wasn't expecting it. But, I gather, neither were you.

ANDREA
It's part of life, Daddy. A wonderful part.

DOHERTY
I guess I can't get used to the idea that Daddy's little girl is grown up and married and having a daughter of her own.

ANDREA
Isn't that the way life's supposed to go?

DOHERTY
That's what I'd always hoped.

ANDREA
How did you know I'm having a daughter?

DOHERTY
I always wanted one. I'd hoped you would, too.

ANDREA
But I can't, Daddy. Don't you remember?

DOHERTY
I – I was trying to forget.

ANDREA
I think you'd better try to remember.

The class looked confused. Spanner seemed pleased. "Okay, that's the text of the scene," he said. "Now let's work on the subtext. What do we know from watching it?"

A young woman in the back raised her hand.

"He's too drunk to know what he's saying to her," she offered.

A second student, a young man, raised his hand. "And the daughter sees he's drunk and starts to lean on him."

Spanner turned to the boy who'd played Doherty. "How did you feel?"

"Confused," he said. "I saw the speech in the middle about daddy's girl growing up and played it for nostalgia, like a sentimental drunk, 'I love you guys'" The class laughed. "But it felt wrong."

"Good," Spanner told him. "I'll tell you why in a minute." He faced the girl. "And you?"

"I was holding my father accountable," she said. "It's hard talking to someone who's drunk. She caught him in, well, not a lie, but something askew."

"Both of you are quite right, as far as you know," Spanner said. "Now let me give you the context, which contains the subtext. In the story, the daughter, Andrea, died when she was a young child and her father—remember, he's a doctor—was powerless to help. What I wrote was a hallucination that Doherty has while operating drunk. He's imagining the daughter he once had and the grandchild he will never have, but he's mixing his facts. Now I want you to do the scene again, right now, right away."

The young man and woman ran the scene again. Same words, but the class watched it devolve right in front of their eyes. When it was over, Spanner chirped, "Train wreck?"

"No kidding," said the boy who played Doherty. "Knowing the backstory, that's all I could think of. I couldn't stop myself."

"What about you?" Spanner asked the girl who played Andrea.

"You took my life away. I realized that my only function was to support him. I could feel myself just mouthing the words this time."

Spanner nodded for the pair to return to their seats, took back the pages, and addressed the room.

"Now you know how important the alliance is between director, writer, and actors," he said. "Actors have to play the moment even though they know what's coming. Directors have to make sure they don't tip their hands. And writers have to create full characters without making them servants to the story."

"And you expect Brendan Forsyth to pull this off?" somebody asked from the middle of the room.

"Of course," Spanner said quickly. "I know he can do it. My job is giving him the fuel for his creative engine. We've talked about how tough it is to play a convincing drunk. Now add to it the details of love, loss, and pride." He smiled. "By the way, thank you for making my words sound better than they looked on the computer."

"Are we going to get invited to a casting call?" the first girl asked.

"Why not?" Spanner said. "I'll be in touch with Roy"—he smiled at the teacher – "just be sure to show up sober."

He left the seminar to applause. In truth, he'd known the scene worked before he brought it in. His real mission had been to start the rumor going around town that the script was a winner and to use the buzz to short circuit any power plays Brendan Forsyth might use to change it. It was a strategic move. Spanner had a good memory.

*   *   *

The first note started as an innocent inquiry at the end of a conference between Forsyth's agent and the producers.

"Does he have to drive an SUV?" the agent asked.

"Why not?" Charlie Greene said.

"Brendan feels that the character would drive something sporty, say, a Porsche." Don Masaroff was an old-timer who brought his client list with him when he'd hopped agencies the year before. He was known as a gentleman and had repped Forsyth since forever and was used to gently nudging producers rather than playing brinksmanship games.

"The man's a middle-aged surgeon," Greene said. "Plus, we've lined up a promotional tie-in with General Motors for free vehicles in exchange for an onscreen credit. A Porsche wouldn't be in character or in the budget."

"Brendan thinks the character should be more daring," Masaroff said, ignoring Greene. "It raises the stakes for his encounters. Besides, a lot of middle aged guys buy a sports car. It's a rite of passage, you know? I did."

"I didn't," Greene said firmly. "But I'll ask Allan. I suppose your client wants it to be red."

"Only for one of them," Masaroff said.

"Excuse me?"

"The one for him should be red. You can use the black one for the picture."

"Wait, wait. Red and black makes two."

"You don't expect him to keep the picture car after principle photography ends, do you?"

"I wasn't planning on him keeping anything," Greene said. "He's already got a limousine at his service for ten weeks. Where's he gonna put the Porsche, in the trunk?"

"Okay then, we agree on two Porsches," Masaroff plowed forward. "Three if you want one too, and four if Adam does. I don't, so you're safe there."

"Where are we gonna find the money in the budget?" Greene asked.

"Easy," Masaroff trailed off. "You and Adam fly coach."

Adam Hoffman returned to the office as Greene was hanging up. He was scowling. "I was hiring Billy Carnahan as first A.D. He worked with Forsyth on that picture about the detective with Alzheimer's. I can never remember the name of it."

"Very Funny. It was *Alibi Ike*."

"That's the one. He says making a picture with Brendan Forsyth is like being nibbled to death by ducks." Hoffman started going through the drawers of their partners desk until he found his inhaler. "Day one he complains about craft services, day two you lay out the snacks he told you he wanted on day one, and on day three he shows up with a shopping bag and clears off the table at wrap. He keeps this up on days four and five until you have to go to his dressing room if you want a bag of pretzels."

"So we'll buy him his own supply. Is that it?"

"Week two, Carnahan says, he starts making off with the props from a hot set."

"You mean before they've finished filming them?"

"That's what a hot set is. Carnahan had the job of visiting Forsyth in his dressing room and 'borrowing' them back. Anything the guy touches, he thinks belongs to him."

"He's getting twenty million against five percent of the distributor's gross and he nicks pretzels and props?"

"So big and yet so petty."

"Not just petty," Greene said. "I just spoke to Masaroff. Let me cut to the chase: do you want a Porsche? Because we're already buying two."

Hoffman didn't flinch. "I'm not surprised. This is Brendan Forsyth's world and we're just living in it. I'll bet he's one of those actors who, when he says, 'I want to make the script my own,' ends up thinking he actually wrote it."

"Who's gonna tell Allan," Greene said, "you or me?"

Hoffman took a long, asthma-reducing snarf on his inhaler. "Why spoil his weekend? Let's give him the pleasure of his own Brendan Forsyth phone call. I'm sure it's on the way."

*　　*　　*

Allan Spanner's phone rang at eight A.M. sharp. "Allan, my old friend," Forsyth awakened him, "I hear you're writing me an award-winning performance."

"I was until four in the morning when I finally fell asleep."

"I like your humor. I hope you put some of it in our script."

"Can I call you back?" Spanner said, ignoring the "our script" he just heard. "If I don't get five hours, I'm a basket case."

"I just wanted to see how we were doing," Forsyth continued, ignoring his old friend's request. "I don't want to overstep, but we found, when we were doing *Capture the Citadel*, that, if we wrote a couple of lines that we could use in the trailer, it helped sell the picture. I wanted to put the idea in your brilliant brain to do that with *Operation Death*."

"You mean write some smart-ass line that gets quoted like 'I'll be back' or 'just do it'?"

"Not smart-ass. Memorable."

"'Memorable,' as in I go to a close-up of you and your blue eyes saying it forcefully before cutting to the next scene?"

"I'm just trying to help us make the best possible movie. We've known each other a long time. Remember the play we did together at the Springfield Melody Tent? If it'd had a couple of memorable lines, it could have been a hit."

"Brendan, the play was *Hamlet*."

"All I want is for you to be open to my ideas. After all, I'm the guy who has to say this shit."

"I'll protect you, Brendan, honest. No forgettable lines like 'To be or not to be.' I promise."

"Stop pulling my leg, Allan. You know what I mean."

The call was over within minutes but it took Allan Spanner another hour to get back to sleep. The sound of grinding teeth always kept him up. Especially when they were his own.

*   *   *

Hoffman wasn't surprised to get the next call. They're too smart to try to play us off against each other, he thought, they probably just want to keep us on our toes.

"Yes, Don?" he answered without looking at Caller ID.

"Hi Adam," the agent chirped. "How's everything going?"

"It would go a lot better if you and your client weren't sticking your noses into everything before there's anything there to stick them into."

"This isn't about Brendan," Masaroff said. "It's about the hair and makeup guys. Have you hired them yet?"

"We haven't hired anybody below the line. We don't have a final script or budget yet."

"Well, when you do, there are a couple of people we've worked with who make Brendan feel comfortable, and we'd like them aboard."

"He has that in his star contract, Don, along with the dressing room and the chef."

"I know, but I mean hair and makeup for the supporting players. Brendan wants everyone to look good."

"I have an idea. Why don't you have Brendan release his hair and makeup people to work on the supporting players?"

"Very funny, Adam. You know that we need to keep his people free for touch-ups, especially in the last third of the story."

"The last third of the story takes place in an operating theatre. His hair and mouth will be covered, and one of his eyes will have a microscopic monitor."

"That's another thing. Does he have to be covered so much? The public wants to see Brendan Forsyth."

"It wouldn't be realistic."

"Sure it would. Have Spanner add a line about a new technology that prevents infection and they're using it for the first time on the President's shrapnel wound so the surgeon can have more freedom."

"You're a good agent, Don," Hoffman said. When he told the story later to Spanner and Greene, all three of them wanted to laugh, but none of them could.

"The one thing we have to keep in mind," Greene sighed, "is that a Brendan Forsyth picture always delivers. He's a juggernaut. Whenever he decides to make a picture, he puts a thousand people to work."

"Including apparently many of his own," Hoffman groaned.

"Including us, too," Spanner reminded. "I'll be finished with the script in another few days. Do we want to make bets who gets the next call?"

Had they made bets, all of them would have lost. The day after the screenplay was sent around, Hoffman got a call from the production designer.

"Where in Mr. Spanner's script does it say that Dr. Doherty's home has dark brown deep pile shag carpeting?" Manny Szapanski asked. His tone was cautious.

"If it does, I must have missed it," said Hoffman. "Are you sure this is for *Operation Death*?"

"Yes," Szapanski went on. "I got a call from Mr. Forsyth himself who said it would be a good idea and he gave me the name of a carpet company I should call."

Hoffman shook his head. "Hold off on ordering anything. The script hasn't been approved yet. I guess he's just trying to be helpful."

"That kind of help I don't need, Adam. It's the kind of help I see when we're striking the sets and ten trucks pull up I've never seen before to haul props and furniture away. If Forsyth's movie apartment doesn't need dark brown deep pile shag carpeting, I'd be willing to bet that one of his own houses does, or maybe an apartment building he owns somewhere."

Hoffman pondered this a moment. He didn't want to play detective, so he told the art director, "Do this for me, Manny. Call the number Forsyth gave you, make nice, say it's too early to place an order, ask them for prices, and forget everything they say."

"In other words, bullshit 'em."

"You got it."

*   *   *

Surprisingly, Allan Spanner's first draft screenplay for *Operation Death* was okayed by the studio with minor notes, easily ignored. This was a testament to the power of having Brendan Forsyth starring in it. "These are all smart people," the VP of Production told his committee as he sent it to budgeting and breakdown. "If there are any problems, they'll fix them along the way." With that in mind, Spanner and Forsyth sat down alone in Forsyth's Topanga Canyon house to go over the script page by page.

"Excuse the mess," the star said. "I'm renovating the place and the carpet guys left samples everywhere."

"You know, I was thinking of showing up at eight A.M. just to give you a taste of your own medicine," Spanner joked.

"The guards would have stopped you," Forsyth smiled, "but I get your point. Only normal hours from now on."

Spanner nodded in assent. "We've known each other too long to play games, Brendan," he said. "Who knows, at some point we might have to fight the producers or the studio for the good of the picture, and we need to be united."

"Right you are," Forsyth agreed. "I need your writing and directing talent to make this another Brendan Forsyth performance, and you need my clout to make the picture in the first place."

Spanner let the comment hang in the air, hoping that his old friend would follow it with an ironic laugh. When none came, he said, "Let's go over the beats. Your entrance is on page three. That gives us the first two pages to set it up and have everybody saying what a brilliant surgeon you are. Then, bang, you come in and prove it."

"Yeah, but I come in drunk," Forsyth said.

"We don't know that until page ten, which gives you the next seven pages to establish the character and his skill set, and then win the audience by helping the nervous intern."

"I saw that," the actor remarked. "It's terrific. She'll make a good impression."

"He," Spanner said. "It's a male intern."

"Why can't she be female?"

"He can't be female because we shouldn't have any hint of sexuality at this point. Doherty has to be almost intimate with him in order to pull him through, and this is the wrong place for the audience to wonder if he has another agenda."

"If it's a male, won't they think Doherty's gay?"

"Why should they?"

"Because—and I don't mean to make a thing of this—but I was *People* Magazine's Sexiest Man in the World twice. Why not exploit that?"

"If I make him a girl, it would. That's my point."

"Brendan Forsyth can play sexy without sex," the star said.

Allan gave in. "Can we at least agree that you'll play it fatherly?"

"Brendan Forsyth will."

"And I bet you already have someone in mind to play her, right?"

"How did you guess?"

Spanner rolled his eyes. "That's why they pay me the medium bucks."

The rest of the read-through went well once Spanner had acceded to Forsyth's casting demand. As the two men parted, Forsyth said, "Allan, I want to say again what a great job you've done. It was a tough book to adapt. I had my assistant read it all the way through and he told me it could never make as good a movie as you've just shown me it will be. Thanks for helping me with this next stage of my career." With that, Forsyth grabbed Spanner and gave him a big hug.

"Thanks," the director said from within the squeeze. "As long as you don't end the intern scene like this, we're gold."

He got in his car and drove to the studio where Greene and Hoffman were waiting to hear what happened.

"We're screwed," Spanner reported.

"Tell," they asked.

"He's nervous about his image. He's at stage four of the five ages of mankind in Hollywood. Here they are:

"Who is Brendan Forsyth?

"Get me Brendan Forsyth.

"We need a Brendan Forsyth type.

"Get me a young Brendan Forsyth.

"Who is Brendan Forsyth?"

Hoffman shook his head. "I knew it was too good to be true. It was too easy to get a green light."

"Do you think you can handle him?" Greene asked. "He's worth a lot of tickets if you can grit your teeth and do it for England."

"I can handle him if you can handle him," Spanner said. "We may have a couple of constructive disagreements during shooting, I expect that, even plan on it. But it's in post-production where the real damage can be done. He may see a first cut and want to meddle with it. He may not like his performance. Let me say that another way: He may see what a skillful, deep, vulnerable performance I intend to drag out, and it may scare the crap out of him. Remember how Burt Reynolds thought he stank in *Boogie Nights* until he started getting his best reviews since *Deliverance*?"

"Let's not panic yet," Greene said unconvincingly. "We have a Brendan Forsyth picture on the fast track from a major studio. Nobody else in the world can say that. How much more can he want before it hurts the picture? And then what do we do?"

Spanner shrugged. "We'll burn that bridge when we come to it."

*   *   *

Pre-production went according to schedule, the schedule being overseen by the studio's hierarchy of department heads, supervisors, and managers. A major Hollywood motion picture studio is a factory. Imagine a car manufacturer in Detroit turning out twelve cars a year, each one an individually designed model, and hoping against the odds that at least three of them will sell enough to bail out the other nine while returning a profit to the investors. The difference, of course, is that people need cars; nobody says the public needs movies, yet it's the job of each film studio's advertising and publicity department to make them think they do at the rate of at least one a month. Now consider that the current Hollywood studio business model has been in place since, roughly, 1920, and they still haven't managed to make a science out of it. For all the focus groups and sequels and franchises and ancillary sales and pre-sales, each picture remains a crap shoot. And somehow the public knows if it's any good before the studio does.

Operation Death moved through the studio like a man digesting a donut: slowly. Casting proceeded apace (including the legacy role for the intern). Costume fittings were routine for a contemporary picture; naturally, Forsyth's contract permitted him to keep his clothes. Sets went up on schedule and, somehow, Dr. Doherty's home, seen in only one quick sequence, was decked out with expensive dark brown deep pile shag carpeting.

Allan Spanner was working with his storyboard artist when his agent reached him and told him to find someplace private to take the call. He chose the men's room.

"Are you sitting down?" Lance Cain asked.

"Don't try to be funny," Spanner said. "What is it?"

"I just got a call from Pete Trimble. You know who he is?"

"He's some kind of newspaper columnist, isn't he?"

"Yeah, he writes for one of the Chicago papers."

"Does he want an interview?"

"He said he was making a formal call to you as a fellow member of the Writers Guild. Under WGA rules, a writer who is hired to write behind another writer has to inform the first writer."

"What are you getting at?" Spanner asked.

"Besides being a newspaper columnist in Chicago, Pete Trimble is an old Illinois friend of Brendan Forsyth. It looks like your old buddy has hired his old buddy to rewrite your script."

"You mean, the one we're starting to shoot on Monday."

"None other."

"Do something about it."

"I am," Cain said. "I've got a call in to Greene and Hoffman. Maybe you should head over to their office."

*   *   *

"Pay no attention to Trimble," Hoffman assured. "You're directing your script."

"You're missing the point," Spanner said. "He doesn't have to put knives in our backs to prove he can go behind them. This guy is doing everything he can to turn a 'go' project into a development deal."

"Maybe Trimble's changes are worth considering," Green chimed in.

"I don't care," Spanner said. "I'll take suggestions from anybody. I encourage it. The best line in my last picture was a wisecrack one of the electricians made. But this has nothing to do with the good of the picture. It has everything to do with the good of Brendan Forsyth. He wants to turn a political thriller into one of his redneck movies. If that was the case, he never should have taken the role."

Spanner ran his fingers through his thinning hair and turned toward the producers' second floor window. Their view from the executive building allowed them to see everybody entering or leaving the main gate, the famous one seen in documentary after documentary. Legend had it that, in one of these second-floor offices, years ago, the mogul who'd founded the company watched the parade of stars leaving after a hard day and lamented to a reporter, "Look at that. This is the only industry where its business assets go home every night."

"This can only get worse," Spanner said, breaking his reverie. "I think I'd better have another one-on-one with Brendan. This can't go on."

*   *   *

The two men met at Cheshire, a new place on Sunset where neither man had ever been. Forsyth was uncomfortable because he wasn't known there, which is why Spanner insisted on it, deeming it neutral territory. Both men ordered drinks which neither of them touched.

"I'm glad you wanted to get together," Forsyth began. "I assume you got word from Pete Trimble."

"I did," Spanner said calmly. "He was compelled to call me under the rules of the Writers Guild. I would have preferred that you call me under the rules of friendship."

"Don't be so thin-skinned," Forsyth said, a little coldly, Spanner thought. "We've come a long way since summer stock. I need to protect my assets."

"I didn't know what that meant when you said that before and I don't know what it means now. What assets?"

"A Brendan Forsyth picture," the actor said. "People expect it."

"This isn't a Brendan Forsyth picture," Spanner said. "It's an Allan Spanner picture starring Brendan Forsyth." He let it sink in, then added, "Are you afraid to stretch as an actor?"

"Stretch, no," Forsyth said. "Snap and break, yes. Remember that FBI picture I made three years ago?" He was referring to *Undercover Thug*, in which he was a brave FBI agent who infiltrated a skinhead organization and brought the leaders to justice."

"I do," Spanner said.

"Wouldn't you call that a stretch? The critics did."

"Sure," said Spanner. "Only you were still playing it safe."

"Like hell. I almost cried when my partner died in that scene."

"You played the only skinhead in the world who had long, perfectly styled hair."

"Because I was the goddamn star!" Forsyth yelled.

Spanner refused to play into him. "You know what that said to me? What it said to me was that you weren't prepared to go the distance for the sake of your art. I was hoping that you would go the distance for me, but perhaps not."

Forsyth turned his cocktail glass. "Funny about people," he said. "I came here hoping to persuade you to compromise, and you start off attacking me for wanting to make a better picture. That's why I brought Pete in. He's working on the car chase."

Spanner froze. "What car chase?"

Forsyth smiled with secret satisfaction. "You missed it, didn't you? There's a perfect place for the car chase."

"*What car chase?*" Spanner repeated.

"Act three. I can't believe you missed it."

"If I missed it, it's because there shouldn't be one. There's no one to chase in act three. You're being driven to the hospital by the Secret Service. You need to operate to save the President's life. They don't know you're drunk on your ass. Who could be chasing you?"

"We could have us drive in separate cars and chase each other."

"That's asinine. Your condition won't play unless you can react to second and third parties. You also have to sneak a snort from your hidden flask so you can drink yourself sober before you get to the O.R. If you drive yourself alone, there's no challenge."

"Get rid of the flask and have him pull off the road on the way back, do a fast pop or two in a bar, and get back in the car."

"Brendan, you're running amok. If you don't want to do the picture, just pull out now and we'll deal with it."

"Don't try and pressure me," Forsyth said through clenched teeth. "I want to do the film! I want to work with you. I want this to be an additional direction for me as an artist. Not a new direction, but a direction on top of my current direction. I want to be multi-directional."

"Then do the script the way I wrote it, the way you and the studio approved it, and the way everybody who reads the book is expecting. I promise I'll protect you in every direction."

Both men fell silent. Forsyth extended his hand.

"You're right," he said. "I panicked. I always do before a big film, and this one's really important. Let's do it."

"Thank you," Spanner said, and handed Forsyth a menu. "Now let's get something to eat."

Forsyth opened his menu. "There is one small change I'd still like you to make as a favor to me."

"What's that?" Spanner asked cautiously.

Forsyth didn't look up from his menu. "Does he have to be a drunk?"

*   *   *

"How do you fire Brendan Forsyth?" Greene asked.

"You don't," Hoffman said, looking over their star's contract. "He has a pay-or-play deal. The studio wanted him so bad, they signed this in the dark."

"Plus the only reason we got fast-track approval is that he said yes," Spanner added. "How do you fire a guy who was the reason you got to make the picture?"

"What if all of us quit instead," Hoffman suggested. The others were silent. "Okay, I apologize," he continued. "I had a sudden attack of artistic principle. It won't happen again."

Spanner perked up. "What if we get Brendan to quit? If he quits, are we obligated to pay him?"

"Not if he's the one who abrogates," Greene said.

"What would make Forsyth quit?" Hoffman asked.

"Apparently my script," Spanner said. "You can't make a picture about an alcoholic who stays on the wagon. That's like making a musical where nobody sings."

"How can we make him pull his own plug?" Hoffman asked.

Spanner gave it some thought. "Ratchet up the stakes. See how far he'll go, and then we go further. Make Dr. Doherty sexually impotent from drinking. Make him steal prescription drugs. Make it that he molested his dead daughter. Get Brendan to blink, not us."

Which is exactly what they did. They not only dug in, they dug deeper. Naturally, the reaction came not from Forsyth but from his agent. "You had to be hard-ass, didn't you?" Masaroff brayed at Greene. "You and your artsy-fartsy movie. This is all your fault. He wouldn't star in it now if you gave him two Porsches and carpeted his entire house."

"Sorry to lose him," Greene lied. "But if this is his decision. . ."

"I'll just move him into any of ten other projects," Masaroff said. "But you guys, you're losing a sweet payday 'cause I wouldn't be surprised if they canceled the picture."

"On the contrary," Greene said, "we're going forward with a new star who respects the script. The studio is fully behind us. You see," he added with a lilt that Masaroff was certain to hear, "they've worked with Forsyth before."

*   *   *

As it happened, Allan Spanner didn't direct *Operation Death*. Hoffman and Greene got the prolific Robert Zorich to direct from a new adaptation by Lew Wrentham that was so sharp and clean that Spanner didn't bother filing for Writers Guild arbitration. He was paid for his unused script but, as a courtesy to the producers, he declined his pay-or-play director's fee. Neither Hoffman nor Greene had ever heard of such largesse and promised that they would produce any future movie he wanted to make. Surprisingly (for Hollywood), they kept their word and, a year later, got behind *In the Matter of Doctor Watson*, a pastiche of the Sherlock Holmes stories that was one of the happiest productions of all their careers.

Operation Death went forward with Ryan Howson, Brendan Forsyth's former co-star, who played the flawed surgeon to personal triumph, winning an Oscar nomination and making an effortless transition from romantic leads to character roles, extending his career by a decade.

Spanner had no regrets about losing *Operation Death*. "I learned a long time ago," he said, "never do a project that you're not totally committed to because, at the end, you will have worked for three years and achieved nothing for it but heartache."

Larry Cooper started other novels but, sadly, never managed to finish one. Pete Trimble continued to write for one of the Chicago papers and, every time Forsyth made a picture, he could count on a couple of weeks' work doctoring its script.

Allan Spanner runs into Brendan Forsyth on occasion. The two old friends reminisce about working together at the Springfield Melody Tent and lie about wanting to work together again, only this time on a project that they both feel comfortable with. It occurs to Allan, who wonders if it also occurs to Brendan, that what they are nostalgic about at such times is not the Springfield Melody Tent, but their youth.

DEAL PICTURE

The Vice President of Production of United General Pictures was being recklessly candid, but I expected nothing else from my former prized student.

"I'd love to buy your pitch," she said, "but all we're making this year is shit." It's a good thing her office had carpeting or she would have heard my jaw hit the floor.

"Is that a compliment?" I asked, quickly putting away my look book and realizing that my project had been shot down by friendly fire even before it taxied, let alone took off.

"Yep," she said, "orders from the top, and not just from the top of the studio, but from the top of the conglomerate that owns us. Make shit."

"This is hard to hear," I said, "coming from the studio that won six Oscars last year out of eighteen nominations. There's no way you could make shit even if you tried."

"Well, we're trying. Awards cost money. Shit doesn't." I waited for her to crack a smile. Nothing doing. Megan Koplowitz sat poker-faced on her thousand-dollar swivel chair, pulling on her five-dollar vapor cigarette, and leafing through the studio's billion-dollar list of fecal matter. "Here's a male bonding cop picture," she said, showing me the logline for *Badge Buddies*:

An older detective on vacation with his family helps a young small-town sheriff solve a crime that's too grizzly for a rural community to deal with.

"It has possibilities," I tap-danced defensively. "It doesn't have to be shit."

"Oh yes it does," she said cheerfully. "You'll see why after you've read this one." She showed me the logline for *Which Witch?*:

An older witch on retreat with her coven helps a novice small-town witch solve a demonic possession that shouldn't be happening in such a rural village.

"We're not sure whether this will be set in the Middle Ages or in modern times," Megan said. "It depends on whether we can recycle costumes from our *Medieval Mayhem* limited streaming series."

I blanched further. "How can the company that won the Emmy for *Medieval Mayhem* make–what did you call it? I wanna be sure."

"Shit."

By now my face wore that expression you get when you've been on hold for twenty minutes with Tech Support and the fourth outsourced guy you start over with says your service contract doesn't cover it.

"If you liked those," Megan said, reflexively flicking the nonexistent ash off her vapor cigarette (it was her first day) "try this one. It's our family animated film for next Fall." The title was *Big Kids*:

A fourth grader goes back to third grade to help the younger class monitor find out who is taking far too much construction paper from the supply closet.

I am not the coolest of writers when faced with aggressive stupidity, but I felt sure Megan knew I was not holding her responsible for what she was showing me. She also knew that I was taking a year's sabbatical to explore more closely the subject I was teaching at University, commercial filmmaking.

"Does somebody have videos of the head of the studio fucking a goat?" I asked. "This isn't just shit, it's diarrhea."

"Yup," Megan said, "and I'm the one who has to make sure it flushes on time and under budget."

I shook my head. "Haven't you ever heard the Hollywood maxim, 'Nobody ever sets out to make a bad picture'?"

"You taught it to me," she said, finally smiling. "But haven't you ever heard the Hollywood reality that a studio has to have one picture going through each stage of its operation at any given time or else it has to eat into its overhead instead of attaching the expenses to pictures?"

"I certainly have," I said. "When I taught it, I called it Feeding the Brontosaurus. But this sounds like Jurassic Park." I calmed somewhat and tried to sound positive. "Can't you hire a good writer to polish what you have?" I confess I was positioning myself to be that polisher.

"Why should we?" Megan shrugged. "Lookit. We know that buddy cop picture's cost X dollars and gross Y dollars with Z marketing costs. Why should we spend more?"

"Because a better picture can gross better."

"There's no guarantee of that," she said, letting the sheath of production papers flop into her upper-left-hand drawer. "No, we're sticking with what we've got. This year we're only making shit." Meeting over.

"Can I take you to lunch?" I said, stalling for more time. "It's the least I can do after you've given me such good material. We can place bets on how many of my film majors switch to art history because it's more commercial."

"Can't travel for lunch," Megan said, "but let me take you to the commissary. Maybe you'll see some stars you can tell your students about."

"You're my star," I said with a real smile, and Megan returned it. We had an understanding, born in mutual cynicism but refined over the years as she had risen from PA to VP and had called me for advice every step of the way. Now she didn't need me any more–I needed her–but the bond remained.

As we were led through the UGP commissary, I couldn't help it, I looked around for famous faces. None today, professor. We were seated in the Blue Room, the private dining suite where studio executives ate and, on colorful occasions, intimidated underlings for sport.

"That is the actual table where Gerald Z. Kline made Vince Bonner get down on all fours and kiss his shoes," Megan said, pointing to an empty banquet table set for twelve. On the wall beside it was a fresco of the studio's first hits back in the 1930s. The Kline-Bonner story was legend (I think I taught it to her) where Bonner, the son of an investor, had dared to criticize one of Kline's personal productions that later went on to win the Academy Award. The day after the Oscars, Kline berated Bonner at lunch and made him crawl from one end of the room to the other to plant one on his Guccis. That afternoon, in revenge, Bonner's father withdrew his investment from the studio. This is what Kline had wanted all along; he fired all of Bonner's relatives and simply went to the bank and, on the strength of his fresh Oscar, got a $100 million line of credit (very big for 1946). In one move he had managed to win a purge, land a fortune, and secure a place in Hollywood lore.

"What do you recommend?" I asked Megan as I opened the menu. "The hardboiled detective sandwich or the baked stuffed shirt?"

"Stick with the boneless chicken," she said. "It's named in honor of spineless executives."

For some reason, I glommed onto the jambalaya. I make it a practice never to eat jambalaya anywhere but in southern Louisiana or my own kitchen because so few cooks know how to make it right. Jambalaya is a stew of leftovers; the word comes from "jumble." You can make a perfectly good jambalaya out of fresh ingredients, but it always tastes better the next day. Something registered in the millisecond that the idea shot through my synapses and I turned to Megan.

"Hey, I have grotesque idea," I said. "The studio is always being asked to do favors for other people. Do other people ever do favors for the studio?"

"You mean like working for free?"

"As a matter of fact, yes," I said. She was intrigued. "I mean writers whose scripts you've bought but decided not to produce, or directors who had three-picture deals but you let them out after the second one, or crew members who were paid for a full week but the picture wrapped on Wednesday."

"I suppose so," she said, "but if a picture wraps early, we celebrate, we don't make people stand around doing nothing just to work off unused salary. We let them keep it as thanks for working fast."

"In other words," I started fantasizing, "you have all these elements for which people owe you their services and you're not collecting the debts."

The waiter took our orders (I asked for the warmed-over plot device and Megan settled on the smash cut transitional salad) and we munched our crudités in silence until her curiosity got the better of her: "What are you getting at, Professor Steuben?"

"Remember how Peter Bogdanovich made *Targets*?" I said. Fortunately, she knew who Bogdanovich was. "Boris Karloff owed Roger Corman two days of shooting after a picture called *The Terror* wrapped early, no surprise there, and he rolled it over so Peter could use Karloff's two days on any picture he could put together."

"Yeah, but Peter and his then-wife Polly Platt had something called talent," Megan said. "What are you going to do with the hacks who owe us commitments?"

"They're not all hacks," I said hopefully, using the word correctly. "Besides, accidents happen. Even a broken clock is right twice a day. The trick will be getting all those broken clocks in sync."

"You're losing me," Megan said.

"Okay, here we go. I'll make you a deal picture.

I bet you that I can make a movie for free if you let me put it together with people who owe obligations that the studio never collected. I'll find you a movie that can be shot a day here and a day there on standing sets or on the streets. Nobody will even know we're doing it until it's done."

To say the least, Megan looked skeptical, so I continued. "I bet stuff walks out the back door all the time here. Props, carpeting, cans of paint, printer paper. You yourself told me that Sergio Castanziis builds a new car into every picture he produces, then drives it home. Well, this is bringing all those chickens back to roost. Remember how in film school we said that you can always count on people to volunteer for one day? This will be that film. At worst, you can shelve it and it won't have cost anything. At best, it will be a streaming novelty. And anyway, how could accidental shit be any worse than the shit you're making on purpose?"

Our food arrived. I was so excited, I couldn't eat, and neither could Megan. At the end of an indigestibly long silence, she said, "All right, you can pull a Spielberg. There's an empty office down the hall from me. I'll get you a phone but no secretary. You'll have a walk-on so you'll have to park in the tourist lot. Pretend you belong here. I'll send a memo that you're going to look at our contracts from the past year. Anything further back wouldn't be fair. You really think you can shoot a whole picture a day here and a day there?"

"Film students do it all the time."

"That was before George Lucas. Prove me wrong."

With that, she signed the tab and we parted, she to her office and I to the panic room I had just opened up in my heart. What the hell had I done? Oh yes: I had promised I could make better shit than the professionals.

The first thing an academic learns when he leaves his ivory tower is that the real world isn't anything like what he's been teaching. When Pauline Kael, for example, returned to *The New Yorker* after a sojourn as a consultant for Paramount in the mid-1970s, she seemed more fed up with studio product than ever and started writing about Hollywood's obvious flaws as if she had discovered them. Fortunately, since I had entered academia after years in the industry, I had no illusions left to shatter other than those that involved the ivory tower itself.

Within a week I had read fifty scripts that the studio owned outright but had shelved. Some had been written by famous writers on the way up, some by once-famous writers on the way down, and others by flavors of the wrong month. I figured roughly that the aggregate amount that had been spent optioning, developing, rewriting, and buying them exceeded thirty million dollars–and not a single page of any of them had been shot. If this waste was typical of every film company, and if the stockholders ever realized the sad extent of it, there would be riots in Beverly Hills.

The amazing thing is that every script had something great in it, but not everywhere. Most had terrific opening scenes that had sold the property in a pitch meeting but blew the second act complications. A few actually had terrific second acts with well-developed characters but the endings didn't pay off. And a very few had endings to die for but the script had long since petered out before it got to them. Many had fascinating characters with nothing to do, and some had wooden characters who weren't strong enough to motivate what happened to them.

In other words, there were solid reasons why each project had been abandoned. So how do so many bad scripts get made anyway? As the producer told the writer, "This is the worst script I've ever read–unless Robert Downey, Jr. wants to do it."

It also struck me that there had to be a way of piecing together all the good parts and cutting out the dross. So what if the picture didn't make sense? There were big enough holes in Indiana Jones to drive the lost ark through, yet you couldn't go out for popcorn for fear of missing one. Why did Tippi Hedren go upstairs into the attic in *The Birds*? Because that's where the birds were, dummy. Why didn't the Indians shoot the horses instead of the driver in *Stagecoach*? Because the picture would have ended thirty minutes early.

I set myself to create a Frankenfilm out of pieces of some twenty scripts. I called it *Jambalaya: The Movie*.

One weekend and a lot of typing later, I had assembled 97 pages that made absolutely no sense but was a great read. I did a Find/Replace to make all the character names consistent, and I changed all the scenes so they would work on standing sets on the studio lot or locations within an hour's travel.

The remarkable thing is that, thanks to writing gurus like Syd Field, Linda Seger, Blake Snyder, and Robert McKee, every script of the last twenty years was pretty much the same anyway, right down to the page number where the plot turns. Combining them was a snap.

As week two started and the gate guard at UGP was starting to recognize me, I moved into my Don Corleone/Bonasera phase. This was where I phoned various directors, cinematographers, actors, grips, prop people, costumers, make-up artists, and other craftspeople to remind them of the debt they owed the studio. Most at least stayed on the phone until I finished; a few hung up on me with a brusque "call my agent." Nobody said yes.

Here is where reverse psychology came into play. The breakthrough came when I changed the pitch to, "How would you like to screw United General Pictures?"

"How long is the waiting line?" I commonly heard. This was my opening. I explained that I was trying to make a guerilla movie on the studio lot, that everybody would know about it except the executives, and that everyone was being asked to work on a favored-nation basis.

"How favored?" one director asked.

"For free," I said.

"That's not favored-nation," he said, "That's Third World." Then he added, "Or maybe Writers Guild."

I had my greatest resistance from actors. "The script makes absolutely no sense," Lisa Lucerne insisted. "Not only is there no character arc, there's no character."

"I couldn't agree with you more," I said. "Will you do it? We can wrap you in one day, two at the most"

"Do I get a limo, a trailer, and my own chef?" she asked.

"Sorry," I said with a smile, "but I can pick you up in my Toyota, set up a chair in the shade, and bring you a salad from Starbucks."

"Why should I even do this?" she asked.

"Two words: *Thrill Killer.*" That was the name of the stinker she'd made for the studio five years ago that got her out of soaps and into medium-budget genre pictures. "You owe it to us to do a cameo reprise of your classic character, Mabel Monahan, the singing seductress. How about it, Lisa? C'mon."

"Um – I dunno."

"I've got Adam Suarez directing."

"Really?" she enthused. "Oh, what the hell! It'll be great to work with Adam again." We set the details.

Then I called Adam Suarez.

"Mr. Suarez," I began, "you don't know me, but I have a commitment from Lisa Lucerne to do a picture for me and she wants you to direct."

"Who is this?" he said.

"It's Norman Steuben," I said. "You hung up on me three days ago, remember?"

"You're the guy trying to make a picture off the back of a truck."

"Yes. How'd you like to do a couple of days directing it? Lisa says she's willing to recreate her role as Mabel Monahan only because you're directing."

"What do I get out of it?" he asked.

"Exactly that: you get out of it, meaning the third picture you owe the studio on your three-picture deal. They signed you on your way up, and you still owe them a picture at your old rate. I can make that go away."

"I see," he said. "When does it start?"

"A day here and a day there," I said. "Whenever we get the chance."

He laughed heartily and said, "What the hell, as long as you have a firm yes from Lisa, it might be fun. It makes as much sense as anything else around here. Send me a script. You sure this lets me off the hook?"

"Absolutely," I said.

And that is how movies get made.

At this point, maybe I should explain what a "deal picture" is. A deal picture is a movie that gets made not because it *should* be made but because it *can* be made. It's a movie that comes together because everybody is in it for the money, or owes a commitment, or something having nothing to do with the quality of the product. It happens all the time–a sequel to a first film that was a flop, a season renewal on a TV show solely to give it enough episodes to syndicate, a low-budget picture because sets from a blockbuster are still standing.

Jambalaya wasn't only a matter of lying to Peter in order to get Paul. Lining up editors was a challenge. If anybody recognizes incoherence, it's the film editor.

"This script is so disjointed, even the page numbers don't help," texted Shirley Baskerville. She was just coming off three years of a TV series and was looking for a feature to help her re-acclimate to longform.

"I prefer to think of it as picaresque," I said. She laughed and told me to come over. She had an editing set-up in her guest house and used it to train AFI fellows and USC interns. "Everybody knows how to edit on their computer these days," she said, "but not the tricks. Why not have the kids do your work, then I'll supervise and press out the air bubbles?" It took no effort to see why Baskerville was considered the earth mother of two generations of editors. Many are the filmmakers who crashed on the couch in her guest house while their first film was being nursed into shape. What Verna Fields was to the film school generation, Shirley Baskerville was to the digital kids.

William Goldman has said that the most exciting day of your life is your first day on a movie set and the most boring day of your life is your second day on a movie set. Goldman never visited *Jambalaya: The Movie* where every day was a first day. As we began scrambling to shoot, something unexpected happened. Both above and below the line people who had long since become jaded by the process of professional filmmaking began to re-discover the euphoria they had felt at the beginning of their careers. Stealing shots while staying ahead of the police was the least of it. Mostly there were the battlefield improvisations. For example, rather than marshal a team of gaffers to light a major scene in a boardroom, one-day cinematographer John Farraday devised a way to shoot it with everybody holding glowing iPhones up to their faces. (Shades of Val Lewton.) When we couldn't persuade Central Costumes to make good on their debt of a wedding gown for a marriage ceremony set in the paved bed of the mighty Los Angeles River, we held the nuptials in ratty sweat clothes (shades of Orson Welles) and credited them anyway as revenge.

"I haven't had this much fun since film school" was a constant expression. Since nobody was getting anything anyway, nobody pulled rank or made demands. And if anybody did get uppity, he or she was given a stern talking-to by somebody bigger who had decided to work a couple days just for the hell of it.

None of this is to say that anyone in the movie business should work for free. It's just that the people who made *Jambalaya: The Movie* had reached a level of success where they could afford to give back. The fact that they owed it anyway didn't create bitterness, it provided relief. Every day was a kind of party with a constantly changing guest list. You never know who would show up.

Everything was going great guns until Megan Koplowitz asked to see footage.

"You *do*?" I asked, stunned. For some reason this possibility had never occurred to me.

"Yes," she said, surprised at my surprise. "I've been hearing rumors and I want to see what you've been up to. If you don't mind, that is" she added sarcastically. We made an after-hours appointment and she came over to the Baskerville bungalow for a work-in-progress screening.

Before we started, I asked her, "What rumors have you been hearing?"

She was blunt: "That you've got a hit on your hands."

"A hit?" I said, "or something that rhymes with hit?"

"Goddamndest thing," Megan said, "but everyone I talk to for the last couple of weeks has been asking me about *Jambalaya: The Movie* and why it isn't on our production charts. They say they've spoken to people who have worked on it and everybody–and I mean *everybody*–tells them that they have no idea what the picture is about but that they had a hell of a time making it. I even got a call from the head of the studio."

"The one with the goat?" I asked.

"Hush," Megan said, becoming unexpectedly serious. A spark ran through me that the student was about to become the teacher. "You don't understand what's happening here. It isn't a matter of commerce, it's about morale. People keep checking their text messages to see if they've been invited to 'come make the movie.' Your movie. We have six other pictures in production right now and nobody gives a shit about any of them.

All anybody wants to do is be in yours and nobody even knows what it is!"

Rather than try to explain anything, I started the playback. We had about forty-five minutes of footage assembled, roughly a third of the script. When it was over, Megan stepped outside of Shirley's guest house, lit a Camel (she'd ditched the vapes by this time), and pronounced, "Your shit is better than our shit."

"You haven't seen all of it," I said. "Wait till we finish. Maybe it will get worse."

"Nah, I've seen more than my share," she shook her head. "I know shit, and my shit can't even touch your shit."

"Now what do we do?" I asked, playing along. Only she wasn't playing along.

"Just keep shooting and we'll see what happens. If success has a thousand fathers but failure is a bastard, the people lining up to take credit for your movie are going to look like the Macy's Thanksgiving Day Parade." Then she said something softly that nearly killed me. "You're making everybody else here look bad. When they find out, I hope they don't make me call off the picture."

"Whoa," I said, gob-smacked. "You mean you'd actually pull the plug because it makes the studio's other movies look worse than they're already supposed to be?"

"That's the size of it," Megan said. "I'm sorry, Norman, I know you wanted to use this as an experiment, and I guess it succeeded in a half-assed way, but –"

"Wait," I said franticly. "Maybe it's half-assed right now, but why not let us finish it so at least it can be completely assed?"

She consented to wait and see, promising to let us move ahead "with the courtesy of deceit." The enormity of the adventure now settled upon me. Somehow, we had managed to make professional filmmaking enjoyable again, and it scared the hell out of the people whose jobs depended on making it into toil. When Samuel Goldwyn said, "pleasant shoots mean pleasant pictures" he meant that, if you had no conflicts while making it, there would be no sparks on the screen. We had proven him wrong: when people enjoy what they're doing, it shows in their work.

I knew what to do. I had to keep the bad news from the crew and the good news from the executives. The fastest way to do that, I thought, was to ask Brendan Christian, the volatile star of *Perseus at the Watering Hole* (who got arrested for throwing a wine bottle at a sommelier), to come to the set. He did, and agreed to have a tantrum that I recorded on iPhone and posted on YouTube to show how unpleasant it was shooting *Jambalaya: The Movie.* In point of fact, we had to shoot the tantrum four or five times because everybody kept breaking up. Who knew Brendan Christian had a sense of humor?

We also planted stories in the trades of discord among the performers and took to Twitter with one actor slamming another. Never mind that we all sat around a swimming pool scripting the tweets. We almost blew the deal when Billy-Sue Martin's put-down of Marisa Sweeney posted be-fore Marisa Sweeney's original insult to Billy-Sue Marin. Before long, *Jambalaya* was being touted as "the most hate-filled set in Hollywood, wherever the hell it is."

Naturally, this attracted the press. So we put them in the movie by turning our cameras around whenever they showed up with theirs. A whole subplot developed involving reporters and video crews appearing in the middle of completely unrelated scenes. Given that the plot of the movie was already somewhere in the orbit of Mars, the interwoven presence of paparazzi strangely seemed to make sense.

We finished *Jambalaya: The Movie* and held the cast and crew screening in the Josh Volpe Screening Room, the biggest on the lot. We needed to. Only then did the General Pictures executives realize what we had done: we had packed more stars and award-winning craftspeople into our film for free than they could have ever afforded if they had hired everyone, even at scale. It was a once-in-a-lifetime assembly. The question was whether the movie would work.

I'll tell you how well it worked: it was a hit in Europe before it was a hit in America. Nobody here doubted that the picture looked great. The trouble was that it made even less sense when it was all put together than when we shot it. It was Rachella Zbigniew in the studio's international division who came up with the solution. She had it dubbed from English into Bulgarian and then subtitled back into English for distribution by General Pictures Classics, the studio's art film division. Thanks to growing public awareness of world cinema, nobody blinked at seeing Brendan Christian, Lisa Lucerne, and other American stars making cameo appearances in a foreign language film. Little did anyone know that it was shot in Hollywood, USA. It cleaned up. Apparently American critics don't think a Bulgarian film has to make sense. (But the Bulgarian critics did. "Няма никакъв смисъл," they all said ["It makes no sense."])

On a more sobering note, the three projects Megan Koplowitz shepherded through the studio–*Badge Buddies*, *Which Witch*, and *Big Kids*–did exactly as much business as the bean counters had predicted, setting in stone the studio's policy of, well, you get the idea. Around town UGP became known as the number one studio for making number two.

As for the lessons learned by producing *Jambalaya: The Movie*, you're reading them. I teach it in my classes as a case study now that I have returned to University after my sabbatical. One student even noticed something that I had not, and wrote about it for her term paper. *Jambalaya: The Movie*, she said, may not have had a story, but it had a backstory:

An older film teacher travels to Hollywood to help a young student out of a jam and together they produce a movie that saves the studio.

A little hyperbolic, perhaps, but highly perceptive and well worth giving her an "A"–and Megan Koplowitz's direct phone number.

.

THE PUBLICIST WHO THOUGHT HE WAS A STAR

Bobby van Arnold wasn't really a criminal, he just knew how to game the system. "It isn't cheating," he insisted, "it's working the loopholes so guys like us can make a living." He underscored his point by poking me in the chest when I handed him my first weekly expense report after he'd hired me. He said, "What's this?" and went through all my neatly arranged figures, doubling them, turning $5 into $10 and $10 into $20, and finally crumpling the receipts. "How the hell can I turn in my expenses when you want to send them this? You want to make me look like a crook?"

"But that's all I spent," I said weakly.

"So what? You think the producer is gonna be happy with a cheapskate publicist? You want him to think we don't care enough about his film to spend the hell out of it? Fill out a new expense report and don't make the same mistake."

Okay, maybe he was more than a little corrupt. Faking expenses was only a part of my job orientation, Bobby said. The man was my mentor. I didn't want to make him look like a crook even though that's what he wanted to turn me into. And he was right; the company was paying me so poorly, I didn't resist. That's how it worked.

Bobby always made a big first impression. Standing six-foot-eight, he dressed like a cowboy with fringe jackets, boots, and a Texas drawl that made him sound both trustworthy and in charge. Our field office in Philadelphia repped the company's releases in the Middle Atlantic region: Pennsylvania, Virginia, West Virginia, Maryland, Delaware, and New York State but not New York City. Bobby hired me straight out of college back in 1970 because he wanted someone who knew the "youth market," which is what older people called the free-spending college kids they both loathed and coveted. Never mind my film school idealism; I quickly learned that movies weren't a job, they were a racket. Bobby made this clear to me right after I turned in my doubled expense report.

"Run down to the Post Office and mail these presskits to Baltimore," he said, handing me a dozen manila envelopes containing 8x10 glossies and press releases for the company's upcoming picture. "And get a receipt." After that, he showed me a round-trip airline ticket to Baltimore made out in his name for the next day. The fact that he could have driven from Philadelphia to Baltimore more easily than getting to and from two airports confused me.

"Why bother to mail the presskits to the newspaper people in Baltimore if you're going there anyway?" I stupidly asked.

"Because I'm not going there," he said. "Baltimore a lovely place. They have white steps and blue crabs. But *The Glory Brigade* is a one-week in-and-out picture that won't benefit from advance work." He let my confusion fester for a few long moments and then said, "Let me show you how to travel on paper. You buy your airline ticket on your credit card. You put it on your expense report for reimbursement. Then you don't go, you cancel your ticket, the fare gets credited back to your credit card, the studio pays you for a trip you didn't take, and and you mail the presskits to everyone that you would have seen in that city if you'd-a gone there."

"Don't you ever have to really go to the city?" I asked, my snotty college boy attitude looking for flaws in the system.

"Of course you do!" he said. "You go there on tour with a celebrity or when there's a new editor or critic you need to schmooze. You make it an *occasion*."

If the studio knew of Bobby's skimming, they looked the other way because he was good at his job. When there was a new star that they wanted to break in, they always started him or her with Bobby who would teach them the ropes. "Never give anyone an autograph on a blank piece of paper," he'd instruct the latest sensation, "because, in a crush of people, you never know what you're signing, and later they can fill in anything from a promissory note to a contract. Never answer a question you don't want to answer. Either say, 'no comment' or ignore it and just say what you want to say. Now let me teach you how to shake hands."

He showed me what he showed them. "Brush everyone's fingertips if you're running a line on the red carpet. If you actually have to shake someone's hand, jam yours all the way against their thumb joint so they won't be able to crush your fingers if they have rings on.

"And never, ever, *ever*" he added, in italics, "get your ass lower than your knees if there's a camera in the room. It makes you look like you're taking a shit in the woods."

Like Willy Loman, Bobby had friends in every walk of life in every city. He knew doormen, newsstand guys, headwaiters, and bartenders. Especially bartenders. We were having a beer after work when he told the bartender, "I bet you five dollars you can't write me a receipt for twenty dollars."

"I bet I can," smiled the bartender, who must have heard this before. He took one of the official receipts out of the center of the pad, rang it up $20, and handed it to Bobby, who said, "I lose," and gave him the fiver.

"Now," he turned to me, "I can either put this on my expense report, give it to you to put on yours, or swap it with a field man for another studio to put on his. Some people trade baseball cards. Publicists trade fake receipts."

The biggest publicity stunt Bobby pulled while I worked for him could have sent both of us to jail. I'm only spilling it now because the statute of limitations has run out. It involved a film called *Panic* and a character called the Panic Man that, I blush to remember, was me.

Panic was a thriller by the gifted Czech director Jan Prokosh. A serial killer stalks the population of a small-town murdering people in the most disturbing manners: he somehow learns what scares them most in the world and uses the knowledge to, literally, frighten them to death. He kills one man by locking him in a public bathroom with a dozen hungry rats. He gives an elderly school teacher a heart attack when he fills her bed with cockroaches. He even sends a transit bus off the road, taking out five passengers, by playing the sound of a Vietnam fire fight for the driver, who was a war veteran and flips out. The audience knows who did it early on, and the tension comes from wondering how a police detective–himself deathly afraid of spiders—will catch the killer before the killer learns of his arachnophobia and strikes first.

Bobby arranged an aggressive "spot the Panic Man" promotion with the town's most powerful radio station. As the eponymous character, I would be assigned to stand at a specific address at a given time of day and the DJ would reveal where I was so some astute listener would find me and win a first-class trip for two to Europe with all expenses paid by World Pictures. It was a hell of a promotion.

As the Panic Man, I wore a transistor radio with an earpiece tuned into the radio station (they've changed their call letters three times since then so why bother to identify them now?). For the first few days I had the time of my life in my three-piece "job interview" suit with a red carnation in the lapel. That was the costume we settled on. People treat you differently if you wear a three-piece suit, especially when it's ninety degrees outdoors in the middle of August. I never had to open a door at hotels or restaurants. Pedestrians stepped aside crossing the street. I got called "sir" by older people. The catch was that identifying me didn't count unless it was within thirty seconds of the radio station announcing my address.

My suspicions began when I realized that they always chose storefronts that didn't have numbers. At first I let it pass; the more on-air promotional announcements that were made before my capture, the more publicity the movie would get. By Friday, however, it was starting to wear thin. My suit needed cleaning. I smelled. Finally, while I was on duty at Broad and Walnut across from the Bellevue-Stratford, the announcer outro'd the tenth rotation of Jim Croce's "Time in a Bottle" and said, "We have a report that the Panic Man is on the prowl again." He read the plug for the film and then said, "The Panic Man is standing across from the city's most famous hotel and if you catch him within thirty seconds from now, the all-expense paid trip to Europe is yours. Now PANIC!"

Within seconds a young woman bear-hugged me from behind and we both tumbled to the pavement. Then a man of about thirty reached down and grabbed my shoulder, shouting, "I win, I win, I saw him first."

"No way," said the woman as I helped her up.

"You pushed me aside!" the man insisted.

"Stop kidding yourself," the woman returned. "I heard the announcer say 'PANIC' and saw the Panic Man. I was the one who got to him, not you."

"You couldn't have heard," the man said. "You don't even have a radio."

The woman said nothing, but held up her purse, which had the radio station coming out of it. "Now let's see your radio," she challenged. The man turned his head to reveal an earpiece. Then they both faced me. "Well?"

"Well, well," I stalled. "I wish I could say that both of you could win, but it wasn't a tie and I have the bruises to prove it." I nodded toward the woman.

"We'll just see about that," the man said, stalking off.

"I suppose he's going to write a strongly worded letter to the *Gazette*," the woman said, chuckling. We introduced ourselves (her name was Catherine) and I said, "We have some paperwork to fill out. Would you care to come with me to my office?"

"Is that an invitation?" she asked.

"Yes," I said. "It's an invitation to come to my office. That's where the paperwork is."

The three of us headed back to the office: she, I, and her smile. When we entered, Bobby begged off of a phone call and he was not smiling. After introducing himself to Catherine, he said to her in his most courtly manner, "Would you have a seat out here, little lady? My assistant and I have to call the studio and let them know we have a winner."

Once we were alone, Bobby said grimly, "are you absolutely sure she got to you first?"

"Not only did she get to me first," I said proudly, "she beat a really obnoxious jerk who lied about it."

Bobby took a deep breath as he weighed something in his head. "That really obnoxious jerk was the son of the radio station sales manager. You see, we had a deal that, in exchange for a large commercial buy on top of the travel promotion, the sales manager and his wife would win the trip to Europe. We had you chasing wild geese all week, but when it came time to actually have a winner, we told Richie-that's the jerk's name-where you'd be. Unfortunately, that young lady got to you first. It's gonna take some fancy footwork to untangle this."

"What's there to untangle?" I asked. "Just give the girl the prize and tell the sales manager sorry."

"You're so young," Bobby said, shaking his head. "The prizes were all reciprocal deals with the radio station. They're in trade for commercials, and unless they go to the sales manager, they don't exist."

"Why can't the studio pay?" I said. "Surely this can't cost more than one day's perks for a movie star."

"The studio can't know about it," Bobby sighed, and for the first time I saw worry lines on his forehead. At that moment, I remembered a lesson from a broadcast ethics class. I knew it was rude, but I couldn't stop myself: "Isn't it illegal to fix a broadcast contest? Like the quiz show scandals of the 1950s?"

No response from Bobby.

I went on, digging myself in deeper, "If we don't make good, Catherine would have every right to bring the matter to the authorities. Why would the sales manager risk his station's license on a deal like this?"

"He didn't," Bobby declared. "*I* did."

A knock at the door broke his reverie. "I'm sorry to interrupt," Catherine said through the door, "but I have to be back at work. Can I give you my name and address so you can get me the paperwork?"

Opening the door, I pasted on a smile and said, "Sure thing." She stared past me at Bobby, who, gentleman that he was, stood and offered his large hand. "How do you do, miss," he said, every pore offering charm. "I'm Robert van Arnold representing World Pictures. May I say congratulations and, by all means, tell us how to find you. We'll want to get photos, announce your name on the air, and make all the arrangements." After I showed her out the door, Bobby said to me, "She seems like a nice girl. Do you think you could get her to change her mind?"

"Not in a million years," I tried joking. "She has a pretty good tackle and I wouldn't be surprised if she also had a lethal left hook."

"This is serious," Bobby said. "The prize has been committed to the sales manager. The tickets and all the reservations are already in his name. It has a cash value of ten thousand dollars if someone had to pay for it and, at this moment, that someone is me."

We closed the office early. I spent all day Saturday worrying and all day Sunday wondering why I had wasted all day Saturday worrying. This wasn't my fault. I had done my job. If anything, I, too, had been used. Worse, nobody even offered me a kickback. Then it struck me that even thinking such thoughts meant that I was already corrupt because my complaint wasn't that I was being used, but that I was being used *for free*.

"Bobby," I called him at home on Sunday night, "I want to do something to help."

"It's too late," he said curtly. "Catherine Whelan—that's her name—left word on the office machine that she's talking to her lawyer because the radio station announced Richie as the winner, not her. She said if we don't make good on the promotion she's going to take it to the District Attorney."

"What happens now?" I asked.

"I'll have to call the studio."

"What are they going to say?"

"Let's put it this way: the phrase 'good work, you're getting a raise' won't be part of the conversation."

"Why didn't you tip me off about the deal?" I heard myself ask.

"Would you have gone along with it?" Bobby said.

"No."

"You're just answered your own question."

Monday morning, Bobby was already in the office when I arrived. "I spoke to the coast last night after we talked," he said. "They're picking up the cost of the second trip.".

"Great!" I said. "Where did they find the money?"

"They told me to give you your notice."

"But I had nothing to do with it!" I protested.

"I didn't say it was your fault," Bobby answered. "But I had to blame someone." He let it sink in. "Don't worry," he said, "you're young. Nobody knows who you are so nobody's gonna saddle you with it. Anyway, never trust anybody who hasn't been fired at least once."

"So now I can now be trusted?"

"I'm just sorry we can't be a team any more. I enjoyed having someone look up to me for the last couple of months."

"You're six-eight," I said. "I couldn't help it. But now I know how small six-eight can be."

"Look, kid," he said in his most avuncular manner, "I'm sorry about this. The publicist is always the second guy to get fired. The first is the caterer. It comes with the territory. Since nobody knows what we do, they never give us credit when we do it well. They all think they get publicity because they're so famous but they never remember that we're the ones who made them that way. It will never get better as long as you stay in this game, so you have to sock it away while you can." He reached into his pocket, peeled off two $100 bills, and handed them to me. "This is from me," he said. "Out of my own pocket."

"Thanks," I said. "I can see this winding up on your expense report as a trip to Maryland."

"Delaware," Bobby corrected with a smile. "Maryland would have been four hundred."

Catherine Whelan pulled back on her threats when the forms and the tickets came through and, from what I heard on the radio, she and her fiancé enjoyed their trip. Nobody ever proved that anything was amiss about the Panic Man contest, but that didn't stop World Pictures from changing its expense account policies. Within three months, the company issued air travel cards to its personnel, meaning that all tickets would be paid by the accounting department rather than by reimbursing employee credit cards. The studio even set up its own travel division to keep the commissions for itself.

The last I heard of Bobby van Arnold he was living with his wife (his children having grown) on the top floor of Hawaii's Watson Hotel for whom he was not only doing publicity but also booking the hotel's entertainment program with the celebrities that he'd befriended in his thirty years in the movie business. I sent him a Christmas card that year and he returned a postcard with a photo of the hotel on the front and a rubber-stamped "greetings from Hawaii" on the message side, no signature.

I held a few more jobs in movie publicity but lost my taste for it when the companies started buying a gross with huge advertising budgets instead of creative publicity stunts. Every now and then, though, I see a headline that makes me wonder if Bobby is back at it. It might be Big Ben playing the James Bond theme, an entire section of Super Bowl fans holding up cards that spell a movie title, or a smart phone that comes loaded with a new album whether you want it or not. That's the kind of thing Bobby van Arnold would do. And even if he didn't, the fact that I think he did says something about a six-foot-eight Texan who wore fringe jackets and could sell a ladies' club a bag of shit.

BAD PENNY

Johnny Clampett was living proof that no good deed goes unpunished. You know the type: someone who only calls you when he needs a favor. The kind of person who's fun to be with but after an hour you start looking at your watch. A loser who wakes up every morning and paints a bullseye on his own head, then blames others for his failures. Someone who doesn't have a mean bone in his body or any common sense. A user. That's Johnny Clampett. Trouble is, I owed him a favor and he never let me forget it.

It wasn't that he shook me down; my own guilt and gratitude did that. When I got tired of lending him a few dollars here and there that I knew I'd never get back, I got him his SAG card so I could put him on the budget whenever I directed a TV show. You've probably seen him. Sometimes he was a reporter who shouted a question in a crowd, sometimes he was a desk clerk helping the stars check in. Often he played the next person in line after a featured player in a convenience store scene. His characters were always named "Man." He wasn't an actor, God knows, but he was always just good looking enough to fit into any scene but not so good looking that he took away from the star. In the old days he could have worked constantly as an extra, but he never wanted a career. He just wanted to book enough hours to keep up his health insurance. Come November, if it looked like he'd fall short, he'd call me out of the blue and ask me to find something in whatever I was shooting, usually a bit part, but sometimes he was so far in the hole he asked for an under-five so he could qualify for coverage. I always came through. A lot of filmmakers take care of old-timers this way, but Johnny wasn't an old-timer.

We met when we were in our twenties and I was a bad boy. I was music director of a heavily formatted top-50 rock radio station in the east and the hits just kept on coming, not only on vinyl but in little amber vials with built-in spoons. It wasn't the record reps that brought the toot, it was Johnny. At first, I wasn't sure who this guy was who hung around the deejays. They all seemed to like him and looked forward to his Friday visits. One day Andy, the afternoon drive guy, made the formal introduction. It was an auspicious meeting; the GM, Jack Whalen, always left early on Fridays so we called Fridays a "Jack-off Day." When Andy got off his air shift, he invited me into Jack's office where Johnny laid out a three-foot line on the glass coffee table, handed me a rolled-up hundred, and said, with a Cheshire smile, "Here, do a couple inches."

Who could say no back then? Then Andy left the room and I realized who and what he was. He asked me if I wanted to become a customer. Naturally, I said yes. But I didn't expect his next question.

"This is important," he said, "I'll only ask this once: Do you want me to be your dealer or your friend?"

It seemed both logical and polite to say, "Friend." I didn't realize it was like inviting Dracula into your house.

Johnny was no hanger-on, I'll give him that. He was always pleasant, always courteous, and always managed to show up at station functions. He could talk with anybody about any topic, and only when I thought back over it did I realize that he never revealed anything about himself. Nobody ever noticed this anomaly because folks in our business tend not to be interested in other people anyway.

He was a great mixer. He used to say that the party didn't start till he got there. At first I thought it was because of the drugs, but he only dealt to a select group of customers and friends. He *was* the party.

He was also careful to have cover jobs. He would stop by my place in good clothes and driving new cars. Always a different one. He told me that they were drive-aways that he was taking from one city to the next. He also showed up at my apartment one night with two beautiful women. "They're working girls," he announced. "We're on our way to a stag party and thought we'd stop by."

"We?" I asked.

"I'm their driver," he said. "I go in with them to make sure there's no trouble." He patted a pistol in his pocket. "You wanna see it?" I declined. Two hours later, they were off to the stag party and I put the linens in the washer.

A few days later he called to ask if I could get tickets to the Steely Dan concert for himself and Mona, one of the girls he had brought over to my place. "I'll pay for them," he assured, "but they're sold out." I squeezed a pair out of the record label and Johnny picked them up at the station. I wished him and Mona a good time.

At three in the morning the phone rang. They say never answer the phone after ten PM but I did, and Johnny was on the other end. His voice was slurred and there was noise in the background.

"I had a little trouble," he said, "nothing major, but I need to be bailed out. You got any cash around?"

He used to keep an envelope with ten thousand dollars in cash as bail in case he got busted, but I didn't want to ask about it on the police station's phone. Instead, I said, "Which precinct?"

His bail was only a couple hundred dollars. "What happened?" I asked as casually as I could manage.

"Oh, I got into a fight outside of the Haymarket." The Haymarket was one of the town's noisier gay bars.

"Were you driving somebody to another stag party?" I said.

"Nah," he said as if it was routine. "I was talking to a friend and some townies started giving us shit, so I clocked them."

"I didn't know you hung around gay bars," I said.

"Best dance music in town," he smiled. "I had Mona with me."

"Are the two of you an item?"

He winked at me. "We are until her husband finds out."

Remember that bullseye Johnny painted on his head? Mona's husband broke a chair over it a week later.

Because I got along with difficult musicians, I got a call from the manager of a group called Fivenicate to come out with them to Los Angeles where they had been signed to a movie. I took a leave of absence from the radio station and baby-sat them through what turned out to be a disastrous shoot. The kid director–fresh from Cinema School–knew everything about the camera and nothing about people. The only thing that kept the band from stalking off the picture was me. When the front office realized that I had saved the production, they made me assistant producer. I looked it up and saw that Billy Wilder said an assistant producer is like a mouse studying to be a rat. I didn't stay for the premiere and, when I returned to New York, Johnny called.

"'Sup?" he said. "I read about you in the trades."

"I didn't know you followed the trades."

"I do now," he said buoyantly. "I'm proud of you. I bet you're gonna blow this town and head west."

"You'd lose," I said. "What I've got here is a career. Out there it would just be a job. As crazy as the music business is, it's the rock of Gibraltar compared to the movies."

Maybe I was feeling full of myself, or maybe I was trying to justify myself to Johnny, but that weekend I scored an eightball from another dealer and decided to celebrate. I hadn't done any in a while and I'd forgotten what it does to you. I

was into my thirtieth hour and the paranoia had set in. I had locked and bolted the door to my apartment, closed the windows, pulled down the shades, and turned off the radio and TV. I didn't want any contact with the outside world. Meanwhile it was a 90-degree August day and I'd turned off the air conditioner because every time the compressor went on, it made me jump. I was sweating, drinking beer, and doing lines, and it all seemed perfectly natural. But I had forgotten to unplug the phone, and it rang. In a panic, I picked up the receiver, dropped it on the floor, scooped it up and said, "Hello?"

"'Sup?" It was Johnny. "Wanna go for a sandwich?"

"I'm not hungry," I said, so wired I must have sounded like those chattering teeth from the joke shop.

"What are you on?" Johnny interrupted.

"Nothing," I lied.

"Bullshit," he said. "I know it isn't mine. Where did you get it?"

"Never mind," I said. "I'm gonna hang up now."

"No you're not," he said. "I'll be over in twenty minutes."

"I won't be here."

"Yes you will. You're paranoid but you'll let me in."

He hung up and I started getting dressed. Oh, yeah, I was in my underwear. Fifteen minutes later Johnny knocked at my door. He was never on time in his life, and now he was early.

"Some people can handle it," he said, collecting my paraphernalia. "You can't. Let's open the windows, turn on the A/C, and get you back to earth."

He stayed with me until I came down. He let me ramble, watched me make lists of the albums I owned, and kept silent while I looked in the fridge every ten minutes as if the contents had somehow changed since the last time I looked. He didn't chastise me or lecture me–he didn't have to–and when he finally put me to bed ten hours later, he hugged me without comment and left. Monday I went to work, threw away the emergency gram I'd hidden in my desk, and have been clean for the last thirty years.

Coincidence of karma, a week later I got offered a six-month job as music liaison for a big studio picture back in LA. It's now or never, I thought, so I quit the radio station and went Hollywood for keeps. One film job led to another and soon I was working at a production company putting pictures together. Mid-level stuff. So what if I never got offered bigger jobs? I was having so much fun, I didn't mind. I married my first wife, Meghan, a terrific person. We'd met over the negotiating table when she held out for a huge payday for her client's spec script, *Duty Calls*. We dated and I was taken with her sense of humor, so I proposed. I miscalculated. I thought she would find it funny when I went down on one knee and asked her to be my first wife. In those words. "First wife." I got my laugh, but she got the last one at our divorce a year later. She showed the same negotiating skills across the alimony table that she'd shown setting up *Duty Calls*.

"'Sup?" I picked up the phone and it was Johnny.

"How did you find me?" I asked.

"Your old radio station," he said. "I still have a few friends there. By the way, they changed their format after you left. Now they play shit."

"You still go there?"

"Not on business. I quit. It's all crack now anyway. Hey, how come you never call?"

"Lemme guess," I said. "What do you need?"

"Is that any way to treat me?" he said. "I don't call just when I want something, do I?"

"You really want me to answer that?" I said. "Besides, I've learned something out here. You can be bosom buddies with someone for years but the first time you ask 'em for a favor, it's the last time you hear from them."

"I'll take that as a no," Johnny laughed. "I just wondered if you needed an assistant."

"I can't afford an assistant," I lied. "Have you gone through all the jobs in the east?"

"This place is tired. Thought I'd change the scenery like you did."

"It was somebody else who changed my scenery, Johnny. With a job."

"Yah," he said, his voice getting sharper. "Just like it was somebody else who got you clean."

"You made your point," I admitted after the truth sunk in. "Okay, why don't you come out for a while, stay in my spare room, and see if you can find work. I can't support you, but I can give you a cot and three hots."

"That's prison talk," he said. "What do you know that I don't?"

"All I know is whatever you taught me."

I had my assistant (yes) make the plane reservations and picked Johnny up at LAX. He arrived without luggage, so we stopped by Ross on the way to my place to buy him something to change into. Next day I started calling around to see who could give him work. A PA job here, a runner there. He was a little old to do those jobs, but at my level I could pull a few favors. People take care of each other out here without asking why. I wondered how long it would take me to pay Johnny back for that August afternoon.

Thinking it over now, I didn't really owe him anything. But I had been raised with a sense of obligation. It gave me a good reputation but it stopped my rise; nobody hands over a company to someone who wants to be liked.

When I planted Johnny in one of my pictures I told him not to acknowledge me on the set lest it show the kind of favoritism that annoys a film crew. He played well with others and Assistant Directors always bumped him up whenever they could. He also learned the day player's trick of blowing his lines after 5 PM so they had to call him back the next day.

One morning he didn't show up to finish a bit for which he had been held over. When frantic phone calls came to naught, they hastily recast the part and had to reshoot his scenes. The producer held it against me. I suppose someone should have called the police but you don't go chasing trouble. Besides, I knew he had to be okay. Guys like him are survivors. And I was right; two weeks later I got a postcard from him from Fort Lauderdale–no phone number or return address – that said he was staying with friends who ran a B&B. That night I took his belongings, including the ones I'd bought, and put them in the garage. I should have thrown them out, but something stopped me.

Six months later I was in bed with my future second ex-wife. It was after ten o'clock and the phone rang. Sheila picked it up before I could tell her not to and handed it to me.

"'Sup." Johnny's voice was slurred. "Who was that?"

"My fiancé," I said sternly. "Where are you?" I was afraid he might be down the block.

"Florida," he said. "I gotta talk to you."

"You are."

"You still got my clothes and stuff?"

"Have you been drinking?"

"Damn right," he said, and belched for effect.

"Call me back when you're sober," I said.

"Wait, don't hang up," he returned. There was panic in his tone, but he recovered. "This place is tired. Can you bring me back out there?"

"Like I said, Johnny," I spoke clearly, "call me in the morning when you're sober. I'm not going to talk to you when you're drunk."

"I gotta get out of here," he said. "You owe me that much."

"I paid you back ages ago," I said, "many times over. I'm sorry, but this is the way it's gotta be."

"I thought we were friends," he said, by now pleading. "Remember?"

"Yeah, I remember. When we met, you asked me if I wanted to be a friend or a customer and I said a friend. I treated you like a friend. The trouble is," I said, feeling my heart beating, "you've always treated me like a customer. Now call me back tomorrow sober or don't call me back at all." I hung up the phone and unplugged all the extensions. I even turned off the answering machine.

"Who was that?" Sheila asked as I got back into bed.

It was getting late and I didn't have time for a long story, so I just said, "Someone I used to know."

Johnny never called back.

A year later I was running the company.

FOUND FOOTAGE

Murder Mountain *is a "found footage" movie that was shot but never found. The gimmick in found footage cinema is that it's made to look like someone captured a horrible event on home video, died while shooting it, and then someone else stumbles across the footage later and tries to piece together what happened. The genre seems to have fairly recent roots in Ruggero Deodato's 1980 horror film* Cannibal Holocaust. *The idea was resurrected in 1999 by* The Blair Witch Project *that cost a paltry $60,000 and grossed over $250 million. Other examples have followed, such as the* Paranormal Activity *franchise, but the genre is antithetical to Hollywood in that the films must, by definition, be made without stars or decent production values.*

Murder Mountain *owes* much *to Cannibal Holocaust as* well *as Blair Witch. Its documentary style, apparently unscripted performances, and unknown actors lend credibility to the contrivance. Where* Murder Mountain *went off the rails, however, is not what went on in front of the camera but the tragedy behind it. The plot of the picture was simple and promotable: four young people scale a killer mountain only to be eaten by a Yeti, and their story is told when a search party later discovers their video equipment and puts the tragic pieces together.*

The plot behind Murder Mountain, *however, was cynical beyond belief. It's told by Brent Major, one of the survivors.*

Day 1: I show up for the table read at Alex's and Sherry's house only to find that there is no script, only an outline.[1] Alex says we'll use the structure that he and his wife, Sherry, devised, but we'll make up our own dialogue. This means that we have to invent our own characters from the ciphers in the outline. I call my agent and explain this to her, but she says (screams), "Jesus Christ, Sherry produced two of the biggest hits of the last decade. I don't care if she tells you walk across the 405 naked and blindfolded, you do it!" So I smile and start to explore "Clint Wayne," the studly yet wise leader of the four-person climbing team. My co-stars are personable. Bobbi MacLaine is the glamour girl who tags along because she wants to be with Clint, and Cheryl Corwin is the tomboy whom he really deserves. Then there's Jack Jacques, funny as hell, who serves as comic relief and naturally is the first person to get eaten by the Yeti. Oh, yeah, there's an Abominable Snowman. Alex says he'll play the Yeti himself in a shag rug with lots of snow clinging to him. It all sounds dreadful but it's a six-week job and we get to go to Alaska.

Day 2: Interesting chat today with Sherry Patterson at the espresso machine. I asked her why she cast me as the lead and she said, as casually

---

1 This is the husband-and-wife team that had made *Alien Army* and *Lusitania,* two special effects blockbusters. Why they had to use their own money for *Murder Mountain* (even though it was only a fraction of their earnings from those other two films) says a lot about how even heavyweights find themselves disadvantaged when dealing with the studios.

as if she was sharpening a pencil, "because you're an unknown." I tell her I've done guest appearances in four popular series, and she said not to take it personally, but all those series were in their fourth or fifth season and had gone through all the really talented guest stars by then.[2] When she saw the I'm-going-to-phone-my-agent look on my face, she called a cast meeting. From the way she and Alex acted as they sat together finishing each other's sentences, it was clear that they had planned to have this talk with us all along, just not this early.

"There's a reason we cast you four kids in our film," she started. "You're at the beginning of your careers. Your faces are not well known, and that is essential. *Murder Mountain* is a found footage film. Found footage films are con games on the audience, but we're taking the con another couple of steps. From the time we leave for Alaska to the time the film is released, none of you will make any other movies or TV shows. Go into hiding. Then we're going to spread word that you were all killed on the mountain and the morbid curiosity factor will send the film through the roof. Of course, after we've made our money back, you'll suddenly emerge from hiding.[3]

"You're not going to really kill us, are you?" Cheryl asked, jokingly.

"Of course not," assured Alex. "We'll leave that to the critics."

Crickets.

"No, seriously," he clamored, "we want to create a horror movie that's also an event."

"What are we going to live on between shooting and the premiere?" Jack asked.

"Unemployment," Sherry said. "But we'll slip you cash stipends under the table. Believe me, the film will cause enough of a sensation that your careers will be worth it."

"Can we at least tell our agent?" Bobbi asked.

"Tell no one," Sherry proclaimed. "If that's going to be a problem, let us know now so we can re-cast."

Days 3-8: Settling affairs, paying rent and utilities in advance, and telling everyone I'm going to a religious retreat and not to call or worry about me. Also getting together with Sherry and Alex to ad lib scenes and develop our characters. I gave Cheryl a call and asked her if she wanted to have dinner to get to know each other better. The evening went well enough; no sparks, but the basis of a good friendship. She's smart and says she wants to be a producer, and is studying Sherry as a role model. Good for her.

---

2 This is a Hollywood truism. Series are front-loaded with performers to whom producers and production owe past favors, so they cast them in the first couple of seasons to pay them off. In later seasons, budgets get tightened and casting directors are less interested in celebrities than warm bodies to play "customer" or "clerk."

3 At most, a film company may pay an actor or actress to hold off making another film that will compete in the marketplace with the one they're shooting. In cases where actual deaths have occurred during a film's production, no responsible producer would exploit that tragic factor.

Day 9: After a week of acting and character exercises we flew to Fairbanks, Alaska. I picked up a couple of postcards at the airport gift shop and then realized I won't be able to mail them because I'm supposed to be in hiding. I don't think they mean for us to stay locked in our apartments when we get home, just not go up for acting jobs. So much for thinking I was finally going to be able to give up waiting tables.[4]

Day 10: First day of principle photography, if you can call it that. Just the four of us out back of the motel in a scene where we're going over maps. Alex handles the camera himself and Sherry runs the audio mixer. Video is so forgiving anyway, but even if it looks like crap, that's okay because it's a found footage movie and doesn't have to look slick. Having a two-person crew also lowers the chances that anybody is going to hassle us for a filming permit. We did, however, get the hairy eyeball from the motel manager until Sherry slipped him some money and said who she was. Until then, all he had seen were two older people taping four younger people in a motel and he clearly thought we were shooting a porno.

Day 11: Took the train to Mount McKinley which is going to serve as Murder Mountain. The Native Alaskans call it Mount Denali, which means

"McKinley" in Alaskan. Just kidding. It means "the high one," and it's pretty impressive. Also impressive is Alex's directing. He knows just what to say to get me, Jack, Bobbi, and Cheryl into dramatic situations by playing our characters (not us) against each other. Cheryl kept throwing me "do you believe this shit?" glances that made me break character. She's getting to me.

Day 12: A little truth came out last night as we were becoming acclimated to the elevation in the hotel bar. Sherry and I got pretty acclimated. She confided in me that this film was their attempt to save their marriage. Her productions had done way better than his and they planned *Murder Mountain* as a way to go off together and recreate the feeling of adventure they'd had when they met in film school. When no studio was interested, they financed it themselves– rather, she financed it herself–and never looked back.

Day 13: Fortunately, we're not going to really climb the mountain, just shoot around its base and find a glacier to double the rest. This relieves all of us. I'm the most fit of the bunch, but I still wasn't looking forward to lugging fifty pounds of climbing gear (including helping with the video equipment) up a 40-degree angle while trying to improvise dialogue. Never mind the axiom about creating the reality of the situation. None of us is an alpinist (I Googled it). Thus, we spent the day shooting a scene in which we talked about climbing the mountain, and Cheryl's character raises

---

4 I've often wondered why so many actors work as servers. It's hard work and grossly underpaid. Then I remember that servers get food, and sometimes meet people who can help their careers. Hollywood being what it is, one of these days some enterprising producer is going to make a movie about waiters and waitresses. The casting call alone should be amazing.

the issue of a legendary Yeti that's supposed to be stalking the peak. To which Jack said, "There's no Yeti–Bigfoot ate him." This will have to pass as comic relief.

Day 14: This isn't Rum Doodle,[5] it's a real frigging mountain. It's hard to match shots when you take one step and then slide across the sagittal plane.[6] It doesn't bother Alex, who keeps shooting and says, "Don't worry, we'll fix it in Post." I didn't think anybody said that any more. They just do it in quiet shame.

Day 20: First day with Alex in the Yeti suit. Finally. All the previous footage is just the four of us walking, talking, and arguing, which is about as exciting as watching security camera footage. Now we get a chance to do action. The first Yeti scene involves the four of us walking and talking and arguing, only now we're being followed by the Yeti. I hope Alex knows what he's doing. He and Sherry sewed a couple of shag rungs into a poncho, slipped it over his head, added a mangy hood, and then blackened his face to hide his features. I think I should be offended. I said that if it doesn't work as a horror film, they can add music and call

it *The Abominable Jazz Singer*. Alex didn't appreciate it, but Cheryl did.[7]

Day 21: Time for Jack to die. It's a Hollywood rule that the best friend always gets killed first. How it happens is, his character leaves the tent to find firewood and gets torn limb from limb. Alex wants to make the first kill as gory as possible to prime the audience. I am thinking that he is also making it as stupid as possible because there is no firewood–or any plant life, for that matter–above the tree line for Jack to find. I don't want to be one of those actors who's always making suggestions and gets branded as a troublemaker.

Day 22: Continuing to shoot the dismemberment of Jack. I now realize how clever Alex and Sherry are. Once Jack's character is dead, he can operate the camera while Alex plays the Yeti and Sherry continues to run audio. I asked Jack why he didn't volunteer to play the Yeti and he said, "Because Alex is really into it."

Day 23: Apparently Bobbi will be the next to go, and it will be during a love scene that she and I are supposed to have on a glacier. Glaciers being made of ice, this means that one of us is going to have to be on the bottom unless we can find a more creative position. Where is the Kama

---

5 An allusion to W.E. Bowman's 1956 cult mountaineering satire, *The Ascent of Rum Doodle*, a majestic peak that rises 40,000 and 1/2 feet above sea level in the country Yogistan.

6 The sagittal plane is an imaginary line drawn between the two actors closest to the camera. The camera must stay within this hemisphere or else screen direction will not match between performers. If "the line" is violated, two actors talking in a scene will appear to be looking elsewhere instead of at each other

7 A reference, of course, to *The Jazz Singer*, the film that ushered in talking pictures, which features a scene where its star Al Jolson sang in blackface. "Blacking up" was a convention of the time that has long since fallen into major disrespect.

Sutra when you really need it (no Wi-Fi on the mountain)? Alex had the idea that, instead of the stock scene from every cheap horror film where the boy and girl are making out in a car on a dark road at night when the killer finds them, this one will be in broad daylight out in the open. I need to get to know Bobbi better if we're going to be making out. Right away she says that she's a Christian. I tell her I respect that, and then she says that we're going to have to fake making out: no kissing, no nudity, and no movement. I ask her if Alex knows about this. She says no. I urge her to tell him as soon as possible. I wish I was playing the love scenes with Cheryl.

Day 25: Bobbi came around, but we lost a day's shooting working it out (and that says a lot since days are twenty hours at this latitude).[8] She and I will nuzzle, fully clothed, and, when it comes to "doing it," we will be together (fully clothed) inside a sleeping bag, rolling around on the glacier. This solves the problem of frostbitten asses. We shot the scene in record time: one hour. But I think we're going to have to loop her dialogue as I don't think her ad-libs "pork me for Jesus" and "lick the sin off my soul" will work in the context of a horror film.

Day 26: Continued the love-and-death scene with the Yeti tearing open the sleeping bag where Bobbi and I are rutting. Alex was indeed "really

into it," using his paws to rip apart the pre-scored side of the bedroll only to expose Bobbi's completely clothed body. Problem: She really has to be naked. Solution (eventually): Sherry doffed her clothes for the good of the film and allowed her back and butt to stand in for Bobbi's. It didn't matter that everything about them looks different; Alex assured his wife that the editing will go so fast that she won't be seen. "Then why did you have me freezing my ass off for forty-five minutes?" she griped as she put her clothes back on. Cheryl ran sound for the rest of the day. I guess there's still tension in the marriage.

Day 27: Predictably, Sherry caught a cold and stayed at base camp. This is to be our last day on actual slopes. We shall move into a warehouse for the remaining scenes. I wish I had some sense of how this movie was going other than that it is running over schedule. Alex is keeping it all in his head. All I know is that it's walk, talk, Yeti; walk, talk, Yeti. The Yeti is going to emerge as the star, if only because he does to all of us what audiences will want to do if the film is as bad as it threatens to be.[9]

Day 28: Cheryl is dead. The poor girl was running audio when the camera swung around toward her, she ducked, trying to stay out of frame,

---

8 Screen Actors Guild rules are absolutely clear how nudity is to be handled in contracting and performing. Unfortunately, the Hollywood sex scandals of 2017 didn't lay down the law about casting.

9 This is a reminder that filmmaking is an ordeal. As Francois Truffaut said, "Making a film is like a stagecoach ride in the old west. When you start, you are hoping for a pleasant trip. By the halfway point, you just hope to survive."

and fell into a crevice in the glacier. The crevice was covered with a snow bridge that gave way when she stepped on it. Horribly–but amazingly–Alex caught it all on video. He immediately set the camera down on the ground (without turning it off, thinking fast) and we all tried to help. Cheryl had fallen deep into a wedge of ice that she couldn't pry herself out of. Jack and I lowered a rope, telling her to grab it and we'd pull her free. She was really wedged in there. When we couldn't pull hard enough, I looked around for Alex to help but he had picked up the camera and was shooting the rescue. "Put down the fucking camera," I yelled. He actually had to think about it. All four of us–Jack, Alex, Bobbi and me–pulled as hard as we could, and Cheryl tried to free herself, to no avail. I said what about dropping her a flare that might melt the ice around her legs. We tried that but she had to stop because it burned her. Suddenly the glacier began to shift. We could feel the ice sheet trembling. We had to jump back or risk falling in ourselves. Then it closed on her. Just like that. It closed on her and swallowed her screams. Meanwhile, the son of a bitch Alex had gone back and picked up his camera and started yelling, "I got it! I got it!" I tried to yank the camera out of his hands but he clutched it to his chest, so I hauled off and walloped him in the face.

*   *   *

Post-Production: The inquest criticized Alex for insensitivity in shooting Cheryl's death video but, as the tragedy was clearly an accident, no criminal charges were filed, although I guess every one of us is guilty in one way or another. I have my own feelings.

We were, of course, immediately released from our promise to avoid acting work. In the backlash, we didn't get any offers anyway. Alex and Sherry collected insurance money on the production and settled civil claims with Cheryl's family. They say they will finish the film to honor her, but that's bullshit; they want to exploit her death and no one can persuade me otherwise.

We held the cast and crew screening (all eight of us, counting the music editor and color timer) in Sherry's and Alex's home. It turns out that, after we wrapped, they shot pickup footage in an ice house to make it look as though it was the Yeti that shoved Cheryl to her death. They asked me to record a voice-over but I declined, so Alex did it in character as the alpinist who discovers the footage years later when the glacier deposits it at the foot of the mountain. (I know, it takes decades for a glacier to flow; go blame global warming.)[10] At least they had the decency to dedicate the movie to her.

Murder Mountain had its public release on video, or tried to. Because it contains a real death, no distributor wanted to touch it, and streaming services like Amazon and Netflix ran the other

---

10 This references the *Alfred Hitchcock Presents* television episode titled "The Crystal Trench," scripted by Stirling Silliphant, in which a widow waits decades for the body of her deceased husband to be deposited by a glacier only to discover that the locket he wears around his neck carries the photograph of another woman.

way. A few people might have caught it on DVD screeners. I have a case of them.

Sherry and Alex are still married, so at least one good thing came out of the experience. On thinking about it, however, I wonder if they're still in love or if it's because a husband and wife can't testify against each other.

GLOSSARY

This glossary is offered as a courtesy to readers who might not be familiar with the language of show business. Everybody knows that show business has its own argot, and not just the words coined by Sime Silverman, who founded the trade paper Variety in 1933. Such terms as Boffo (a box office hit), ducat (ticket), bow (premiere), ankle (quit), Blighty (England), tub thump (publicize), nabes (neighborhood theatres), and a hundred other colorful expressions are lovingly referred to as "Variety-eze" for their cheeky descriptions of concepts that insiders know and outsiders only think they do.

The entertainment industry is different now. It has become assimilated in the way that the children of immigrants reject their old world roots and seek to blend in to their new country. Today's Hollywood is world-wide, conglomeratized, and soulless. It's an animal that demands a new lexicon, and here it is along with some old favorites worth remembering:

Algorithm. Perhaps the most frightening word in the entertainment business these days. A program by which companies like Netflix feed scripts and project proposals into their computer in search of whether the project meets their needs. It is an attempt to remove the human element from commercial decision-making. The computer analyzes the words in the proposal against a secret protocol and uses it to consider the potential for projects. Nobody knows exactly what the algorithm is, where it lives, or what it likes to feed on, but it's spreading. (NOTE: A prototype called "Discovery Dan" was supposedly used by Discovery Networks to analyze producer submissions against a profile of a typical viewer who is late 30s, is married with two kids, likes pork rinds, and fixes his car in his driveway.)

Assistant Producer: A mouse studying to be a rat (Source: Billy Wilder)

Bandwidth: Financial and/or mental resources, as in "my company doesn't have the bandwidth to produce your film" or "he doesn't have the bandwidth to understand your script."

Buying a Gross: The practice of spending vast amounts of advertising money to lure audiences to see a new movie, often in excess of what can be recouped.

Cattle Call: Holding open auditions for an acting role to anybody who wants to show up and try for it. It has another meaning for writers (see Disney Cattle Call).

CBJ (Complimentary Blow Job): Spending the first five minutes of a business meeting praising the most powerful or famous person in the room. Offered right after the complimentary bottled water.

Courtesy of Deceit, The: Protecting your boss by lying to him about your actions, thus giving him deniability.

Critic: Journalists who tell you what movies to spend your money on even though they see them for free. Lately seasoned professional critics have been replaced by bloggers who think film history began with *Ferris Bueller's Day Off.* "Like eunuchs in a harem; they know how it's done, they've seen it done every day, but they're unable to do it themselves." (Source: Brendan Behan)

Critic-proof: A film that is such a commercial sop to the public that no review, good or bad (but particularly bad) can damage it. (See also: Buying a Gross)

Disney Cattle Call: Inviting a succession of writers to pitch their idea of how they'd script a studio-owned property. In the end, the studio hires none of them, but gives the best ideas from each of them to their own chosen writer.

DNA (as in "the DNA of a project"): The thematic essence of a film or TV series. Used as a guide against which all ideas are compared, accepted, or rejected. Example: If the DNA of a serious horror movie is zombies, having them sing a romantic ballad would not be in the DNA.

Embryos in Three-Piece Suits: Writer Larry Gelbart's description of young television and film executives who know how to keep their job but not how to do it. (See also: 27-year-old Jasons)

Encouraged to Death: When everybody tells you how great you are but nobody gives you a job to prove it.

Eyewash: Publicity or other activity performed to stroke someone's ego, usually a star, director, or producer, that does absolutely nothing for the good of their production.

Feeding the Brontosaurus: The process of having a series of productions moving through a studio's departments in succession (i.e.: development, budgeting, casting, costumes, set construction, shooting, editing, scoring, mixing, distribution, etc.). In this way, a studio can attach the expense of each department to the budget of the film rather than be forced to charge the expense to overhead, which would affect the stockholders. The imagery is that, when a brontosaurus eats, it takes a long time for the food to make it from one end out the other.

Finger Up the Pulse of the Public: Applied to a filmmaker who instinctively knows what the public wants to see based on meeting its lowest common denominator of taste.

500-pound Gorilla: Someone who gets what he wants by virtue of his or her commercial clout or corporate position rather than whether he is right, wrong, or talented.

Flavor of the Month: A temporarily hot property. Refers to an old advertising campaign for Baskin-Robbins ice cream.

Franchise: A film containing characters and situations that can generate sequels, each of which contains the elements that made its predecessor popular without allowing the main characters to change enough to make the public lose interest. This is what makes a TV series work, except when it's applied to movies it's called a franchise and is considered as a new thing.

Go-Away Money: Cash paid to someone who is forced off a project that he or she may have nurtured for years but that a heavyweight (See: 500-pound gorilla) wants all the credit for. In another profession this would be called hush money and would often involved an NDA (Non-Disclosure Agreement).

I don't have him: A phrase used by Assistants when their bosses are getting involved in something they shouldn't, and the Assistant wants to keep the caller from connecting. (See also: #Me Too)

Lights (green, red, yellow, brown):
Green-light: Formal okay to go into production on a project;
Red-light: Pulling the plug on a project;
Yellow-light: Tenuous approval if certain aspects are met
Brown-light: When a project turns to shit.

"Make the Project My Own": A phrase used by actors and directors when they want to immerse themselves in a project to the point of feeling emotionally close to it. Unfortunately for the writer, this usually means that the actor or director comes to believe he wrote the script.

Martini Shot: The last camera set-up and take of the day, after which those who participated are entitled to a celebratory drink. (See also: Wrap Beers)

Mash-Up: Combining two or more film genres into one that reflects the appeal of each. Example: a Zombie musical. (Hmmm, not bad. Forget what you read about DNA, above.)

MeToo'ed: Someone, usually male, being accused by a subordinate, usually female, of inappropriate behavior, usually sexual.

Monkey Points: Income based on net profits. Monkey points are assigned with alacrity to people who do not know what either Monkey Points or alacrity mean. (See also: Nyet profits)

Net, the: Not referring to the Internet but, rather, to the concept of net profits, which is equally ephemera, as in, "nothing gets caught in the Net."

Non-no No: Dodging the stigma of saying "No" to a project by making it impossible for the other person to say "Yes." Example: a director doesn't want to do a particular script but also doesn't want a reputation of being choosey, so he demands a fee higher than the producer can afford. In this way, the director has forced the producer instead of him to say No. Warning: If the producer says yes, there go two years of your life on a project you don't want to do.

Nyet Profits: Using the Russian word for "No" ("nyet") as a pun on "net profits," meaning "no profits." See: Monkey Points.

Pass: A neutral-sounding word for declining to be involved in a project in a town where no one wants to get the reputation for saying "No" (See also: Non-no No).

Pizza Thursdays: A contrivance by which male executives post fake casting notices for actresses just so they can meet attractive women. Rumored to have begun on a TV series whose female star was an ageing actress who demanded that no young women be added to the cast. She had Thursdays off, and that's when her male cast and crew sent out for pizza and female wannabes.

Pocket Pass: When someone to whom a project has been submitted cannot say Yes and so merely fails to respond in the belief that he or she would rather be thought of as an asshole than a no-sayer. NOTE: This can also refer to someone who lacks the ability to get projects produced but keeps asking to read scripts anyway to prevent people finding out that he or she is dead in the industry. A major time-waster.

Producer: When Joseph L. Mankiewicz moved to MGM, he told MGM head Louis B. Mayer that he wanted to be a director. Mayer insisted that Mankiewicz become a producer first, explaining, "You have to learn to crawl before you can walk," which Mankiewicz later said was the best description of a producer that he ever heard.

Producer's Incentive: If a producer can bring in a project ahead of schedule and under budget he is often allowed to keep the unspent money.

Reboot: A remake. You can call it by whatever high-tech sounding term you want, but a reboot is still a remake and everybody knows it.

Service Interview: Meeting with someone for no reason other than both parties can say that they have had a meeting. Nothing is expected to come out of such an encounter except name-dropping rights. (See also: Vice-President in charge of relatives.)

Shopping Agreement: A contract by which a producer gets permission from a writer to try to raise money on his script without paying the customary option fee. This allows producers to take advantage of desperate writers. The Writers Guild of America discourages the practice, yet nevertheless has a Shopping Agreement template on its website.

Slate: A collection of film projects proposed as a studio's output by a production executive, as in, "I'm sticking a group of otherwise unconnected projects together and calling it my slate." Often said approximately three years before they get shitcanned.

Soft Pass: De facto turning down a project by not responding to it, rudely tying up everyone waiting for an answer, even a No. (See also: Pocket Pass)

Spielbergville: Generic suburban community in which statistically average people are the subjects of appealing stories. Named after the early films of Steven Spielberg who set them there.

Studioed: The practice of removing original, unusual, or exceptional aspects from a film when test audiences find the movie too challenging. This can also refer to filmmakers who are forced to shoot a new ending because a test audience is confused or disappointed by their original vision. Notable examples of studioed films include Pretty Woman, Little Shop of Horrors, and, most famously, Fatal Attraction.

Tentpole: A single, large-budget picture -- often a franchise -- whose box office success is expected to prop up the finances of its distributor for several months as it plays off.

Third Person Innocent: A form of grammar in which the reflexive case is used so that nobody is forced to be referred to in the first or second person. Example: Rather than say, "You dropped a case of light bulbs," the third person innocent would be, "A case of light bulbs was dropped."

27-year-old Jasons: Mid-level agents, network managers, studio development people, and other individuals who go to the same trainers, hang out at the same bars, drink the same trendy cocktails, wear the same clothing line, and make their decisions based on market research rather than personal taste or courage. They know little of the history of their own profession, were all raised on TV and comic books, are virtually interchangeable, and will continue to hire each other throughout their generation.

Verticals: The various levels of corporate managers and executives, many of them superfluous, who are inserted between your job and getting your job done.

Vice President in Charge of Relatives: Someone who is hired solely to placate people with whom the executives do not want to be bothered. This can include filmmakers whose movies are flopping, students to whom the executive gave his card on career day, meaningful one-night stands, etc.

Wrap Beers: Courtesy brewski provided by the producer to crew members at the end of a day's hard work.

Writer: The first person to work on a film and the last person to get credited. The only one who creates; everybody else just interprets. "Theirs may be the kingdom," Billy Wilder said of the studios, "but ours is the power and the glory."

EXTENSION CREDIT PAGE:

Some of the stories in this anthology were first published under different titles (shown in parentheses). Please see below for their original titles for purposes of copyright registration. Stories marked (*) were created for Hollywood Dementia but have not appeared there as of this writing. The date of first publication for each illustration is the same as for their matched stories with the following exceptions that were created for other stories: Frontispiece (originally for "The Minder, Part 1," August 14, 2018); "Walt's Last Wishes" (originally for "Mickey Mouse and Sewer Rat," August 22, 2017); and "Bad Penny" (originally for "Burning Desire, Part 2," June 12, 2018).

Age of Anxiety (October 18, 2015)

Bad Penny*

Bernie Beats the Greylist (as "Ageless Anxiety," July 5, 2016)

Christmas Picture (as "Nobody Does Christmas Like the Jews," December 18, 2017)

A Cocktail of Fear (August 27, 2017)

Collateral Damage*

Critical Thinking (as "Critical Mass," February 10, 2016)

The Curious Case of "Rapture in Rimini" (as "Rapture in Rimini," August 25, 2015)

Deal Picture (as "Jumbalaya," December 1, 2015)

Firing Forsyth (September 24-26, 2018)

Found Footage*

Glossary*

Group Marvelous*

Herschel the Horrible (as "Revenge, Thy Name is Oscar," February 20, 2017)

I Want to Thank the Academy (December 30, 2015)

Memo from the Corner Office (February 23, 2016)

Night Shoot (September 6, 2017)

Nobody's Oscar (January 12, 2016)

Only Scoundrels (November 1, 2017)

The Publicist Who Thought He Was a Star (as "The Publicist," June 19, 2018)

Trigger Warning (February 26, 2019)

Walt's Last Wishes (December 19, 2016)

THE AUTHOR

Nat Segaloff has been a studio publicist and film critic (not at the same time), playwright, celebrity ghost writer, college teacher, TV producer, and broadcaster who, over the years, collected dozens of true Hollywood stories that he disguised, some more thinly than others, for Hollywood and Venal, His many books and documentaries include biographies of Arthur Penn, William Friedkin, Stan Lee, John Belushi, Harlan Ellison, Larry King, and Stirling Silliphant. His plays include the Waldorf Conference (co-written with Arnie Reisman and Daniel M. Kimmel) and Closets. He co-founded the science fiction production company Alien Voices with John de Lancie and Leonard Nimoy, and is currently writing the biography of Shari Lewis & Lamb Chop with Shari's daughter (who is Lamb Chop's new mom) Mallory Lewis. He lives in Los Angeles and has given up expecting people to return his calls.

THE ARTIST

Thomas Warming has worked for more than twenty years as an illustrator and concept designer for film, computer games, children's books, graphic novels and advertising campaigns. As an author/illustrator, his children's books are released in Scandinavia and Korea. Warming still enjoys a longlasting work relationship with Nikki Finke, providing illustrations for her Hollywood fiction site, Hollywood Dementia. Warming works in a diverse range of styles, preferring acrylic paint for analog and Photoshop for digital illustration.

Also by this author from Bear Manor Media.

Final Cuts

NAT SEGALOFF

The untold stories behind Hollywood swan songs.

ISBN 1-59393-233-2

$24.95

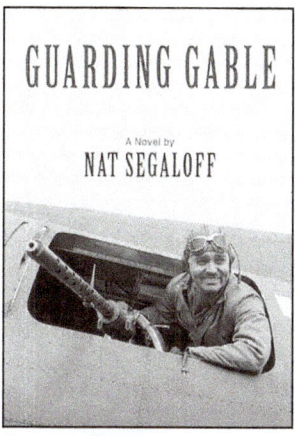

Guarding Gable

NAT SEGALOFF

A novel on Gable's high flying WW2 days.

ISBN 978-1-62933-406-6

$19.95

Screen Saver: Private Stories of Public Hollywood

NAT SEGALOFF

Hollywood's most glamorous people are far from glitzy when far from home.

ISBN 978-1593939582

$20.00

Screen Saver Too: Hollywood Strikes Back

NAT SEGALOFF

More private stories of public Hollywood, a memoir by former movie press agent-turned-film critic/producer.

ISBN 978-1-62933-199-7

$20.00

Available on audiobook from Bear Manor Audio and other providers.